All's Fair

by Jay Mulling

Copyright 2026

To Valeria and Lauren
And all the other people out there who said "yes,
and" to teaching middle schoolers math.

Acknowledgements

It's always strange to get to the point, in a manuscript's life, where it's time to pull the plug and publish. For independent authors, the point can feel all the more arbitrary. I wrote this book a year and a half ago and let it sit for a good long while before coming back and deciding that it would be the next project to launch into the world.

While the book isn't, overall, particularly sad, I wrote it as a grief novel. I was going through one of the bigger losses of my life and used the pages of *All's Fair* to process my heartbreak. I realize that "writing a romcom to process death" is, perhaps, one of the most Enneagram 7 things I've ever done, but, well. Here we are. If any of you are also grieving loved ones, when you pick up this book, I hope that the characters are able to give some comfort by the end.

As ever, I couldn't have gotten to this point without the help of my friends and family. I'd like to thank my alpha and beta readers for their continuous support and encouragement. For reading every new manuscript I toss into their inbox, really, and answering my billion-and-one follow-up questions every time we workshop new pages. I'd like to thank my sister, too, even though her insistence on reading at three speed meant she missed, like, half the jokes. I'd also like to thank my sensitivity reader. I appreciate the time and energy you gave to a complete stranger and her random, imagined world of high school teachers.

I would like to acknowledge that, while my main character is Mexican-American, I am very much a white lady. I went back and forth on whether or not this was appropriate but, at the end of the day, most of my novels are inspired by friends and the friend I based Bea on is one of the strongest, snarkiest Latina educators from southern California I've ever met and it felt disingenuous to white-wash her existence. "Authors writing outside of their experiences of identity" is very much an ongoing question and I look forward to continuing to think through the meaning of diversity and inclusion in the literary world.

Lastly, thank you to the educators out there. Teaching children is a nigh impossible job—and that's *with* all the right resources. The emotional and physical labor that goes into raising up these generations of humans is incalculable (though I really wish someone would try, maybe then salaries might come close to actually compensating teachers). Thank you, thank you, thank you for all that you've done, are doing, and will do.

And, scene.

Chapter One

I read recently that millennials aren't having as much sex as previous generations. Like, a statistically significant lack of "as much sex." The article gave a whole bunch of reasons why thirty-somethings aren't getting it on with their similarly sex-deprived peers. Some of the reasons were compelling. Many seemed wide of the mark. By the end of this particular research rabbit hole, I couldn't help but feel like nobody had actually asked a millennial. At least, nobody had asked a millennial who wasn't some manosphere bruh complaining about porn and how much easier women had it on dating apps.

Because, here's the thing: I can tell you exactly why millennials aren't having as much sex as previous generations. And it begins and it ends with a single question—a single, stupid question— that has us all sweating bullets and running to the nearest diagnostic apparatus we can find.

"What do you want?" Ugh.
Story time.

***

I had gone on a date with this guy. He was a hot trans man who showed up wearing argyle suspenders and had way too much working knowledge of barcode inventory systems. Read: exactly my type. I was also very horny, so he had that going for him as well. Point being, we were at his place sometime after nine PM and doing what soon-to-be lovers do.

He eventually asked if I wanted to go to his bedroom, which I obviously did want to do. As previously mentioned, he was very hot. An adept kisser, too, and in that creative, exploratory way that heavily implied "good times forthcoming."

We got up, I did the sexy backwards walk where I was sort of kissing him, sort of trying to take my pants off, and sort of trying not to trip over his rug. We stumbled into the bedroom. He disengaged long enough to close the door behind us. Turned back to face me, breathless, and asked the dreaded question.

"What do you like?"

"What do you like" is, of course, an interesting query, and for many reasons. On one level, it's polite. The question is aware of the relational dynamics of intercourse and wants to make it clear that open communication will be a key feature of all forthcoming hanky panky. On another level, it's modest. It's not assuming it can please you without any guidance. It's acknowledging that it is not, indeed, a sex god, and that you probably know your body best, anyway.

Those first two levels did not occur to me, in that particular moment, and had to be explained by trusted friends after the fact. Indeed, what I heard was something more like what I would attribute to the third, fourth, and fifth levels of the "what do you like" question, which go as follows:

The third level is full of fear and anxiety. It hears the "what do you like" and assumes the person asking the question wants explicit, well-researched responses. It assumes this because only somebody with fairly good social and sexual awareness would ask such a question, surely, which means that they probably have been partying on the sex positivity train for some time, now. Which is also intimidating, because that train is full of kinks and cuffs and all sorts of other things you mostly just don't think about. Not in a judgmental way. It just really isn't your thing. But this person, well. It might be their thing. A realization that transforms the fear into anxiety. What if they like something you don't. What if they need you to be more specific than you have language for. Or worse, what if they start diagnosing you, when you fail to self-identify, and halfway through the night you end up with a praise kink.

What if, god forbid, they want to *talk* through it all. Nothing quite brings a person out of their body like another person requiring a personalized commentary of the libidinal proceedings.

The fourth level is almost the worst. The fourth level is looking down at yourself, frowning, and remembering that you are thirty-one years old. It's remembering that you followed a stranger home after a few hours of chatting at a dimly-lit gastropub. It's remembering that the blanket on his couch hadn't been folded. That, worse, he had had a picture of him and his sister framed on the wall. It's remembering that you're thirty-one years old, standing half-naked in a stranger's bedroom, and trying to answer a fairly simple and mostly performative question. And you can't. It's realizing you can't answer the damn question. It's realizing you don't know what you like.

The fifth level is the actual worst. Because, you do know what you like, of course you do. But it has almost nothing to do with sex. And has nothing at all to do with the person standing in front of you, asking the question.

The fifth level is also the actual worst because it is the one I actually gave voice to, when push came to shove. And it just really wasn't my finest moment.

"What…do I like?" I just sort of stared at him, then. Because it was after nine on a Thursday. Way after my bedtime. Way after a lot of times, actually. Never thought I'd be wandering aimlessly through bachelorhood past thirty.

"Yes, what do you like," he said again, leaning against the door. I'd stripped him down to his binder and boxers a whole ten minutes ago and, while it is neither here nor there, I need you to know that this man had smiling cacti printed across his underwear. "And do you want the lights on or off?"

"Um…" was I supposed to have an opinion?

He stepped towards me. Reached towards me, too. Ready to resume. "Tell me what you want, Beatrice."

That killed the mood. Killed it dead. Which was a real bummer, too, because I had worn my sexy bra for this date. Well, had been wearing. It was currently being worn by one of his lampshades.

I went from zero to fifth level in under a second. I was suddenly nothing more or less than a lonely woman in a stranger's apartment, too existential for casual hookups and too tired to play the dating game. The worst part was that I had been the one to suggest we go back to his place. I had been the one to turn what could have been a perfectly lovely first date into this trainwreck.

"What... I want," I said, breathing, staring at nothing. "I ..." I floated somewhere above my body, watching, curious, and wondered if I was going to let the roar of half-formed thoughts flooding my brain answer his question. I certainly hoped not. They were a little loud, for starters, and had the general outline of a night-ruining monologue.

"I want a field, Hedi." Welp. Night-ruining monologue it was.

"Interesting," he said, his hands stalling on their route down my back.

"I want a field with Mr. Darcy at dawn after he's walked through dew and fog to hold me. To just hold me." I made a mental note to never, ever, under any circumstances *ever* go on a first date while in the follicular phase ever again. "I want 'financial savvy and a generally team-spirited disposition.' Serious and aloof is not as sexy as it thinks it is. I want that moment after a hangout with friends where everybody had fun, and laughed, and I look over at my lover and know that they had fun, too, and wasn't it as easy as breathing to have all of my people in one room together?" This was the point at which Hedi stopped trying to kiss my neck. He sat down on the bed, aware of where this night was going. I sat down beside him.

"I want years of trust and friendship and respect and secret little smiles, all for me, and golden August days spent on a dusty picnic blanket. I want to be loved. I want to be fucked. In under twenty minutes, usually. I don't want dirty talk and I don't want to fake orgasms. I don't like having to pretend hookups are about orgasms—I can do that just fine by myself—when really, sometimes, I just want a hot, sweaty body on top of me. Like an x-rated weighted blanket. I want it, Hedi, but not how it can be got, right here, right now. Is what I'm getting at." I sighed and hoped that my shirt wouldn't be too hard to find. I stood up.

"So... I shouldn't have asked about preferences, I take it?"

"I guess I'll go," I said, too embarrassed to look at him.

"Do you want a snack?"

"What?"

"Are you hungry?" I did look at him, then. He was trying very hard not to smile. I scowled.

"No, thank you."

'Are you sure?"

13

"What, do I *seem* hungry?" He put up his hands.

"No, no, I would never say that."

I wandered back into the living room, found my shirt, and pulled it on. He followed me out.

"I know you're going to, but you really don't have to leave. We could watch a movie. You've put me in the mood for Pride and Prejudice."

I rolled my eyes.

"I don't need any more friends," I said, tugging one shoe on, then the other. "Thank you, though."

"But if you don't make new friends how are you going to fall in love with your erstwhile bestie?"

He did have a point. It didn't help that it was a point my mother was fond of making.

"Besides, *you* might not need new friends," he went on, crouching down beside his DVD collection and unashamedly browsing. I supposed he really was going to watch a movie after I left. "But I am very much on the market."

"Why?" I don't know why, but it made me sad to think of people trying to survive this life without any friends. Actually, I guess I do know why it made me sad. Because it's sad.

"Oh, nothing tragic, don't worry. I'm not one of your sexy aloof loners. I just moved recently, is all. Unpacked the last box on Monday."

I finished tying the first shoe.

"Jumped on the apps pretty fast?"

He shrugged.

"My job doesn't start for another few weeks. I haven't done an app in a while, but, well. Why not?"

I nodded. Indeed.

"Working out well for you, I see," I said. I tried to convey the apology with my words and face. He seemed like a nice enough guy. He laughed.

"Perfectly, actually. You're the first person I met up with. Probably the last, too. No offense. But I don't think I have the energy for it."

I couldn't help but laugh. I felt bad and funny and a little bit attacked, all at the same time. I finished tying my other shoe and stood, wallet in hand, phone in pocket, keys ready to go.

"So, I shouldn't call you?" he asked, looking me up and down.

"You'll do just fine," I said, trying not to feel heavy and ancient and so unspeakably sad.

"So if I run into you, should I say hi, or …?"

"Are you planning on stalking me?"

"Somebody thinks highly of themselves."

I grinned.

"Apparently." I turned to go. "Welcome to SoCal, Hedi. You're going to do just fine."

I was halfway home and ten minutes into an increasingly devolving phone call with my sister when I realized I'd left my bra on his lampshade.

Chapter Two

The Queen's Will: Prologue

So there was this queen in ye olde olde who people really liked and who was really good at all of the things good queens are supposed to be good at. And it was all fine and fun, et cetera, but then one day this warlock swooped in and stole her away. Warlocks, am I right? Anyway, he stole her away and it was very bad and she was very sad and of course he put her in a tower, because where else do warlocks put queens, and he told her he'd let her go if she willed her kingdom over. She noped that pretty quick and he got pretty mad about it and they argued about it basically all the time.

He was pretty sure he would break her will, in the end. He didn't. She was a good queen, like we said, and placed her people before her desire to get out of his stinky, godawful tower. Time passed. Like, a lot of time. Probably fifty years, if we're being honest, but she'd lost track of it long before then.

The world around them got older. They did not. Warlocks don't really age, so him not getting older didn't surprise anyone. She, on the other hand ... well, she was supposed to get old and die, wasn't she, and he was to get his kingdom one way or the other.

It turns out, some Queen's wills are a magic all their own. It kept her alive. It kept her people free.

But queens can't live forever in towers, can they? Not even the ones who can live forever.

I frowned down at the lines, wondering who in the world thought that was an acceptable ending for a piece in the student paper I'd bothered to read all the way through to the end.

"But...what?" I asked, staring up at my Advanced Theater students. Twelve, this year, and all absolute nerds. Some were sun-drenched, their skin saturated with August. Some looked like they hadn't crawled out of their room-caves since May. They all had purple bags under their eyes. I suspected none had had to be anywhere before 9 AM in quite a while. "Why are we printing this in the school paper? And also, like, what happened to the queen?"

"Ms. Suré, we already told you," Belen said, sighing, managing a look of long sufferance that belied her seventeen years. "Mr. Holson assigned some French poem for summer reading. And then he told us we could either write an essay about it or write an epic 'reimagining the story.' Obviously nobody wrote the essay."

"Katy Herkle wrote the essay," Claudia piped up. I glanced at her. She had grown three inches over the summer. It was a little shocking. Not terribly shocking, or anything. I'd been teaching high schoolers for six years, by this point. I knew the drill.

"Yes, well, Katy would, so," Belen muttered. She and Katy were neck-in-neck for valedictorian. Katy's mom kept asking the school to recalculate the GPAs. The administrators were always gossiping about it. I swallowed hard and reminded myself that it wouldn't do to laugh at my children. Not to their faces, anyway.

"Okay, very well," I said, placing the newspaper back down on my desk, "but that doesn't explain why one of your classmate's stories is appearing in the school paper."

Belen frowned, pretty sure that that explained exactly why one of her classmate's poems had appeared in a new front-page column entitled *"The Queen's Will."* A little paragraph beneath it told the school it would be a regularly appearing column and would under *no* circumstances end as horribly as the original, *Yonec*, what was *wrong* with Marie de France.

"We all were editing our epics at Rag'N'Roll Camp," Hugo offered. "Rag'N'Roll Camp" took place the first week of August and was when everybody who worked on the school's newspaper frantically got together and pitched the rag for Day One—how all the teachers referred to the first day of school—and after which point all of the student editors scrambled for two weeks to get their paper written, formatted, printed, and distributed in time for that first, screeching bell toll of the new school year.

"It was more fun than we thought," Hugo went on, "because we all hated the poem. Or, loved hating it. The lovers die at the end, very *Romeo and Juliet*. So dramatic. We needed more material for the newspaper, anyway, and Frances thought a regular column might be fun. Coach Roberts didn't say no, so." He gestured towards the newspaper.

I couldn't help but think Coach Roberts hadn't been fully listening when giving this the green light. She was in charge of varsity basketball, the school's newspaper, and Geometry. Not all of them were priorities. The woman just really loved her triangles.

"Shocking," I said, sitting back in my chair. My students were supposed to be picking out monologues. Instead, they were huddled around my desk, passing my plate of banana muffins around like a communion tray, and waiting for me to crack and accidentally say something terribly insightful or delightfully juicy. Whichever came first.

First period—Advanced Theater—was full of my third and fourth year students. There weren't enough students to make up two separate "Theater Three" and "Theater Four" classes so they all just got put in "advanced," which made it very difficult to recycle material, is all I'm saying. I'd known these fifteen-, sixteen-, seventeen-, and eighteen-year-olds for years, by this point, which meant they were all perfectly secure in their "what's she going to do, fire me?" classroom status. Which was fine by me, of course. Safe, secure spaces led to better character exploration.

"Whose epic did you pick?" I directed that question to Hugo and Belen, who both also sat on the newspaper's editorial board. Hugo grinned as Belen shook her head.

"Can't tell," she said, before remembering that that wasn't the line she was supposed to be feeding people. "I mean, I don't know."

"Smooth."

Some of the other children snickered. Belen rolled her eyes and huffed a little too defensively.

"Do you…do you like it?" Noel blurted out. She was 5'3", which always surprised me. Her manic presence tended to fill whichever room she was in. Kind of like an electrical storm.

"I do," I said, nodding, reminding myself that modeling positive feedback had been my New Semester's Resolution. "I'm very excited to read a year's worth of reimagined French poetry."

"We couldn't decide between poetry and prose," Sophia told me. "Because, you know, the original was in verse, of course. But what if some of the characters are lower class?" She paused, waiting for me to laugh at her kissass comedy. I of course obliged, saintly teacher that I am.

"Oh my gosh," Noel breathed, "not everything is about Shakespeare, Sophia."

"Now, now," I said, "Noel, we don't blaspheme in this house—" that got laughs from everybody who wanted an A in the class—"and we also don't cut Sophia down. Offstage, anyway. You know the rules. Would you like to throw a gauntlet?"

Noel shook her head vigorously. She hated stage combat.

"I didn't think so." I nodded my head towards Sophia. Noel sighed.

"Sophia, I'm sorry that I cut you down offstage. Will you accept my apology?"

Sophia was trying very hard to look like she trusted my preferred methods of mediation. Which was bold of her to do, seeing as I didn't even trust my preferred methods of mediation. It worked short term, well enough, but I sort of had this suspicion that this would be coming up in their therapy sessions, ten years from now.

"Of course," Sophia said, staring at the desk.

"But also, Sophia's right," Hugo rolled right along, "well, sort of. Most of it won't be in verse, is what I mean. The... um, anonymous author is collaborating with... um, themselves, and, um, some of themselves don't want to rhyme all the time."

Not a few of his peers laughed, myself included.

"Very fun," I said, looking back down at the paper. "Now, shoo. I need monologues, people, monologues."

They did not shoo. They did tell me all about this short film they had shot, over the summer, and wanted to know if we could incorporate videography into theater, this year. I made a mental note to start figuring out how in the world editing software worked, told them to write a budget and proposal, and more or less accepted that

23

this was going to be "a thing" for at least the next six weeks.

"How do you make a budget?" Belen asked, taking this as seriously as she took anything. Which was to say, very seriously.

"And people say we don't learn useful things in the arts," I muttered to myself, walking up to the whiteboard. The students hurriedly filed into the first two rows of desks, ripping notebooks from backpacks and pens from each other—why was there always a shortage of pens?—and staring me down with an intensity I didn't realize a lesson on budgets could ever possibly elicit.

"First things first," I said, uncapping a brand new blue marker. I inhaled, just a little, before reveling in how lightly I was able to write. The slightest touch, and ink spilled forth, clear and stark against the deep-cleaned whiteboard. Oh, the magic of that first-day-back look and smell.

"Unless you're an olympic athlete, the per diem is your friend." They actually scribbled that down, which reminded me that, well, you know. I always forget to limit the sarcasm and referential humor when around students. Always re-learn it real quick, each August.

"So, children," I said, dirtying up the big, clean board, "budgets. Otherwise known as 'how to coax money out of the earmarked octopus.'" They wrote that down too, but it was more okay because half of them had taken Ms. Faye's AP U.S. History class, last year, and, after they had read about the Gilded Age, had had a running joke about Octopi for two entire months. If you don't know what I'm talking about, it's okay. I barely know what I'm talking about, either. They kept trying to explain why it was funny. I figured out belatedly that I would never understand. That they were just going to keep explaining until I laughed. So, I laughed. A statement which, quite honestly, just about sums up my career as a high school teacher in the public school system.

Chapter Three

"I forget," Yvonne said, eyes wide and blank, "I always forget." She was staring at nothing, her hands resting on a half-opened container of yogurt.

Three of us were sitting in the teacher's lounge, hours later, and trying very hard not to look like we'd just survived a 48-hour medical rotation.

"We'll get that stamina back in no time. We always do." That was Stacy, the fourth person in the room. She didn't look tired at all. She looked like she'd spent her summer waking up at five in the morning for trail runs, drinking healthy green smoothies, and reading up on current 'best practices of inclusive classrooms.' So, she looked like she always looked, is what I'm saying.

"Shut up, Stacy," I muttered, telling myself to drink water. Telling myself not to go for that third cup of coffee. Telling myself that Day One was way too early to break the two-cup habit I had spent months cultivating.

"Aww, missed you too, Bea," she said, smiling. I groaned.

"How big is it, this year?" Paul, the choir teacher, asked.

"Forty. Five. Students," I groaned again. "And that's just one section. They broke Theater One into two classes." They usually did. "The next section's got another forty." Paul nodded sympathetically.

"You?" I asked.

"Fifty-two," he said, "All in one, though. Because of course I can manage fifty-two thirteen-year-olds. That makes sense." He sighed. "And of course, again, most of the girls insist they're altos. None of the boys want to be baritones. And half of them were too shy to do the parts audition, anyway." He shrugged. "So, you know, the usual."

"The usual." We all said it like a toast.

"Do you need help with that?" I asked Yvonne, staring at her yogurt. She didn't seem to hear me. I took the yogurt, opened it for her, and handed it back, spoon in and ready to go.

"The state passed a law incentivizing this new method of algebra instruction," Yvonne said, mindlessly eating her yogurt. "Diana signed us up for it." The only thing I'll say about our principal,

Diana, is that she's *very* good at coaxing money out of the earmarked octopus.

"She told me two weeks ago. I bought one of those self-teaching workbooks. It didn't work." She said it so quietly, so despairingly, like she'd seen her own tombstone. Stacy burst out laughing before she could catch herself. I bit my lips, not wanting to break rank and join the smoothie-guzzling jogger. Solidarity, and whatnot.

"I would offer to help," Paul said, spreading peanut butter over his celery, "but I can't math anymore, so."

Stacy nodded, wiping her eyes.

"If it's anything other than calculating a twenty-five percent gratuity, I can't, either."

I looked up from my berries, eyes wide.

"Twenty-five?" I asked, glancing from person to person, "is that what we're at, now? I've just been doing twenty."

Stacy shrugged. Yvonne didn't seem to hear me. Paul looked at me like I'd murdered a small bunny.

"Karma's a bitch," was all he said.

"Uuuughhh," I muttered, pinching the bridge of my nose. I couldn't keep up with the world, sometimes. Just when I thought I could afford to be generous, the tip expectation went up.

"No, according to the sophomores, Karma is a boyfriend," Stacy said, folding up her cloth napkin. It had little daisies on it. I don't know why, but Stacy's napkins always made me so weirdly happy.

"What?" Yvonne asked, zipping up the lunch box her son had outgrown three years ago. It was covered in little animations from something called 'Minecraft.'

"It's a Taylor Swift song," Paul told Yvonne, knowing the poor woman would never get there on her own. "From that album that just came out."

"Just?" I asked, brow raised. He rolled his eyes.

"Like, six years ago," he said, "which still fully qualifies as 'just' in Teacher Time."

"That's not right," I said, "you know it's not. Teacher time should be faster than regular time, not slower. The children keep us well-informed. We just feel slow and ancient by comparison."

"Ya, so, relatively speaking, our time moves slower."

"That doesn't—no, Paul, it—" but I couldn't think of anything else to say. My brain was too fried and I had to save what was left for my tech classes and forty-student second section of Theater One.

"How're the flowers?" I asked Stacy. She smiled. Of course she smiled.

"Most are lovely. Some students didn't press them right, though, and they're covered in mold. But it's sort of funny, because they didn't realize it was mold. They just thought that's what pressed wildflowers looked like."

"Yep. That sounds *real* funny," Paul agreed. Well, 'agreed.'

"Poo-poo on my parade all you want, Paul," Stacy said, standing and stretching, "It's great fertilizer." We all groaned. Stacy, if you hadn't guessed, taught first-year biology and environmental science, which was an elective science course for juniors and seniors. She always assigned an extra credit wildflower project over the summer for her elective course. Which all the nerds did, of course. I mean, these were the types of children who had chosen to fill elective periods with *more* science. Of *course* they did the extra credit. I grinned. Belen was in that class. Pretty sure Katy Herkle was, too.

Chapter Four

"Oh—" control it control it control it—
"interesting choice, Nando!" I made a mental note
never to do a "Yes, And" warm-up with unvetted
fourteen-year-olds. I blamed social media for
making this child believe he could turn a dog park
scenario into an active shooter awareness session.
"That's all the time we have, today."

I wasn't going to be saved by the bell.
Indeed, we still had ten minutes left in this class
period. But this was a yes, and situation, wasn't it?
And sometimes we just had to make things happen.

"Okay, students, I want you to take out your
notebooks and write about the way you're feeling,
right here, right now, and how you think this feeling
will grow and change. How you think your craft
will change, the more we work on staying in our
bodies and trusting our reactions."

Sometimes being a theater teacher gave you
a lot of leeway in how seriously people took you

and your assignments. I tried to imagine Stacy telling her students to journal about the way their biology lab had made them feel.

Needless to say, every single one of my forty-two—forty-*two*— students grabbed out their notebooks and began writing in earnest. I briefly wondered what I'd ever done to command such respect and obedience.

I didn't have much time for such wonderings, though, because our principal appeared in my doorway. I tried not to cringe. It's not like I was already in trouble. It's not like I was *ever* in trouble, I amended—I was an employee, not a student—and, besides, was on, like, five committees that involved this woman.

I did cringe, then. I hoped she wasn't here about the Back To School Trivia Night. That idea was dead in the water and none of my co-chairs had had the courage to tell Diana yet.

"Keep writing, I'll be just outside," I said, hurrying through a row of desks towards our increasingly impatient principal. "You're dismissed when the bell rings."

"Bea!" Diana exclaimed as if she hadn't just seen me this morning. And passive aggressively told me my student's needed to do better at their UIL meets, this year, didn't I know that funding for the arts was on the line. I was pretty sure it wasn't. I was also pretty sure—and by 'pretty sure' I mean 'one hundred percent certain'—that ticket sales from our spring musicals more than paid for our program. "Bea, how's it going?"

"Oh, you know," I said, reminding myself that I wasn't allowed to curse on school property, "what's up?"

"Funny you should ask," she said, her eyes already in that middle-distant place where she kept her 'next on the to-do list' list. "You're a new teacher mentor, this year."

"Oh." Oh. "I thought that you were joking about that." Oh, shit.

"Hmm, well, super wasn't," she said, shifting her weight from foot-to-foot. "Anyway, I noticed you didn't respond to my email, last night." She'd sent it at midnight, to be clear. "I just wanted to confirm that you'd be available to your mentee after the school day, today. Don't forget. The school will comp meals and a drink for each of you."

"Wonderful."

"Up to fifteen dollars per capita, anyway."

"Yummy."

"Excellent." Diana glanced at her watch. "The name of the game is teacher retention, Bea. The better you do, the better we'll be." The bell did ring, then. Which was a real bummer, because I had my whole 'we aren't the problem and we aren't the solution' monologue all cued up and ready to go.

"I've matched you with a lovely lady," Diana said, walking backwards and away, "the new English teacher. I think you'll really hit it off. I told all mentees to meet their partners in the teacher's lounge after school. Please don't be late." I died a little, watching her leave. Don't get me wrong, I don't hate my job. I actually love it, if you must know. But the line between love and hate is thin, in some professions, and the ledge was always somewhere within stumbling distance.

I internally grumbled the entire way back to my desk. I dragged my feet a little, too, because there were no students around to pay attention— they only had four and a half minutes to sprint a quarter mile to their next class, use the restroom, and catch up on the latest post-lunch goss—and sometimes embodying my feelings helped get them out of my GD body. And by "GD" I mean "Garland Damned" because obviously that woman's rendition of Old Man River will always and forever haunt me.

One of the benefits of being an arts teacher is that our hallway—and by "our" I mean the material and performing arts teachers—is in the furthest corridor of the school and tucked conveniently behind the Performing Arts Center (the place with the big stage and all the upholstered chairs). Dicky, the material arts teacher, had long ago dubbed this hallway the "Rainbows and Glitter Hall," which had been shortened to "RAG Hall" years before I'd arrived on the scene.

Another benefit is that our classrooms, unlike most other classrooms, never changed custody (e.g., if you're the art teacher you're the one who is always going to need the room with the fumigator and furnace). The music hall—think choir and band—also benefitted from this phenomena because, like, who else is going to need soundproofed practice rooms and carpet capable of absorbing a brass section's worth of spit? Everyone else had to hike out what they'd brought in, as the backpackers say. Yes, even their poo. Schools certainly qualify as conservation zones.

Point being, the classroom I was in, just then, was the one I had been in since I'd first landed this job, six years ago. It was just to the right of the art room and just across the hall from Shop—where we build our sets—which was, of course, just to the left of the backstage door.

As I stomped back to my desk I thought about how I'd more or less entrenched, in this room, how my "tidying things up so that the Big Clean"— the end-of-school-year cleaning—"could reach all the nooks and crannies" had grown less and less thorough, over the years. How two Mays ago I had asked Natalie—the bringer of Big Clean—if she could just pretend like she'd fumigated my desk so that I didn't actually have to find a new home for all the Knicks and Knacks and also years of papers and plays that seemed valuable now but would become kindling in a heartbeat if I actually had to purge my possessions for, say, a cross-country move or the zombie apocalypse. Natalie had said no. I'd handed her a dozen browned butter cookies. She'd thrown in a "keep the posters on the wall, too" bonus. Which meant that the posters papering my walls had been there for twenty-four entire months, by this point, and looked all the better for it. Goblin King Bowie wouldn't have survived another move, if I'm being honest. My upper year students had decided, four years ago, that rubbing his face was good luck. They traced their little adolescent fingers across his laminated jaw before each performance while chanting that their wills were as strong and their kingdoms as great. Beside him, the women of *Chicago* declared that their dirty rotten men had "had it coming." Which was, of course, not the main takeaway of that particular poster. If Diana asks, it's a cultural artifact about feminine rage. But I'm pretty sure forty percent of my graduates can trace their sapphic beginnings to that still of the Merry Murderesses of the Cook County Jail.

The whole east wall was covered in costume fails because yes, we made our own costumes and no, not every oopsie was a salvageable oopsie. I'm sure there's some universe where I have the prowess to resuscitate anything. It's the same universe where I spin my own wool and attend all the crafts fairs in a fifty mile radius of my homestead. It's not this one, though, and this me has no idea how to get stage blood out of a white frock. Which is, subsequently, why our Night of the Living Dead wardrobe lives proudly displayed along a clothesline spanning the entire back wall of the classroom.

Each year, my Advanced Theater students create a shrine in one of the room's four corners. The shrine corner was empty, currently—my students took their shrines very seriously and spent about a month lobbying, planning, and executing—except for the odd assortment of five- and ten-dollar plant stands I'd thrifted over the years for shrine display purposes.

The west wall was papered in show bills from plays our department had done since I'd been here. Students had scratched their signatures across the surfaces of the bills. I was pretty sure I'd be able to sell a few of them for thousands of dollars, one day. I already had two former students in daytime television. One, you've even heard of. I'm not saying I'm about to quit my day job, or anything. Just saying I've got a pension-padding plan in place.

I finally—*finally*—made it back to my desk. I didn't realize dragging my feet could be so exhausting but there I was, utterly spent, collapsing into my chair.

"Ms. Suré," somebody whispered. I almost shat my pants. I did look up, wondering how the hell I'd overlooked a whole ass student.

I hadn't, though, a fact which had me wondering how I hadn't even made it through the first day before having a break with reality. I was most surprised by how unsurprised I was, if I'm being honest.

"Ms. Suré, Ms. Suré."

I almost failed every student in every one of my classes, then and there. I didn't, of course. I did grab my phone from the cup I'd tossed it in at the beginning of the day. The phone that was now whispering my name to me, over and over. I looked down at the screen, still mostly confused, to see that my sister was calling me. I answered.

"I'm at work," I said, "and I think my seniors need a good scare."

"What?"

"They've grown far too confident. I think they think they're above punishment."

"Isn't it your job to give them confidence?"

"Oh, sweet summer child. Have I taught you nothing?"

My sweet December-born might-as-well-have-been-older-than-me sister sighed into the phone.

"I'm on a lunch break, Bea, and thought I'd check in about this weekend." This weekend? "Are you still bringing the cake?" Oh. Right.

"Yes, yes, sorry," I said, looking up as next period's tech theater students began to file in. This was Tech 3 and 4, which meant that there were five of them, that they were all best friends, and that they didn't need any direction from me to occupy themselves productively. "Of course I'll be there, Lena. And with cake, too." It was a cousin's gender reveal, so, you know. There were no circumstances under which Lena would show up alone. This was our cousin's first baby, for starters, and also the word around the rumor mill was that she'd invited upwards of eighty people. It seemed like one of those things that would just insist on being overwhelming from every possible angle.

"Excellent. I'll see you there. Unless you need a ride?"

She was the world's worst driver so, no.

"Thanks, but I'm good. No need to add a half an hour to your commute."

"Okay." Somebody started shouting about probate on her end.

"Got to go," she said, sighing. "This guardianship doesn't know the meaning of lunch break."

"Yikes."

"And Bea," she said, her shoes click-clacking in the background, "you could always grade them on a curve. I've never been so humbled."

I imagined Katy Herkle's mother would love that.

"I'm not sure my seniors could survive that much cortisol. They're sensitive little bees."

"Hmm." She hung up. She wasn't one of those "good bye" or "I love you" sorts of people.

"Pete," I called, beckoning over the six-foot-one sixteen-year-old who had, without prompting, begun sketching the set design for that fall's play. We hadn't even picked the play yet. "Come here a minute." He walked over. It took him two steps to do so. "Pete, I hear you're no stranger to a good prank." He tried not to look too proud of himself.

"I have a variety of skillsets that I can, upon occasion, make available to friends and family. For the right price, anyway." I refrained from asking nobody in particular what the kids were watching, these days. "What's up?"

"I need a proportionate response to this," I said, holding out my phone and playing him my new phone alert. My whispered name filled the room, eerily raspy and pitched just low enough to evade identification. Chris and Nathaniel looked up, then, our conversation officially more interesting than the sound equipment they were stalking on eBay.

Pete took my phone and held it to his ear, letting the alert play over and over and over again. I couldn't tell if he was doing it for dramatic effect or if this really was part of his creative process. He walked away with my phone, then, and sat down in what was now an exhaustive circle of his peers. Lu and Lex had wandered over, fifteen seconds ago, only too prepared to start an all-out prank war with the "Dramatics," as they called them.

"Give us an hour," he finally said, pulling out his sketchbook. This was beginning to feel about a thousand degrees more ominous than I'd intended. I smiled. All's fair, and all that jazz.

Chapter Five

I was halfway to the parking lot and all the way through planning my takeout dinner order when I remembered that I was supposed to be picking up my mentee from the teacher's lounge. I cried a little, kissed my imaginary pho good-bye, and rushed back into the school.

"Oh, Bea," Stacy called as I passed D Hall. She left the science corridor and jogged to catch up. "I was just about to text you. Diana told me you'd also signed up for the mentorship program, but then I saw you leaving, and—" she sneezed, then, which I was pretty sure she deserved. Nobody got to be that energetic and happy without a few environmental repercussions. Balance is key to a well-running universe. So They say.

"Yes, well."

She actually waited for me to go on. I supposed she was the sort of person who gave excuses the benefit of the doubt. She never made them, after all, unless they were actively hospitalizing her or a loved one. In my memory, she'd only ever missed three days of school. All three of those days had been spent tending to her sick, grape-eating dog.

"Feeling good about this year?" I asked. It was that or begin a three-minute lamentation about the lack of fried shallots in my life.

"Oh, excellent, excellent," she said, bouncing up the stairs beside me. I briefly considered tripping her. "They split the students into three bio classes, this year. Last year it was just two thirty-student sections, which was difficult when it came around to doing labs. There's only so much equipment, you know. This way, everyone fits at the tables. Scalpels only have to be shared amongst groups of three, instead of six or seven." I couldn't see how a lower scalpel-to-adolescent ratio was anybody's preferred outcome. Then again, Stacy did drink wheatgrass every morning.

"How many new teachers do we have, this year?" I asked, stepping out of the way of a group of girls rushing off to band practice. I barely evaded getting impaled on an oboe case. Them corners be sharp. I internally scowled, remembering that another year of school meant another year of working with Mr. Sunderson, the band director. Goddess, I hated him. Just, ugh.

43

"I think twelve," Stacy said. Which meant there were twelve. "Six teachers retired last year, three moved, and Diana decided to afford three more. Margaret now has a co-teacher." I did a little dance for Margaret, then and there. That poor saint of a woman had been requesting help the entire time I'd been here. She ran the Essential Academics program and had one aid for twenty students, which I'm pretty sure wasn't even legal.

We turned a corner and were hit with the smell of burnt coffee and leftover donuts. We reached the teacher's lounge a second later.

"Well," Stacy said, holding the door open for me, "this will be fun." She really meant it, too.

Not all places feel the same, in this life. Some hold no meaning to us, for starters. We haven't lived in them, loved in them, breathed in them. The corners aren't filled with our memories and the floors aren't filled with our footprints.

But then, there are some places that we've never even been to that feel immediately like home. Thin places, places where the material reality separating this life from all lives is threadbare, where you can breathe in and out and share breath with whatever eternity is just past the tips of your fingers.

And then there are haunted places, places that have known so many tortured souls that they have begun to see themselves as the torturer. People have become trapped, in these places, have poured their blood into the floorboards and their tears into the laminated countertops. They have invested themselves so wholly into their miserable geography that they are the place. That the place is them. Thin places eschew time, perhaps, but haunted places collapse time. They hold their pasts, presents, and futures together in their strange, suffocating grip. Poltergeists beget poltergeists, you know. They don't like being left alone in their own hauntings.

The teacher's lounge is all three of these places, and all at once. It is a lived-in space, filled with so much of a teacher's life that it feels familiar and safe. Ick.

It is a thin place, too, in the weirdest of ways. I blame the fact that high schools are places of transition, of children overflowing with all of their potential futures. It's not our fault some of the rooms are on the liminal side of things.

The teacher's lounge is also haunted. I feel like that doesn't need further explanation.

Point being, I stepped into the teacher's lounge, that afternoon, and was hit with the familiar sense of dread and homecoming, security and possibility, life and death, death and life. And before you say anything about melodrama, I will remind you that you did sign up for a story narrated by a high school theater teacher, so. You know.

The rubber, blue-speckled floors still shone with their summer wax. Five circular tables stood mostly empty, at present, except for the fresh bouquets Stacy and Cassandra, the office assistant, had handpicked and arranged early that morning. The room didn't yet smell like that one forgotten Tupperware of miscellaneous lunch and the people didn't yet feel like sleep-deprived hyenas. The vinyl green loveseat sat under the windowsill, sagging as always, and the rack of purple mats we'd stolen from the elementary school when the principal abolished nap time still stood shoved against the wall beside the microwave. The mats were neatly ordered and crisply rolled, which wouldn't last long. You'd better believe we used those suckers. A box of half eaten donuts and a pot of fresh coffee were the only things adorning the countertop beside the shared fridge. That countertop was the only thing that stayed tidy, as anything put on it was fair game and the only people more desperate for free snacks than high schoolers were their teachers.

"Bea?"

I wondered how many times Diana had said my name before I came to.

"Hmm?"

"I said, good afternoon, Bea."

Stacy had already abandoned me, off talking to some twenty-two-year-old blonde who looked too happy to be alive. I grinned, wondering how long it would take them to start matching outfits on accident. Or, better yet, on purpose. There were a few other pairs chatting over coffee, but I assumed most of the mentors had whisked their novices off as quickly as they could. Fifteen bucks can almost cover two beers, after all. Carpe diem.

"Yeah, yeah. Where's this English teacher I've been promised."

"Oh. Um." Diana wouldn't make eye contact with me. "She's…decided teaching isn't for her."

"No kidding? How many periods in?"

"Um. Two."

If I'm being completely honest, I can't remember the last time I'd heard of a teacher who quit after the first day. The first week? Absolutely. First month? Sometimes. The first year? They can't abscond fast enough. But the first *day*? *What*?

"That's not going to count against my mentor stats, right?" I asked. Diana gave me what I assumed authors mean when they write "withering glare."

"So you're saying I'm free to go," I said, tugging at my backpack strap. I'd never made the transition to whatever it is people use when they

47

don't use backpacks. It'd just been me and Gilbert, these past twelve years, and I didn't see why that ever had to change. Except the right backpack strap did have a tendency of coming undone, as it was now, and was more mended thread than original material, by this point.

"Absolutely not," Diana barked. And then, remembering that I wasn't an adolescent trying to break school rules, a quieter, "no, that won't be necessary. We were a few mentors short, anyway." She looked at her clipboard. "He's not here yet. I don't think bus duty has ended—" the door opened behind me and I knew my pho-starved fate had been sealed.

"Sorry I'm late," someone said from behind me. Someone who sounded familiar, of course, because, of course. I turned around, my stomach twitching, and stared at my newest colleague.

Fuck.

"Glad you could make it!" Diana said, checking off what turned out to be the last name on her list. "Hedi, this is Beatrice Suré, our Theater Arts teacher. Bea, this is Hedi Dictine, Margaret's salvation. Her words, not mine."

He looked as surprised as I felt. He wasn't feeling his surprise the same, though. He was grinning, for starters, and his stupid eyes were glittering in the fluorescent light of our thrice-haunted lounge. I wondered what my face looked like. Somewhere between "flabbergasted" and "fuuuuuuck," based off of the way his grin kept growing.

"Well, that's everyone accounted for," Diana said, "I'm off. Don't forget to keep your receipts, people." And without another word—without so much as a "yes, you've been entrapped, time for me to go have wine with my wife and laugh at all of you suckers"—she abandoned us to our fates.

Rare are the moments when I've lost all my words. They do happen, though. Now was one of those times. It's not every day your boss starts a mentorship program and matches you with the only man on staff who's seen your boobs. Which is, perhaps, the best argument against hook-up culture I have yet encountered.

Hedi just stood there, politely, patiently, waiting for me to feel all of my feelings. We both moved to the side as Stacy and her mini-me skipped through the door, off to run a 5k together. Not before Stacy introduced herself to Hedi, though, and introduced us all to Anita. And then it was just us and two people I vaguely thought worked in the foreign language department.

"You moved for a *teaching* job?" I finally managed. He shrugged, still smiling, as he stared at the nap mats.

"No. I moved because I needed to be closer to family."

"You're a teacher."

"According to my I-9." He finally looked away from the mats, his face having fallen somewhere between "thoughtful" and "damn oh damn I am so tired, damn." "Thank goodness for national teacher shortages. Makes getting jobs in new places pretty straightforward."

"Mmhmm." He could speak for himself. I had to fight for my stage. "So you're a teacher."

"I think we've already covered that one."

Part of me was still panicking. I felt weirdly exposed—like, nakedly exposed—in my place of employment. Part of me was a little miffed that he was hotter than I remembered him being. I mean, that hardly seemed fair. And part of me was a little bit pleased with myself. I'd started questioning myself, in the days following "The Incident," and was glad to see that I hadn't actually been willing to crawl into bed with just anybody. He certainly wasn't just anybody. Not with that hair and that... face. And those eyes. Those eyes that had gone back to laughing at me.

"I don't remember you being this quiet," he said, brow raised, lips twitching back up, up, up.

"Ex*cuse* me," I huffed, pulling at my backpack's strap.

"Oh, sorry, we're pretending nothing happened. I can do that, too."

I decided it was time to start drinking fifteen dollars worth of beer.

"Well, first of all, nothing *did* happen," I said.

"You wound."

"Second," I said, holding out my arm, gesturing for him to lead the way out of the door. He didn't get the memo. When he continued to just stand there, I asked, "sorry, but, did you want to stay here?"

"Oh, you were going to follow through with this? I sort of assumed…" he trailed off at whatever it was my face must have been doing.

"I am no *quitter,*" I managed, raging, furious, spitting mad, a true hellcat, through and through, "and am a *professional,* mores the point, and third, will have to sit on *another* committee if I don't participate in this program."

"I won't tell if you don't."

"And, fourthly," I said, bringing up my hand to belatedly tick off these excellent points of mine, "I am no *liar.*"

"Ah." He glanced through the doorway and into the dark hall beyond. "Well, I don't know. I've already made so many new friends, today. Not sure I need another one."

I pretended like I wasn't about to drown in shame.

"I'm sorry about that," I said, walking out of the lounge. "I was an asshole, you were a perfect gentleman, and that was a bad night."

"So the thing that happened was both nothing and bad."

"Are you coming or not?"

"Can nothing even be bad?"

I turned to face him. He was leaning against the doorframe, his shirtsleeves rolled up, his tie slightly loosened. I pretended like it wasn't the most attractive thing I'd seen in months. I pretended like I didn't want to run my fingers under his suspenders. Because of course he was wearing suspenders.

"Obviously nothing can be bad. If you worked for something but got nothing then you'd say that was a bad turn. It'd be bad."

"I wouldn't say I got *nothing,*" he mused, brushing his fingers through his hair. I tried not to blush. Funnily enough, blushes don't seem to care too much about wills and wants. "Oh, sorry, is that the sort of thing I'm not supposed to say? What are the rules, again? I believe I cut you off at 'second.'"

It took me a moment to catch up with his train of thought.

"I can't remember the second," I said, beckoning him forward. "Now, either jilt me or join me, but I'm leaving. School's out, we aren't rehearsing anything, and I ate my lunch at 10:45."

"Lead the way," he said, finally stepping into the hall. I felt something loosen in my chest. Which was funny, because some other places were getting all sorts of knotted in all sorts of ways. "You're the mentor."

"And don't you forget it."

"Oh, also, did you want your bra back?"

Chapter Six

They told me "pick a place under the sun"
"Pick?" I asked, "from what? Places I have none."
"Because you won't pick one," they said, voice tight
they say lots of things. Some are bound to be right.

—the words of the hawk who had wheeled
the world, around, around, and wandered whether
he'd ever find himself a home again.

"Brilliant," I said, putting the paper down, "I think somebody miscounted the feet in that last line, though." I hoped they decided to stick to prose for all future installations.

"What?" Sophia shrieked, ripping the paper from my hand and utterly outing herself. Belen snickered.

"But did you read the story underneath?" Hugo asked. "We were trying out a verse overview and a prose...uh, view, I guess?" He frowned. I turned to Noel, leaving Hugo to contemplate the various opposites of "overviews." "So what's the dirt on that new English teacher?"

"Ms. *Suré,*" Noel coughed, choking on the swig of coffee she'd just thrown back.

"Anybody ever tell you kids shouldn't drink that much coffee?"

"Anybody ever tell you kids shouldn't be pressured into gossiping?" Belen tossed back.

"Says who?"

Belen rolled her eyes. That was her go-to when she couldn't think of anything else to say.

"Says the people who also think it's a bad idea for employees to use their positions of power to pressure underlings into doing things they wouldn't otherwise feel comfortable doing," Angela piped up. She was sitting at an actual desk—most everyone else had elected to strew bean bags about in the desk-free portion at the back of the classroom —and was doing the actual assignment. Which was combing through the online library of plays and flagging every one she thought we might be interested in doing.

"What she said," Belen agreed, staring at Angela's back. She had a look on her face that, quite frankly, I'd never seen there before. Not even on stage. Which really says a lot, because I'd been clinically evaluating this girl's every expression for going on four years, by this point, and had really thought I'd seen them all. It was something between scrutiny, perhaps. Interest. Jealousy? Curiosity. I don't know. It wasn't a soft look. Wasn't a hard look, either. Wasn't—

Belen noticed me noticing her and looked away. I catalogued her expression and decided I'd circle back, if it came up again.

"Why do you want to know about Ms. Brown?" Claudia asked, scribbling notes about *Paganini* across her legal pad and only half paying attention to her surroundings. "She seems nice enough. She seems way better than Mr. Naem, anyway." Mr. Naem, one of our English 2 teachers, hated kids. He also hated reading, but that seemed somehow less relevant. You know its bad when "hates reading" isn't an English teacher's biggest problem.

"Oh, sweet Claudia," Hugo said, patting her on the hand, "you don't know, do you." Claudia looked up from the stack of plays she'd been flipping through, her eyes slightly crossed.

"What?"

"She quit, my little cygnet," he said, squeezing her fingers. I wondered if he'd ever bothered explaining his nickname for her to her. I'd only gotten there after some phonetic wrangling and google voice-to-texts. "She's already left us."

Claudia actually looked upset. She looked up at me, her recently elongated limbs poking out from the hot pink bean bag at awkward, adolescent angles.

"But why?" She asked. I mustered every ounce of drama I possessed—well, not really, we'll put it at forty percent—and turned to face Belen.

"That's what I was *trying* to find *out*," I said. "Before being so *rudely* accused of abusing my authority."

Angela twisted in her chair, her dark cloud of curls exaggerating her every movement. She watched me. Her expression *was* soft, though.

"Abuse is such a strong word," she said. She was one of those quiet talkers. Like, even when she was projecting loud enough for an entire auditorium to hear her, her voice seemed no harsher than a murmur. Paul and I tried not to type cast her as every manic pixie we ever needed but, well. She'd played her fair share of Ramona Flowers, is all I'm saying.

Belen actively didn't look at her, this time. Like, too actively. Like, actively enough for me to think maybe I knew a thing or two, after all.

"It is," I said, frowning at the title Hugo had just starred. Did he even know what *August: Osage County* was about? "And words only have the meaning we give them. Best not divest the mean

57

ones of their matter." See. I taught things. "Now, about this English teacher."

"But why would she quit?" Claudia asked, her eyes a little too wide, a little too panicked. She loved reading. She loved school. Mr. Naem had made her question all of that. We were all pretty sure she couldn't do a repeat of a Mr. Naem.

"She walked out after second period," Sophia said, "though it really wasn't anything dramatic, Ms. Suré. Why do you care?"

"Ouch," I said, swiveling to face Sophia, who had, apparently, recovered from her metric mishap. She sat wedged between two bookcases and was doing her absolute best to look like she wasn't working on next period's math homework.

"It's just, you did go on and on, this summer, about how we shouldn't pester you for teacher tea," Hugo said, filling in the blanks for me. "This feels a little…" he refrained from calling me a hypocrite, at least.

To be fair, I had been legally obligated to keep my mouth shut, this past year, as the drama Hugo was referring to had involved police, two lawsuits, and an ex-vice principal who was no longer allowed within one hundred feet of any school building, and most certainly not this one. It turns out not all school administrators have scruples about embezzling tens of thousands of dollars from the school district.

What none of us teachers had realized, of course, was that none of our students would jump to "embezzling" as the alleged crime. All they knew was that he'd been arrested, one night—a story that the sophomore who lived across the street from him and saw the whole thing probably told two hundred times, by the end of May—and fired the next day. I don't know why us employees hadn't realized the children were all going to assume it had been for a sex crime. Alas, they'd spent the better part of the summer trying to figure out who he'd been abusing and why the school wasn't saying anything about it.

Oops.

Regardless, when the state finally held his preliminary hearing, students attended en masse. When they realized we'd kept them in the dark for months over an embezzling scheme, they'd been… well, upset doesn't quite capture it. Irritated? Vindictive.

"Right," I said, sighing, sitting back in my chair and wondering what I had done to deserve such principled children.

"So she's not coming back?" Claudia asked, her eyes a little misty.

"Don't worry. Mimi told me that sub who's always passing out candy is covering until they find a permanent replacement."

"Oh," Claudia said, immediately brightening up. "The one who filled in when Ms. Ba had her baby?"

"I think?"

"That's fine, I guess." And so it was. I guess.

"But what *happened*—"

Belen grinned at me. It was a wicked little thing.

"Ms. Suré, we don't get to know everything we want to know."

I had, of course, said that exact thing approximately three weeks ago.

"Life is about learning to live in the mystery."

I hated teenagers.

"So you don't know, is what you're saying," I sighed, sitting back in my chair and reading Hugo's list of plays over his shoulder. The boy was in a mood, apparently. I supposed they always were.

"It really wasn't that big of a deal," Sophia called from her crevice, more than willing to rise to the challenge. "A student was hurrying past her desk to grab a tissue—nosebleed, have you met Meg? She always gets them—anyway, she tripped over the teacher's purse and a bunch of things fell

out. Of the purse, I mean. Apparently Ms. Brown
carries her vibrator around wherever she goes."

How the *fuck* was Sophia old enough to
know what that was.

"Oh." Garland damned, I would have left
and never looked back, too. "Well. That would do
it." Half of the students were blushing. Half were
snickering. Belen was glaring at Sophia, who was
too busy trying to make geometry work to notice.

"Turns out it's not a closed shop after all," I
said to the senior, miming the "there, there" pat with
my hand. "Makes it hard to hold the picket line."
Belen rolled her eyes a third time. Because she had
been too good of a student in Ms. Faye's APUSH
class and knew full well that that had been an
excellent union joke. Was how I interpreted the
look, anyway.

"Ms. Suré," Angela asked, frowning,
tugging idly on a curl. "You can't get fired for that,
right?"

"Well," I said, adding yet another thing to
the ever-running "things I didn't know I'd need to
know" list. "I guess it depends." We did live in the
great state of California. You know, the one where
sex education actually existed. "I don't think she
would have." I wished briefly that she'd have made
it through the day. I wondered if I could have talked
her down from quitting, had she shown up for our

61

first mentorship meeting. Which, of course, had me thinking about Hedi, which, of course, had me squirming up a storm.

"Ms. Suré," Angela asked, her eyes lost somewhere in the middle distance. I mean, there was a reason she kept getting typecast. "You would never quit, right?"

"Don't be ridiculous," Hugo sniffed, starring his fifth "depression in the midwest" play. "We would literally die. She would never condemn us to such a fate." His sharp little cheekbones cut actual holes in the air as he snapped his head around to look up at me. "She would *never.* Do. That," he said again. "Death. Literal death."

"While you know that I do live for these little compliments," I said, rearranging some papers on my desk and otherwise avoiding eye contact— no, it never does get easier to take compliments, no matter how melodramatic of a package they arrive in—"I really need you to stop threatening death, Hugo. There needs to be a few steps between 'everything's fine' and 'the most final thing.' You know?"

"Speak for yourself," Hugo sniffed again, his eyes falling back to his list of plays, "Some of us can't escape our extremes."

"Which is why we won't be doing *that* one,*" I said, pulling the pages from his binder and deciding to just go ahead and suspend his suggesting privileges. "We don't do plays with suicide, Hugo."

"What would it take for you to quit?" Belen asked, apropos of nothing. I gave her a flat stare.

"I thought you enjoyed this class?" I asked, deciding that providing her with the itemized list of every time I'd ever almost quit wasn't actually what she wanted, in this moment.

"I do!" She hurried, the surprise on her face genuine. "That's not—I didn't mean—"

She was saved by the bell.

"I want everybody's top three play suggestions tomorrow," I said. "Be prepared to pitch them to the class. Rehearsals start next week, people. Area is in a month." Some people ran out—Sophia's class was on the other side of campus—and some people meandered on by, waving, asking a few follow-up questions on their way. Belen stayed behind, though. She had newspaper, next, and the students had long ago decided that Coach Roberts and I were telekinetically connected. They assumed I could mentally ring her up and tell her I had the student she was looking for.

"Is everything all right?" I asked. If she had been more than a teenager I would have said something more along the lines of "who pissed in your peanuts this morning," but, well. She was

63

seventeen. I was thirty-one. Children be moody, is all I'm saying, and I be very much under multiple legal obligations to not verbally abuse them.

"Why haven't you read the story, yet?"

I would have spat coffee had I been drinking any, just then.

"This is about the *newspaper* project?" And here I thought her cat had died.

"Well, everybody *is* still mad about Vice Principal Rodgers," She said, tucking a stray hair back under her headband. "You not talking about it didn't make the whole thing more appropriate. It just made it more confusing."

"That, my darling Belen, should be on one of these school posters," I said, scanning my walls for an opening.

"But that's not... I mean, I didn't mean to be...whatever, or anything." I wondered if I'd have to have fewer of these conversations if I were a math teacher. I was pretty sure students never bothered to explain their attitudes to Yvonne. "We're working really hard on this, I guess. Not saying it shows, or anything."

"Stop self-deprecating. Continue with your story."

"Right. Okay. Well, so we're working really hard on this, and I'm having...so much fun, actually. But it's also...like... I feel like I'm running around the school naked, or something. I didn't even feel this exposed when I had to kiss Gabriel during *Into the Woods.* And that was...like, actually in front of people." And Gabriel was, like, actually hot, was what she didn't say. She and Hugo had smacked about a dozen times on stage, too, but the boy had song-and-danced his way out of the closet when he was eight and kissing him...well, it probably was never as intimidating as kissing the heterosexual, took-his-team-to-nationals-in-fencing senior. Which she'd never thanked me for, by the way.

"Makes perfect sense to me," I said, trying not to think about how Hedi had walked into the teacher's lounge before school, that morning, and I'd immediately checked my shirt to make sure it was still on. "What you're doing *is* good, Belen," I went on, making a mental note to start collecting the paper first thing in the morning so that I could have positive feedback ready to go by the time first period came around. "And this is going to feel different than acting. It's a different sort of stage. You're used to using other peoples' words to tell a story. Same in newspaper, probably. You get to write what you think, of course, but you center each piece around interviews with other people. In this," I said, gesturing towards the newspaper on my desk, "it's just you. Even though you're still, you know, cowering behind anonymity." She rolled her eyes for a billionth time. "You've never put your own words to the test, before. And our words, well. They do come from those intimate places, don't they."

Belen looked like she wanted to either dismiss me for being so ridiculously intense, mock me for being such an absolute bleeding heart, or maybe, just maybe, take notes. I got that look a lot.

"Yeah," was what she finally said. "Yeah, they do. It's weird."

Ah, the eloquence of youth.

"Are your classmates talking about it?"

"You really haven't read it, have you."

"What?" What did that mean?

"I think Mr. Holson's seniors, at least, are getting into it. Which is pretty fun. Three different people asked if they could submit installments."

I suddenly very much regretted not having finished the piece. Installments?

"But nobody's complimented the style, yet. It's like they don't know how hard it is—"

"Out," I said, pointing towards the door.

"What? Ms. Suré—"

"Here I was, thinking you'd been ridiculed for your art. But no, you just haven't received the right sort of *praise,* I can*not*—"

She was grinning. She was, study habits aside, the best prima donna I'd ever had.

"Ms. Suré, I thought we were having a moment."

"I"m going to tell Coach Roberts you left my room an hour ago."

She waved the comment away, knowing it for the non-threat that it was.

"Of course," she said, zipping her binder into her backpack. "Please also tell her that I like her class way better, while you're at it."

"Ungrateful wretch."

Belen almost began leaving the room, too. She stalled, though, and got stuck. Kind of like when I say I like cliff jumping, get all the way up to the top, and realize I have no idea how to talk myself into stepping off the ledge.

"Yes?" I asked, refraining from reaching for the school's paper.

"I was wondering…" she let it hang, though. It brought me all the way back to that cliff, staring down at the waves, thirty feet below, a single swimmer shouting up that it was perfectly safe.

"Yes?" I prompted, putting my "perfectly serious and incredibly empathetic" face all the way on.

"Nothing," she murmured, backing away. "I just…nothing, I guess." She turned to go.

"Belen," I called, feeling like, yet again, I knew a thing or two about these children. She

67

paused, her eyes on her toes. And then she did look up. Because she was the Prima Donna, and the Prima Donna does not look at her toes. "Belen, if you ever want to talk about anything, you know that I'm here, right?"

She nodded.

"I do, Ms. Suré," she said. "Thank you."

Chapter Seven

As we said, dear reader, there was a queen, once. She'd been taken by a mighty warlock and locked within his tower. Why? Excellent question. First, because warlocks are evil and more or less constitutionally predisposed to locking people away. Don't ask us why. It's just sort of their thing. Second, because he wanted this queen's kingdom. It had some excellent coastal properties and the best gooseberry jam you've never had. That, and some of the strongest lay lines known to their world. If you don't know what a lay line is, don't worry. A recent school survey indicated that fifty percent of the student body has played a D&D campaign in the past year. So, make a friend, ask your questions, and know that this warlock was looking for some easy magic.

The warlock took the queen years before the start of this particular tale. He locked her in his enchanted tower and vowed to release her only once she'd named him heir to her throne. She refused. He entrenched. They circled each other, day and night, waiting, watching, wondering when the other's will would waver. They never did.

Fifty years passed—yes, fifty—and the warlock was dismayed to discover that the queen had some power of her own. She never aged, he saw, never wrinkled, never grayed, never bent so much as an inch under the weight of time.

"For what do you live?" He sneered, one day. "For whom do you cling to life?"

"Myself, thank you very much," the queen sniffed, "and maybe look in the mirror, once in a while. Pretty sure the only reason you've clung to immortality is the big 'ol Y-O-U."

Warlock hissed—he was at his wit's end, after all, which is a place sparsely populated with words—and jumped from the tower. Unfortunately for the queen, he had dissolved into shadow and night before hitting the ground. He was off, then, to check in on his other warlocky machinations. The queen wondered how many towers the man had. For he was just a man, she had decided, and nothing more.

She watched the sunlight slide through the window and told herself it was about three in the afternoon. She knew she had roughly two days of alone time, when Warlock left, and didn't want to waste a second.

"Time for a nap," she said, smiling, taking herself off to bed. She never slept as well, when he was there, and liked to get in a good twenty or so hours when he absconded.

She opened her door, ready to zzz, and froze. On her pillow lay a hawk. A giant, gasping hawk, its breast red with blood. She frowned. Never in all these fifty years had anyone other than herself or Warlock been in or out of this tower. She hadn't thought it was possible.

"Please, mistress," the hawk wheezed—yes, it's a talking hawk, that's super normal in stories like this—"please help me. I have been mightily wounded, I think, and cannot seem to fix it on my own. Please."

The queen frowned from window to pillow to hawk and back, wondering if this was trick or true.

"Troubled hawk," she began . . .

....

That's it, for now! But don't worry, the next installment will come out in next week's paper! Meanwhile, we want to know what you think! Is the hawk a trick or true? Cut out this section of the paper, circle your answer, and leave it in the comment's box beside room 241. While you're at it,

71

"Fascinating," I said, looking up from *We The People*. Because of course the OG newspaper students hadn't wanted to work anything related to the *school* into the title, like it's name or mascot or, I don't know, school colors. Those students had been way before my time, though, and I could only guess at their particular disdain of Señora Diablo, our school's horse mascot. I had once asked my students what was wrong with the horse. They asked me why the devil had to be a lady. And, furthermore, why students had to be represented by the devil. I asked them why they didn't want to have fun with that. They asked me why I was a pagan gender essentialist.

Needless to say, we hadn't gotten much work done during that particular class day.

"Are people writing in?" I asked Maya. That is, Coach Roberts. That is, my work best friend. I'd gone to her classroom after the last bell had rung and we'd both just sort of gotten stuck. Which was fine by me, of course. The newspaper room was half windows, smelled like freshly printed paper—I wonder why—and had three ergonomic chairs. I don't know how she'd pulled that off. I think maybe Maya had a cousin who made chairs, or something.

"You wouldn't believe it," she said, pointing towards a cardboard box full of paper slips. Some had been torn, some had been cut, some hadn't even been taken from the newspaper. "They've gotten more 'reader responses' in the past day than most of them have in their entire time here."

"More than the dress code poll?"

"More than the dress code poll," Mara affirmed. We both briefly remembered that time, three years ago, when newspaper seniors had asked the AFAB population to write in about all the times they'd been dress coded. The series of pieces they'd produced, after, had caused a minor sensation.

Maya was a tall Black woman with muscles for days and the sort of rare smile that made you work twelve times harder to get one out of her. I'd exercised with her once. It was all I'd ever needed to simultaneously understand the draw of BDSM and to know that it would never be for me. We started working for Clayton High the same year, sat beside each other during the one-day new teacher training, and been best "work" friends ever since. We put the "work" in quotes because that was what we called each other for about two years before both of us realized that we didn't have a life outside of work and that we were actually just each other's best normal friends, too, which led to, like, a month-long spiral on the nature of life and where it's lived and why it's full of all these little human-made boxes. I'll let you work out the balance on who was doing most of the spiraling.

"Do you know where they're going with it?" I asked, pulling the comments box towards me. "A pink hawk?" I asked, cackling, reading the first slip I saw. Maya nodded.

"Oh, there are some fun ones, in there. And I don't know where they're going with it. They just told me they were revising the epic *Yonec* and that they'd keep it PG-13. I told them I didn't care what rating the Motion Picture Association would give it, I still had to read it in advance. I don't know what sort of smut they think they're trying to sneak in there but they sure didn't want my censorship. What a bunch of dorks."

I smiled, reading through the slips. People had crammed quite a bit more than just "true," "trick," and "lime green" into the space left by the journalism students. Entire arcs had been scribbled between the printed lines.

"This is so fun," I said. "It's like AO3. But for a grade. And not porn."

"Yet," Maya muttered, staring at the giant stack of papers she apparently already had to grade. For the fifteenth time that hour, I remembered how much I loved my job. Monologues were so much easier to grade than freshman reviews of *Atlantic* articles.

"How much fun they're having with this makes me think they haven't *found* AO3 yet."

"That would be shocking," I said, looking up from a ripped corner of notebook paper calling for an enemies-to-lovers plot line. "These are full-blown internet babies."

"I know, I know. But they've got their own dank corners of the web to worm through. I hate to say it, Bea, but I think AO3…it might be an old people thing."

I collapsed onto the floor. The absolute agony.

"Hey," Maya said, staring out the window, "have your students been asking about Jim?" Jim was aforementioned ex-VP and had, as previously demonstrated, appeared several times in that day's conversations.

"Yeah," I said, pulling myself back into Ergonomic Chair, no. 2. "Did your students also think it was a sex thing?"

"Super duper did."

"Yikes."

"I think maybe we should ask Diana if we can… oh, I don't know, work around the gag rule,"

Maya said, checking her watch. "Are you hungry? I think I might actually be dying."

I tossed her a Lara Bar—the superior bar, through and through, and I won't hear a word otherwise—and stood.

"How do you feel about pho?"

"Pho-ntastic," she said, smiling, standing as well. And standing well, I would like to add. The woman had perfect posture.

I snapped three times—food based puns were one of the higher forms of humor, after all, and deserved the full triple—and waited as she locked up behind us.

"So tell me about the newbs," she said, walking at a pace that belied her frame. Slowly, I mean, and without any sense of having a place to be. It had been the strangest thing about her, for a while. I mean, I'd seen her sprint up and down the court with her players. I'd seen her jump up and down during a particularly animated geometry lesson. I'd also seen her box—don't ask, it was a weird phase that neither of us talk about—and knew her footwork could be, in a word, swift. But walking? Not a care in the world.

"Oh," I said, thinking that I'd rather not. "I take it you heard about the vibrator?"

"Who hasn't."

"Your precious students wouldn't let me in on that one, by the way."

"Yeah, me neither. They're really intent on this high horse of theirs. I had to get it out of Elena." Ms. Faye. "Can't say I've ever carried a rabbit around in my purse."

"It was a *rabbit?*"

"Oh my gosh, same. I realize there's, like, a whole bunch of other things going on with that… episode, or whatever, but I can't stop thinking about the fact that it was a rabbit? What is that about?"

"Gosh."

"Gosh." We both sighed. We'd finally made it to the end of the building and had just stepped into the sweltering heat of a late August parking lot.

"But I want to hear about the *other* ones, Bea. Should I be going out of my way to walk through any particular halls?" She wasn't as cloistered as me—her Newspaper room was on the second floor, after all, and surrounded by English classrooms. But she didn't sit on as many committees—teaching two classes and coaching a third comes with certain perks—and she tended to use her lunchtime for naps.

"Pin it," I said, arriving at my car. "Unless you want to carpool?" She shook her head.

"So they seem fine," I said, unpinning our conversation about twelve minutes later. We were sitting in our corner booth at the very back of *Curry On*. The whole restaurant was "keep calm" posters with various "ands" attached. The menu came with an explanation of the relationship between the curries they served and the British imperialism that brought them to us. We always ordered off of the Vietnamese side. I didn't know if it was because their vermicelli was frickin good or if it was because I didn't want to be confused for an imperialist shill.

"There's two new world history teachers," I said, giving the seven-page menu a once-over before deciding I was indeed going to get the same thing I always got. "One of them has an accent, too."

Maya peaked up from her menu. She ordered the same thing every time, too, but was less committed to the efficiency of consistency. She liked to peruse, is what I mean. I think it was her way of warming up for the meal.

"Accent, you say?" She asked, the nonchalance dialed up by about ten. "What sort of accent?"

"I thought you'd sworn off dating teachers."

"Um, Bea, who said anything about dating? Am I not allowed to ask innocently after the international origins of a new colleague? What if they need help settling into our Californian ways?"

"It was a Canadian sort of accent," I said, trying to keep a straight face. Maya tried to keep a straight face, too. She did the nose flair-wiggle and everything.

"Ugh," she said, her face melting into utter disappointment, "you are the absolute worst."

"I do believe you mean 'you are the absolute worst, eh.'" She threw a chopstick at me. I didn't duck. There was a sweet-seeming elderly couple, behind us, and if I didn't take the blow it would hit the nice lady right in the scarf-wrapped head.

I didn't bother telling Maya that Mr. Abeni Alfie, the twenty-three year old golden retriever from Harvard Diana had just hired, was Canadian by way of Nigeria. I'm not saying Maya has a type, but, well. She absolutely has a type. It was a longer game, this way, but the payoff—which would hopefully involve me being a wallflower the day she randomly ran into the new hire after some passing period bathroom break—would be so much sweeter. I would be able see her short-circuit in real time and everything.

"So who'd you get paired with?" She asked, finally putting her menu down.

"The new special education teacher," I said, reminding myself not to look away, twitch, or otherwise show weakness. It didn't work. She squinted at me.

"Were they...nice?" She asked, feeling me out.

"He was," I said.

"Cute?"

"Can't say I noticed."

She rolled her eyes.

"So, very." She sat back in her booth. "What's his name?"

"Mr. Dictine." She just stared at me, confused, trying to figure out what it was I was so obviously hiding. "Hedi Dictine."

The woman spewed water. I don't know why I hadn't waited for her to swallow, but, well. Hindsight is 20/20.

"Wow, Bea," she choked, cackling, her eyes watering, "wow, any reason in particular why that name would sound familiar?"

I, obviously, had told her about the failed date. I tell her about all the dates, actually, and she does the same. We also share our locations and make jokes about skin suits, so, you know. Just your stereotypical millennial daters trying not to die, out there.

"I *know*," I muttered, wiping water from my face, "I mean, what are the *odds*?"

"Did you not ask him what he did for *work*?" She was still laugh-hacking up water. I hoped she drowned.

"I mean…" I mean, it hadn't been that long of an interview, if you know what I mean. "We didn't really get around to work before… moving the night along." It had just been one of those perfect storm sort of nights. I don't know why *he* was so willing, I guess, but I had been ovulating and lonely and he had been so incredibly beautiful. I mean, everything. Voice, hair, face, that joke about Sondheim, shoulders. Hips? I didn't know hips could be attractive, but, there we were. And—

"Oh, *God,* Bea," Maya interrupted my thoughts, "really? I'm not saying we're too old for hook-ups but for God's sake, at least do a *cursory* LinkedIn search."

"Wow, Maya," I said, suddenly very interested in my chopsticks' paper wrapper, "that sounds an awful lot like slut shaming." I couldn't even keep a straight face.

"Out. Of. Control," she muttered, flicking a sugar packet at me. It was just constant violence with this one. Witness me, Reader, and the abuses I have suffered at this woman's hands. "So he's hot enough to lure you back to his place without knowing whether or not he was gainfully employed but not hot enough to complete the seduction? How does that make sense?"

"Oh, he was hot enough for that, too. That one was one hundred percent a 'me thing,'" I muttered, straightening as the waiter came over. We ordered two bowls of the best pho you've never had —unless you've had pho with a peanut satay-inspired broth and perfectly fried triangles of tofu, in which case, am I right or am I right?—before Maya bore back down upon me.

"So like...did you give him a special welcome to Clayton High, or—"

"*MAYA I SWEAR TO TVEIT IF YOU FINISH—*"

The nice lady behind me actually shushed us. I decided I'd let the next chopstick fly true.

"But like... seeing him again," Maya stage whispered, staring daggers at the old fuckers, "did it make you... feel anything in particular? How royally did you foreclose any possibility of future shenanigans when you left, that night?"

I sighed. It was a long sigh. Three ages of men rose and fell during the course of that sigh.

"Very much completely, I fear," I said, "I feel like it's already been resold at auction, is how foreclosed I foreclosed it."

"Booo."

"I mean, not really. Can't go around fucking fellow teachers." Something about not screwing where you ate.

"Yeah. Just *almost* fucking *almost* teachers, apparently." She wasn't wrong.

"Besides, he was perfectly nice about it, yesterday. I don't think it was that big of a deal." I would say something like "only in the 21st Century could somebody claim that getting naked with a near stranger who turns out to be your new coworker wasn't a big deal" but I double majored in history, way back when, and am fully aware of the fact that casual orgies have happened in every century this good, green earth has ever known, so. There. Not a big deal.

"Oh? What did y'all do?" She was making "I don't believe you for a second and will milk this for all its salacious worth until you give me someone else to tease you about" eyes.

"Nothing, actually," I said, sighing again, watching forlornly as our waiter passed our table, tray laden with ambrosia and nectar, and served the ancient assholes behind us. "We were about to go get a beer but then his mother called. He rain-checked?" I had been sad by how sad I'd been, the day prior, when he'd looked up from his phone, eyes distracted, and told me he had to go. There had been a thirty second window where I thought it had been an excuse, too, before I had decided that he didn't strike me as the type to make excuses.

"Sorry…his…his mother?"

I nodded. "He moved across the country to be closer to her, I think. I didn't get the details—shut up—but I think she's pretty sick."

"Oh," Maya said, revising her seconds-old opinion that this stranger whom she'd never met was some sort of failure to launch. Which I was pretty sure we weren't allowed to say anymore, anyway. "Aww. Poor man. Poor mama, actually. That's so sad."

"Yeah." It was sad. I wondered If that mean old lady would split her meal with me. I felt positively faint with hunger. "What a way to start a year."

"I'm sure it feels more like a middle, when that's what's on your plate." Wow I really wished I had something on my plate. "You should follow up with him. Like, actually uncheck the raincheck. Or whatever it's called when you reconvene after rain has checked a thing."

I glanced at Maya, brow raised.

"I don't know how you got the newspaper gig."

"It wasn't 'got' so much as 'thrust into my unsuspecting lap.'"

Eww.

"Eww."

"Yeah, I regretted 'thrust' the moment I—oh thank god." Our food had arrived. We didn't breathe for ten full minutes. Which I actually kind of think is some sort of record.

Chapter Eight

When we were eight and ten, my little sister Lena started hoarding green legos. I didn't notice, at first. I'm not sure I actually ever would have, had someone else not pointed it out. I had never thought to mentally catalogue my building materials, for starters, and wasn't what one could call an "observant child." My lego forests simply started growing blue leaves and all of my lego dinosaurs became purple. I thought nothing of the fact that twenty-eight percent of our lego sets were suddenly missing.

When our parents found the box of green plastic toys under Lena's bed, they laughed for about ten seconds before realizing that that probably wasn't normal behavior. They asked her why she'd put them there. She'd told them it was because the yellows and greens weren't allowed to touch. They asked her why not, but she couldn't say. She'd started crying, though, and insisting. She'd lost it when my dad had started to put the greens back in with the rest—he'd stopped immediately, don't worry—and screamed that something bad would happen if they touched. My parents tried to ask her what bad thing would happen, but she couldn't answer that, either.

Point being, my sister was diagnosed with OCD when she was 8. She went on some of the worst drugs I've ever seen in action for a month before my mother screamed at the doctor that baby girls weren't supposed to flatline in corners all day, that her daughter wasn't better, just quieter, and how dare that doctor suggest the two were the same. Second point being, they found a new doctor. A child's psychiatrist, thankfully. The second cocktail worked and the fourth cocktail had her feeling better. Not normal—recall that normal, for her, was thinking that green touching yellow would introduce a miscellaneous plague into our household—but alive, happy, and well.

And so it was that I learned, from a young age, when it was and was not okay to insist on doing things "your own way." I learned how to calm my overstimulated sister down and how to cheer my overwhelmed parents up. I figured out when it was okay to take up space and when I needed to give mine to someone else. Not in a sad way. Just, a true way. And, against every fiber of my being, I learned how to use the damn spreadsheet. Because we love our fucking family, don't we, and our fucking family loves their fuckety fucking spreadsheets. In college, most people—at least, most people interested in self discovery—get excited to learn about things like star signs, Myers briggs scores, and enneagram numbers. My "aha" moment came when somebody explained to me that there was such a thing as a "type B" person. I actually cried. I had never felt so seen.

  Our father died from cancer right before Lena hit puberty. Things became unmanageable, for a while. Grief consumed us, of course, and then teenaged hormones flooded Lena's delicate ecosystem. Leaving the house became an impossible task. Lena's therapist recommended that we start breaking activities down into a spreadsheet. Don't ask me how. Don't ask me why. I mean, I could certainly explain the latter, but I don't really feel like #educating, right now, and am confident most answers can be found with a quick google. Anyway, my special snowflake family doesn't only have a family text thread but also a shared google sheets account. A google sheets account where I recently regained naming privileges, I might add. Which was why this Saturday's gender reveal party spreadsheet had been titled "We Really Don't Have To Go, See Contingency Plans in Cells C1-C8,

Doesn't The Aquarium Sound More Fun." I had checked the spreadsheet one last time before leaving and saw that Lena had left a title edit. I clicked on the box, curious as to what she might have said. "Don't forget the cake," it read.

"Jokes on you," I had muttered to my sheets app, "Marie doesn't even want cake."

I had called my cousin that Wednesday to make sure nobody had developed any gluten allergies since the Fourth of July—the last time I'd been tapped in to bake for a family shindig—and she had said our Tia Rosa was making the cake, actually, and did I mind making accent *cup*cakes? I balked at the plurality of "cupcakes" and double-checked how many she thought she would need. She just sort of mumbled about "oh, as many as you can make, make sure to check in with my mother" and then hung up as quickly as she could manage. I set a timer, gave myself five minutes to rage about how nobody knew the market value of baked goods —or the market value of teachers, for that matter— and took a shot of mezcal. I then calmly texted Stacy, who showed up twenty-four minutes later, full of natural energy and over the moon to assist with the preparation of a hundred cupcakes, didn't that sound fun. She promptly proceeded to organize the next three hours in a way that produced enough cupcakes for at least eighty guests. Which, by her estimation, was about one hundred and forty, actually, but don't worry, Bea, Anita's on her way with extra ingredients. That was around the time I took the second shot of mezcal. Stacy agreed to let me make her a drink, too, but that woman only consumes alcohol in .5 oz increments.

Anita showed up. That's about all I have to say about that. But also, who helps a stranger with a baking crisis on a Friday night? A psychopath?

It turns out psychopaths can be incredibly handy when they're in your corner.

Anita's first week had gone well enough, I learned, though she was, predictably, exhausted. Stacy and I "here, here'd" that—which I thought was ripe, Stacy was literally showing no signs of weakness—before folding another three cups of cocoa powder into the bucket of batter. By the time they were stumbling back down my drive at midnight—yes, midnight—I had promised them a "thank you thank you thank you" dinner, in the coming weeks. There's also a good chance I had sworn over my unborn child. I'm still a little fuzzy on the details.

All that to say, I super hadn't forgotten Marie's cake. Geez, Lena. I checked over the rest of the spreadsheet, made sure I hadn't actually forgotten anything, updated the cell where I was supposed to write in what I'd ended up wearing—a sage potato sack—and by that I mean one of those formless dresses that stops around your knees—and got on the road. I arrived at Marie's twenty minutes later and very nearly aborted the mission, then and there. Cars lined her entire neighborhood, dozens of people were actively entering her front door, and the noise from the backyard rager was overwhelming.

"No, you shouldn't have worn that," Lena said, appearing from nowhere. "I've told you, Beatrice, you can't wear loose dresses to baby showers. People will ask when you're due."

"But it's so fun watching them squirm," I said, staring at the backseat where I had stacked the twelve cupcake containers. Twelve. The idea of picking up a single one felt utterly impossible, by this point in my personal cupcake hell.

"Hey," I called to the nearest passing stranger. A teenage boy who, thankfully, had three teenaged siblings. Or cousins. Or maybe they all just happened to be walking in together. "Can you help carry these inside?" It's hard to say no to a pregnant woman, of course, and they were only too willing to help, the respectful little men that they were. "And put this one in the fridge," I said, taking out a small container with a single, special cupcake I'd made, all by myself. I'd drawn skulls and crossbones over the lid and suggested in two languages and no uncertain terms that stealing

91

would result in a painful, painful end. The tallest one took the container from my hands with as much dignity as he could muster before scampering off to put it in the nearest refrigerator.

The boys recruited five of their closest friends and before I could even shed a single tear over being mistaken for a tia I was staring at an empty backseat.

"Thank God," I said, dabbing at my eyes, leaning against the car. I stared at Lena, who had showed up in black slacks and a black button-down. I grabbed the black blazer from where it lay, perfectly folded, over her arm and carefully laid it over my front seat.

"Can't believe you critiqued my ensemble," I muttered, closing my door and pushing myself towards the fourth circle of hell. "You're a piece of white cardboard away from being mistaken for the priest."

"Hardly," Lena said, frowning at me, "I'm a woman." She looked down at herself. She, like me, hadn't inherited much in the way of curves. Which was very stupid, because our mother literally had the most banging set of boobs you've ever seen. And her butt? Don't get me started. The woman stopped traffic when she wore her denim jeans.

"I always wanted to be a priest," Lena mused, fingering her collar. I took her hand in mine before she got any ideas about buttoning her shirt all the way to the top.

"Yes, well," I said, taking a deep breath, "you are terribly good at orders."

"No, I'm good at ord*er*," she corrected.

"I rest my case."

We clung to each other as we entered a people-to-square-foot ratio that could not possibly have passed fire safety standards. We rushed into the backyard as quickly as humanly possible, our ear drums on the line, and updated the spreadsheet to reflect our new "twenty minutes from now" departure time.

Our cousin Diego pulled us into the corner he and his sister, Mira, had staked out. It was behind a lemon tree and very well shaded, which was a major plus. Not saying I'm weak, or anything. Just saying I can't handle SoCal August afternoons as well as I once did.

"Are we even allowed to do gender reveals anymore?" Mira grumped, opening what was certainly not her first can of white wine.

"Evidently," Lena said, staring at the tree. She leaned forward, after a few seconds, and sniffed it.

"When did you become an arborist?" I asked, staring at the beer Diego had handed me and wondering if I was actually going to commit to twelve entire ounces of a brand of lager I've been told I'm not allowed to shit on anymore.

"Oh, shove it," she said, straightening, "trees smell interesting." And she was a compulsive sniffer, is all I'm saying. "I take it Pia got hold of the guest list." We all peaked around our lemon tree.

"Evidently," Mira tossed back, leaning against the fence.

"Surprised she talked Joey into letting us stand on his grass," I said, feeling sorry for my poor uncle. He was a lawn dad. If you've ever stayed in the suburbs, you know exactly who I'm talking about. If you haven't, just imagine the type of person who mows at diagonals, has a vendetta against squirrels, and sings to grass patches when they start looking a touch yellow.

"I think she slipped a Benzo into his juice this morning," Diego said, staring at my unopened beer. I handed it back to him.

"I'm going to brave the ice chests," I said, scanning the yard until I found the pyramid of borrowed, mismatched coolers ringing one side of the covered patio where a bunch of seven-year-olds were playing giant jenga

"Anybody want anything?"

Mira held up the can of wine, the almost universal sign for "another, thanks." I stepped back into the chaos.

Chapter Nine

The thing about giant Mexican families is that we throw giant Mexican parties. An outside observer familiar with the concept of "family party" might think it would be safe to assume that the guest lists would remain stable, through the years, only changing with marriages and children. The reality is much more fluid, of course, as, frequently, people who received invites only make up about one-third to one-half of those in attendance. The rest is a motley crew of people who are being dated by the invitee, people who were trying to make Saturday plans with the invitee and were told "we just have to stop at a family thing real quick on the way to the beach," people who are being babysat by the invitee, and people who were in the general vicinity of the invitee when said invitee opened the texted e-vite. "Oh, great. Another baby shower." *looks up.* "Hey, you don't have plans this weekend, do you? There'll be homemade sopapillas." Or, depending on the audience, "free beer."

This, of course, is not an exhaustive list of guest extras, but merely provided to illustrate the fact that I weaved through about forty-two people on my way to the drinks station, recognized seven, and was asked by an eighth who I had come with. And then I was milling about the coolers and trying to remember what I had come for.

I had to hand it to Marie. Well, Pia, probably. Marie's mother had always excelled at throwing parties. Besides the mismatched coolers, everything was on theme. Pastels, everywhere. Tall circle tables wrapped in burlap and pink, here, and burlap and blue, there, and everything draped in baby's breath. A massive table had been set under the shade of the patio. It was laid with fourteen different charcuterie boards of varying themes—so varying, indeed, that I assumed some of the people who had made them had not understood the assignment—each of which was bordered by plates and platters of party food. An even larger table had been set inside.

I wondered which aunts had been ordered to make which charcuterie boards. What had those conversations even looked like? "What's a charcuterie board?" "It's when you put the food on a fancy board." "A fancy board? What's wrong with the pan?" "Nothing, Ma, it's just what people do, now." "What is a fancy board, anyway?" "It's like a cutting board. Like, a wooden cutting board." "Madre de dios." "Ay, Ma. It's just what people do, now." I was pretty sure the twenty-year-old plastic cutting board piled high with pulled pork and fry bread had been my Aunt Josey's contribution. A good two dozen of my cupcakes had been dispersed across four baby blue three-tier dessert stands. I smiled. They looked much better than the crumbling brownie squares beside them. I tried not to preen too much but, like, suck it, Gerald. Flower petals lay strewn throughout it all, light pink and bright blue, whispery and whimsical, so well-woven into the spread that some people definitely thought they were edible.

I finally remembered why I was standing in front of a half K's worth of canned booze. I started peaking under lids, looking for wine, and was not at all surprised to discover that they were, of course, in the last ice chest I checked. I fished around in the melting ice, lost a few fingers to frostbite, and wondered why Pia never bought enough chardonnay. There would be eighty cans of merlot left—because nobody except Joey drinks ice-cold merlot out of a *can*, geez, people—and two pinot grigios, but only because they had hidden themselves under a pile of aforementioned and utterly unwanted red.

"I would say 'what are the odds,' but, well. Half of Chino is here, so, pretty good, actually."

I straightened up so fast that I almost passed out. Once enough blood had returned to my brain for me to see again, I discovered that I would never escape my sins. Just kidding.

"Hedi," I said, my vision swimming, my fingers dripping, my heart pounding, my libido—actually, never mind. And then, "Oh fucking hell, are we related?"

Hedi frowned, not quite following. And then the brayingest bray of a donkey's bray—and by that, I mean, he guffawed—leapt from his lips. Truly, I hadn't thought people actually made that sound in real life. The man honked, people, and it was weirdly attractive. Most unfortunately so, actually, since I had yet to clear the "shit, is this incestuous?" hurdle.

"Answer me, man," I said, reaching behind me and pulling out the first can my fingers could find. A frigid merlot, it turned out. I handed it to Hedi and tried again. A pinot Grigio, this time. Good enough for me.

"But watching you sweat is such fun," he said, staring at the merlot and doing his very best not to look confused. He shrugged, popped the tab, and took a sip. "My mom is Marie's godmother."

I actually felt my knees buckle, a little. I held the cold can against my cheek and decided I should count my blessings, more often. 1. Alive, 2. healthy, 3. gainfully employed, and 4. has never once almost slept with a family member.

"Is she here?" I asked, trying not to notice how the quarter sleeves on Hedi's black t-shirt stopped just at the swell of his biceps.

"Hmm? Oh, my mom?" He asked, stepping to the side as a gaggle of young-20s descended upon the alcohol. "No."

"Oh?" I raised a brow. "Not feeling well? Or has she developed some magical superpower where she's capable of saying no to family events?"

"You don't like these parties?" He asked, dodging the question like a little question-dodging ninja.

"Of course I do, but complaining about them is half the fun. Now, stop deflecting and answer me." He'd said enough, in the few encounters we had already had, for me to put two and two together and know that his mother was unwell. But he'd never actually come out and told me what exactly the problem was and, well. It felt a little too stoic, which I am more or less morally opposed to.

He smiled a smaller, tighter smile, his eyes sliding from mine to the can he held in his hands. "It would seem we've been caught out," he told the merlot. I tried to keep a straight face, tried not to fall for his "diffusing tension with comedy" trick.

"Her meds haven't been treating the MS as well as they once did. She can't really walk, most days, and she's given up driving. My sister lives with her, but she just started a new program— nursing, go figure—and can't do it alone anymore. Honestly, I should have moved back sooner. I just... well, homecomings can be disorienting. I mean, I've been home before now, of course. Have slipped in and out for holidays and quick trips. But moving back... well, when you move back, your mom wants you to come to things like this. And nobody here... well, I never bothered reintroducing myself to anyone here, after I left." He shrugged. "Anyway. It's not some big sob story, Bea, don't look at me like that."

I, naturally, did what I always do when people succinctly say their devastating truths: I began to babble.

"I'm so sorry," I said, reaching forward to squeeze his arm. I re-thought the gesture, halfway through, and just stood there, my hand half-outstretched, before pulling it back to cup my quickly warming can. His eyes glittered in the sun as they followed the progression of my indecisive digits. His eyes... well, they mocked me. Yes, eyes can mock a person, no, I wasn't projecting my own feelings. "If there's anything I can do, just let me know. I can cook? What does she like? Is she allergic to anything? I—"

"Thank you," Hedi interrupted, his whole face mocking me, now. "That's a very... well, strange offer, quite frankly, considering that I barely know you. And that, you know, we're not friends."

"Says who?" I scoffed.

"You. Literally, you."

"I really thought we'd be able to move past that faster, my darling protege," I said, flicking a stray chip of ice from the top of my can. "Besides, I'm offering as your mentor. I'm pretty sure 'assisting with mothers' falls well within the job description."

"Mmhmm." I was also pretty sure it was one such of these "mmhmms" that had propelled me into his bedroom in the first place. "Bea?"

"Huh—what?" I asked, trying to remember what in the world we had been talking about.

"My eyes are up here." Of course they were. Where else would they be? I ripped my gaze from his forearms to look into aforementioned eyes. They were still mocking me. "Thank you." His voice was so quiet, sometimes.

"It's no trouble to make eye contact," I said, waving the comment away. He blinked a few times, trying, I imagined, to see whether or not I was being serious. I kept as straight a face as I could manage.

"I meant about the offer to—oh, you were joking," he said, rolling his eyes. I assumed the snickering into my pinot is what tipped him off, but who's to say?

"I really do mean it, though," I said. "If you ever need anything, I'm here. A lot of us, actually. I mean from school," I added belatedly, realizing we were currently surrounded by "lots of us." "I don't know what coming back is like, for you, or if you have people from growing up who you feel safe with, but—" But, I was babbling again. I sighed. "Anyway. You get my point. I'm here. Inconsistent though such statements may be with previous character sketches."

"You would be fun to sketch," he said, studying my face with exaggerated curiosity. I refrained from asking him if sketching women was one of his moves. I refrained for a variety of reasons, of course, not the most of which was that it would absolutely have worked and not the least of which was that now I was revisiting every snapshot of memory I had from his place and trying to remember if I'd seen any portraits of sketched women.

"I do feel supported, by the way," he said, breaking the quiet. "By you all, I mean. Julien's started a happy hour for the new teachers after work once a week. Stacy brought me dinner, last Thursday.

"That bitch," I sighed. Hedi's lip quirked.

"Oh? Is there some super secret veteran teacher reason to dislike her?"

"Other than the fact that she makes everyone else look bad?"

"Oh, yes. I did get that impression. But she also made me an entire pan of sweet potato enchiladas, so. I'm afraid my loyalty has been bought."

Sweet potato enchiladas weren't even that hard to make. Anybody could make sweet potato enchiladas. I bet she didn't even put green chilis in them, the absolute coward.

"That's okay," I said, jumping out of the way as five ten-year-olds burst past, hollering about who-knows-what. "I can play a long game." Hedi just sort of stared. His jaw worked a little, too, before settling into the "hanging open" position. I eventually realized my mistake.

"As your *mentor*," I clarified, "it's in my best interest to usurp whatever hold those other loser teachers have over you. Can't have you corrupted because of a little enchilada dependency.

What did *you* think I meant?" I pushed forward, though, increasingly realizing that he was faultlessly honest and overly sincere and that, thirdly, I didn't want him to speak certain things out loud, a girl was trying to keep her panties on. "Anyway, I promised my cousin a top off. Would you like to mingle or shall I show you our hideout?" I scooted back to the wine cooler and grabbed out a couple more cans.

"Considering I know nobody here except Marie, who seems a little busy, and her parents, who keep trying to set me up with their nice, single nephews, I'm going to go with the hideout option, if you don't mind."

I cringed and gave him my best "god, sorry about that," look. He shrugged it off. I assumed he did that a lot. I offered him my arm, tried not to giggle when he took it, and pulled him towards our lemon sanctuary.

***

The funny thing about gender reveal parties is that sometimes you try to save money by outsourcing all of the labor to friends and family which means that you ask an aunty to make your "reveal" cake without making sure she understands what a "reveal" cake is. Ha, ha.

Our Aunt Rosa—well, great-aunt, probably, the woman was eighty-seven—has made cakes for just about every wedding and birthday and engagement party she's attended in the past half century. They are delicious. They are gorgeous. They could go for hundreds of dollars on the open market. She's never charged any of us a dime.

Rosa doesn't speak very much English, though, and Marie doesn't speak on phones—yes, she's the sort of millennial who thinks that is acceptable behavior—and I can only imagine what the conversation about the cake sounded like, in the weeks leading up to this party. Marie doing her best to explain "gender reveal" in broken Spanish as quickly as possible, Rosa trying to act like she understood what she assumed was English, and both parties overjoyed by the cessation of the call. What I don't have to imagine is the fallout, though, because I was present and accounted for and have the spreadsheet to prove it.

We all gathered around the table Pia had put in the middle of the backyard for exactly this purpose. Hedi had, predictably, done too well with my cousins, who wouldn't stop bothering him about living on the east coast. Diego was being a little too smiley, too—because bisexuals are the actual worst, truly, and god Diego stop being such a thirsty bitch —and Mira was being a little too "so what's my

106

cousin actually like at work, I'm so excited to finally have an inside perspective." Lena, of course, knew exactly who Hedi was. I'd called her on the way home from that first and only date, after all, and panicked for an entire two hours about walking out on the first good person I'd met up with in years after having had a "Breakdown in B minor." And I'd called her again, of course, on the way home from the first day of school, when I updated her on what was apparently becoming a saga.

Lena was a little scary, sometimes, and today was no exception. And by that I mean she interacted with Hedi kindly, compassionately, and without a single whiff of "oh my gosh you're the person my sister was a total witch to that one time, tell me more, and also she really needs that bra back. She has, like, two real brassieres to her name." I blamed law school.

Anyway, we eventually got gathered with the other hundred some-odd guests. The cake—five entire tiers of a rose-themed masterpiece, replete with actual blossoms and blooms—had been arranged upon the table, moments prior, and Marie and Steve, her husband, stood just to one side, smiling, teary-eyed, their hands clasped jointly around a single serving knife.

"Ready?" Steve asked the crowd, "has everybody placed their bets? Who thinks it's a girl?" People hooted and hollered. Mira grumbled under her breath about cishet normativity. Diego just booed. Nobody heard him, though, because Steve had just asked the mandatory "and who thinks it's a boy?" follow-up and one hundred people had begun shouting their manifold opinions. To be clear, they didn't all want Marie's unborn fetus to have a dick. They just had opinions about little boys, plenty of which involved the superiority of little girls but that, apparently, hadn't been worth voicing before there was a masculine other to push against.

"Shall we?" Steve shouted. The crowd went wild. I wondered if Steve had been a circus performer in another life.

"Here's to hoping it's triplets," I whispered into Hedi's ear. He grinned. Leaned over, too, and whispered back, "well, that'd be one way to get a third gender in."

I laughed. "Wow, enough with the trans agenda, already."

We were interrupted by the cake cutting. The expecting couple sliced in, faces split with anticipation. They pulled their piece from the top tier, their breaths held, their eyes wide. They went right on holding their breaths, then, and, funnily enough, their eyes only got wider. Frownier, too, as they stared at their plate of cake. Steve glanced towards Rosa's masterpiece, next. This, of course, mitigated some of his confusion. He stood there, staring into the cream-filled center—the green cream-filled center—and did his absolute darnedest to keep from laughing. His wife burst into tears.

Pia rushed over to Tia Rosa, then, as the crowd of a half billion onlookers tried to keep it together. "Por qué es verde?" She whispered, why is it green?

Rosa frowned. "Por qué no? Ella pidió un pastel de bebé." Why not? She asked for a baby cake? our resident octogenarian baker told her niece. "El verde puede ir en cualquier dirección." Green can go either way.

Diego spat water. Rosa was beginning to stiffen, then, knowing that Marie was upset about the cake but not knowing why. "Pintamos todas tus habitaciones de verde," she insisted to Pia. We painted all of your rooms green.

Pia, for her part, was too tired to laugh and too amused to do anything else.

"She's saying she made a baby cake, like Marie asked for," I whispered to Hedi, "and picked a green filling because green can go either way."

"Thank you," Hedi whispered back, "but I do speak Spanish."

Right, right.

"No recibiste la carpeta?" Pia asked. Did you not get the folder? Rosa nodded, her mouth

109

tight, her eyes fixed straight ahead. On the cake she'd spent days making, undoubtedly, the cake that was more beautiful, more finely detailed, than anything I'd ever worn, much less eaten.

"Si, chica," Rosa bit off, "pero no veo que tiene que ver eso con un pastel." She didn't see what that had to do with a cake.

People were trying very, very hard not to laugh. A little bit because Marie was weeping openly but mostly because Rosa was a proud woman—rightly so, in my humble opinion—and would think we were all laughing at her.

"Tienes la carpeta?" Marie wailed, wanting to know if Rosa still had the doctor's folder. Rosa shook her head, her weathered hands clutching at each other. Pia took her arm, smiling.

"Es muy bonito," she said, gesturing towards the cake, "y huele delicioso."

"What's happening?" Steve asked, finally cracking. I wondered what it was like, being him.

"She doesn't know if it's a boy or a girl," Marie cried, "and didn't bring the scan. Now we won't be able to find out until…until…" but words failed my darling cousin, just then. I blamed the pregnancy hormones.

"Que?" Rosa asked Pia, tsk-clucking in the way only women of a certain age can pull off, "Es por eso que está llorando?" That's why she's crying? "Ella no sabe que es una niña?"

Marie screamed. Steve panicked, understandably, before half a dozen people shouted "it's a girl!" and saved the poor man a few gray hairs. He did start crying, then, and held his wife, and chattered on and on and on about how their baby was going to be the most perfect little niña in the whole damn world. And then we all devolved into the hilarity we'd been holding at bay for the past thirty seconds.

"I think," I croaked, clutching at the stitch in my side, "I think I peed myself, a little."

"Not going to lie," Lena said, dabbing at her eyes, "that's one of the funniest things I've seen, all week."

"Low bar," I countered, "pun intended."

"Are you glad you came?" Diego asked Hedi.

"Of course," he said, watching Rosa shuffle towards the house.

"Come on," I told him, beckoning for him to follow me. And then, to Lena, "I'll be right back, then we can go get an actual lunch." She was a vegan, ethically opposed to finger foods, and allergic to corn, which was just about the worst thing I'd ever heard of.

"Wait, I want to come," Diego whined, staring from Lena to me to Hedi and back. Mira nodded vigorously. I made a "take it up with my sister" gesture and left them, walking towards the house. The house was mostly empty, just then, as everyone was still outside getting slices of Rosa's cake. I looked around at the scattered remains of what had once been and would be again a hopping party. I hurried through Pia's beautiful—if currently overrun—kitchen, pretended not to notice how much I liked marble countertops, and opened the fridge. I had to dig around for a solid forty-five seconds before I was able to find my skull-covered container. I smiled. The tiny teenaged cousin had done his job well, hiding the cupcake behind two rows of pickled condiments and fancy mustards.

"Is that…permanent marker?" Hedi asked, staring at the lid.

"Well, death is pretty permanent, so," I said, grabbing a fork before leaving the kitchen. I walked into the living room, where Rosa and my abuela sat on a couch and chatted about a baby's baptism they were going to the next day.

"Buenas tardes," I said, hugging each woman, "Qué travesuras están haciendo?"

"Estás embarazada?" Abuela asked Rosa. Hedi coughed politely behind me. I just smiled and rubbed my stomach in that way pregnant women do.

"No," Rosa said, "todas las solteronas usan vestidos así." Apparently, all spinsters wore dresses like mine, these days.

"And to think, I brought y'all cake," I muttered. I opened the container—Rosa didn't need to see my skulls—and handed her a single cupcake. It was a dark, dark chocolate filled with raspberries and cream and decorated with a ganache that had taken three tries to set. I'd shaped the ganache into a single rose, just as Rosa had taught me. "Para usted, Tia."

"Nada para mi?" Nothing for me, my grandmother asked, grinning, her jet-black hair haloing around her face in a way that made her look like a pixy.

"No, Abuela. Ella es mi favorita." My grandmother cackled. Rosa, for her part, was looking a little misty-eyed.

"Es muy hermosa, chica," she said, staring at the cupcake. Suck. It. Gilbert. "Y tu tambien."

"Antención, hermana," Abuela snapped at Rosa, "Tenemos un guapo extraño entre nosotros." Focus, sister, she said, we have a handsome stranger among us.

My grandmother was openly ogling Hedi, who was, very adorably, blushing from head to toe.

113

"Quien es el? Finalmente has traído a un hombre a casa?" Who is this? Have you finally brought a man home?

I winked at my grandmother. Rubbed the top of my stomach again, too.

"Si, abuela. Pero puede ser que necesite atraparlo."

I could hear Hedi mutter something along the lines of "dear god, Bea, they'll think I'm a scoundrel" behind me. I mean, who even says scoundrel?

"Buena chica," my Tia said, patting my arm. My grandmother had gone back to cackling. She gestured for Hedi to come nearer, too, and held out her arms. Hedi stepped forward, letting her take his hands in hers.

"Me llamo Hedi, Señora," he said, "Señora," he said to Rosa, "Su pastel fue el mas hermoso que he visto." The cake was the most beautiful thing he had ever seen. And then, to both, "Carmen es mi madre. Madrina de Marie." Carmen was his mother. Marie's godmother.

"Que lindas," Abuela said, pretending like she had any idea who any of those people were. I would have been shocked if she could pick Marie out of a lineup. "Bueno, bueno. Vuelve cuando quieras. Quiero bisnietas." Come back whenever you want, she said, I want great-grandchildren.

"Ay, Abuela," I said, swatting her hands away, freeing him from her grip, "ya tienes bisnietas." You have great-grandchildren.

"Si, si, pero quiero los tuyos." Yes, yes, but I want yours.

"Si, yo tambien," Tia Rosa seconded. "Ya le hiciste pastel? Eso te conseguira sus bebes." Have you made him cake yet? That will get you his children.

"Ya nos vamos," I said, kissing each cackling woman on the forehead before rushing us out of there.

"They are out of control," I said, blinking, the sun sudden and sharp after the cool tones of Pia's living room.

"Takes one to know one," Hedí countered, smiling, his eyes on his feet. "Thank you, by the way."

"I mean, threatening entrapment is just another Saturday. Usually it's for financial gain, though. Any chance you're secretly a billionaire?"

"None, unfortunately. And take the compliment." Thankfully, we were accosted by a starving Lena and a drunkish Diego before I had to do anything overly sincere, like admit to noticing him notice Rosa's disappointment and sadness and knowing he wanted to make the older woman feel better but not knowing how to go about doing so

115

and, upon noticing him noticing, deciding to invite him to participate in my emotional uplift scheme, just because I could.

Mira, funnily enough, was already in my car.

"I guess I'm driving," I said, wondering when, if ever, I would tire of good deeding. I made a mental note to ask Father Hoang if saints knew they were saints while they walked this world.

Chapter Ten

Yes, dear Reader, a green hawk lay upon her pillow, neon-bright and covered in blood. Our stolid queen hadn't realized such a color existed in nature, so fluorescent was this particular shade. "Troubled Hawk," our queen did say, stepping forth, wary, suspecting a trap. "Troubled Hawk, how came you this way?"

"On wings," the hawk gasped, pretty sure he was going to die—if you haven't yet noticed, he's bleeding out—"how else?"

The queen stared at him. Sort of how mothers stare at teenaged children when said children respond to earnest questions by stating the obvious and said mothers can't tell whether their child is being sincere, if thick, or giving an "attitude," as it is called in households across America.

"I suppose the wind, too," the hawk went on, withering under such a look. He, too, had had a

mother. He knew what was up. "And a window was involved. Yours, I'd imagine, if this be your room."

She nodded. She walked over to the window and tried to lean out. As ever, the magic of this place kept her from peeping any further than the edge of the windowsill. All around was naught but sky and sun.

"What does it look like, from the other side?" she wondered.

"I'm kind of dying over here," the hawk whimpered, seeing stars. He wondered if now was the time to start praying to his god.

"You know this is a warlock's tower, right?" she asked, still lost in her own thoughts. "You've fluttered into a war of attrition, Hawk."

"I wouldn't say 'fluttered' so much as 'fell into whilst death spiraling," the Hawk choked out.

"How can I know that you aren't one of his minio—"

"Lady, I'm dying here, less talking, more helping. Chop chop."

Such language would normally have resulted in some sort of corporal punishment. She hadn't been an executey queen, or anything, but she had frequently required poorly mannered courtiers to wear those scratchy shirts made from animal hair that monks and nuns also sometimes wear when they're trying to mortify their flesh. If you don't know what that means, a recent survey has shown that sixty percent of this student body was baptized Catholic. Ask a neighbor, make a friend. Don't mortify your flesh.

She didn't have any hair shirts that would fit this hawk, though. While she was appraising his dimensions she was reminded that he was still bleeding out. And all over her pillow, no less.

"Well, wallop," she said. "Wallop," in this world, is what people say when they're cursing their circumstances. There are plenty of corollaries in our own world but we have been assured that we are under no circumstances allowed to reprint them in our school's paper. "Wallop," she said again, trying to remember what she knew about accipitrine first aid. Those memories were pretty blurry, though. It had been over fifty years since she'd needed them, after all, and we've been told that things stop sticking so well after about twenty-five.

"Oh!" the Queen said, remembering something. "Hang tight, Hawk," she said, hurrying from her chambers.

"Guuurrgg—" he gurgled, more or less dead by this point.

The thing the queen had remembered was that she was in a warlock's tower, which meant that the library was filled with warlock books and that those books were filled with warlock magic. This

*particular warlock was, quite usefully, obsessed
with order, which made finding a book on bird first
aid a simple matter of reading through the finding
aid—a fifty pound tome chained to a lectern at the
very front of the cold, arching corridor. And then
referencing the map on the wall, orienting herself,
and following the color-coded arrows until she
found four books that might be useful. She didn't
bring them back to her room—all of the covers had
been spelled to alert the warlock when they were
being stolen—but she did rip the relevant pages out
—because she'd learned, long ago, that the warlock
hadn't bothered to spell the individual pages, too,
because that would have taken literally hundreds of
thousands of hours and he figured nobody was
going to make it that far anyway.*

*She hurried back to her bedroom. Well, sort
of hurried. She also sort of got distracted by one of
the cartoons that had been doodled into the
marginalia of one of the ripped pages. We won't go
into detail about said doodle. We'll just say you'd
have gotten a detention, had you been caught
scribing a similar doodle into your English lit
textbook.*

*She did eventually reach our lime green
bird, of course, and did eventually whisper five or
so incantations over his more or less dead body. She
waited. She was, like, extremely patient, if you'll*

*recall. He waited, too, but he wasn't exactly
conscious, at the moment, so we're not sure it even
counts as waiting.*

*And then his blood was twisting about atop
the pillow, was spinning itself into a tighter, thicker
stream, was pulling itself out of the feathers and
fabric until, in one fell "schloop," it sucked itself
back into his body. A few magic stitches across his
verdant breast, and he was good as new.*

*He woke up hacking—they always do—and
had to be given a little gulp of something spicy from
Queen's bedside "water" cup.*

*"Queen," he rasped, gazing down at his
would-be corpse, "you have saved me after all.
Thank you." And then, "cut it a little close, don't you
think?"*

*Queen shrugged. He'd taken a tone with her,
after all, and she didn't mind if he suffered just a
little.*

*"Now tell me, Hawk, how you came to be
bleeding out on my bed."*

*"Of course," the hawk said, testing first one
wing, then the other. He spread his wings across the
pillow, wondering that they should still work. "But
first, I think a little wardrobe change is in order."*

*She had no idea what he was talking about
for maybe two seconds. And then he was growing
and changing and molting, everywhere, until*

suddenly he wasn't a bird, but a man, and still just lying there. He seemed a little smug about it, too.

What does this one look like? We won't limit his beauty with words. Just know that he was beautiful, Dear Reader. Like, the most *beautiful. Like, picture the most attractive person you can think of, run them through the vampire glow-up algorithm, then put him in a tunic. Not because tunics are especially cute, or anything. Just, he's supposed to also be vaguely medieval, and we narrowed it down to "tunic" and "habit" and the one that showed off the biceps won out.*

"Sorry about the blood," he said, glancing at her newly clean pillow, "I didn't realize how bad it was until I was just about dead, I guess."

The queen, for her part, was doing her very best not to pass out. She wasn't sure why fainting was what her body was going with, just then. She wasn't sure she'd ever actually even passed out.

"How—" she tried, one knee buckling, "why? Who...who are you?"

"No one important," the man said, rising, "yet."

Good morning, Clayton High! We hope you enjoyed our latest installment of For the Love of A

Hawk. Your write-ins last week were AWESOME!
Thank you for helping us envision our neon hero.
For next week's edition, we want you to help us
name our new protagonist! Leave your suggestions
for Hawk's name in the comments box outside room
241.

"It feels…" I didn't know how to say "like three different people were fighting over the keyboard" without sounding like a bitch.

"Like the biggest argument in my newspaper class last week was whether it's more important for the characters to sound 'old' or 'relatable?' Yeah, tell me about it," Maya said, pinching the bridge of her nose. "They have split into factions, Bea. Factions. Those kids…they literally orchestrated a formal debate, today, and spent at least thirty minutes researching medieval French. So. That was a good use of everybody's time."

I couldn't disagree.

"Are you a little concerned that an FMC in what appears to be a fairy romance just met the most attractive man she's ever seen in her magically elongated life?" I asked, wondering why it was so hard to spin in a circle and snack on mazipán at the same time.

"Sorry, was that English?" Maya asked, putting a foot out and catching my toe, mid-spin. I almost fell out of the chair. The room spun around me as my ears adjusted to my sudden stillness.

"I think?" I said, going back over what I'd just said. And then I was grinning. "Oh, that's right. You don't read fairy smut." She was more of a Hockey Romance girlie.

"Is this that ACOTAR thing you keep talking about."

I felt a good giggle coming on.

"Something like that," I said, standing. The back-to-school assembly was almost over, after all, and my tech students, though self-sufficient, had grown accustomed to my supervisory presence.

"God," Maya muttered, standing as well. We could hear the distant thunder of seven hundred students exiting the gymnasium. "I did see them with copies of Rockinghorse Winner, earlier today, but I was hoping it was an English Lit assignment. Now some of their censorship questions make more sense. Nasty little fuckers."

"All I'm saying," I said, slipping my feet back into my shoes and dropping the half-eaten packet of De La Rosa candies back into my backpack, "is that if I were reading this for my book club, I'd expect a wild, dirty, and potentially religious sexual encounter in the next hundred pages."

I don't think I've ever seen somebody roll their eyes so hard.

"And you wonder why I don't want to join your bookclub," she muttered. I scoffed. It was a pretty good scoff, too. I'd been practicing. I was glad to see my hard work was paying off.

"First of all, you'd love it," I said, stalling in the doorway, "second of all," but I didn't actually have a second of all. That I could tell her, anyway. There was an incredibly marriageable neurosurgeon in my book club and I'd been trying to figure out a way to set her up with him for months. I'd tried luring her to our meetings, over the summer, but she kept going on about not being interested in the books we kept picking. I couldn't just lead with "you don't actually have to read the books, Maya, we barely talk about them anyway, it's an excuse to hang out at a cocktail bar." Because Maya is very good at homework and is, furthermore, a chronic completionist and, lastly, would balk at the idea of a club where you didn't do the one thing the club is meant to do.

"Toodles," I said, realizing the horde had fully descended and that I was going to be late to my own class if I didn't leave right then.

The joys of the second Monday of the semester are manifold. Mostly, though, it's the first "real" Monday of the school year and you get to see all of your sleepy, hormonal darlings try not to blame anything with a pulse for their current state of exhaustion. The energy high schoolers bring to Monday mornings would have you thinking they had been thanklessly working for "the man" for decades. That they had a piece-of-shit husband who'd run out on them, months prior, and a colicky baby who caught every single virus there ever was and was, subsequently, never well enough to make it through a single day of daycare. You'd think that they had a teenager who blamed them for their dad leaving and, to top all of the interpersonal drama off, a boss who had only given one percent pay raises ever since "that" recession. Literally, one student came in quoting 9-to-5. And I don't mean the song. She'd watched the movie twice through, that weekend, and fully converted to second wave feminism.

Of course, my tech students had been exhausted since their tenth birthdays and had come out of the womb with a coffee addiction. That "Monday" mood was their everyday mood, which they reflected in their wardrobes, which were all black, all the time. They didn't really wear makeup, though, which was funny to me and also undoubtedly the reason none of them ever got written off as "emo." No under-eyeliner here. Just a whole bunch of sleepy sighs and determined, hyper-fixating stares. And determined they were. These fifteen-year-olds had to build four different sets each year. We're talking hammer and nail, lumber and paint, people. Last year they had a forty-eight hour turnaround on a treehouse after Paul decided the platform we'd been using really wasn't "doing it for him." They did it in thirty-six. These are the students who create entire wardrobes from single ideas, who know how to apply make-up for every occasion, be it "princess" or "corpse." They are constantly researching historical periods for set details and architecture manuals for…well, safety standards. Because accidents don't happen in this PAC, people. These are the children who know how to mic a cast of forty people and mix the sound in ways that made our at times off-key choral arrangements sound fun and fancy free. I don't even know how they do the lights—I never quite learned, once we updated the system, and they had it under control in less than two hours. I didn't really see the point, after that. They do all this, and all while managing two dozen of the most high-strung Dramatics their fifteen-hundred student school had to offer. All this to say, I understand why every day is Monday, for them. And they absolutely love it.

"What do you have for me, Pete?" I asked, pouring water into the diner-style coffee pot I'd shoved into a far corner. I made the full twelve cups, too, because these children were fiends. I sometimes wondered if coffee was the sort of consumable parents had to sign wavers for. I was always making mental notes to "ask someone" but it was exactly the sort of thing I never thought about until I wasn't around anybody to ask.

"Well, at first we were thinking something small. Commensurate to the initial offense, as you suggested." I turned from the coffee pot and saw that my five darlings had actually huddled up behind me. Like, right behind me. Like, it was all I could do not to yelp. Or laugh. Or both. I mirrored their game faces and prayed that they weren't about to suggest criminal activity.

"But nothing small seemed worthwhile," Pete went on. I was briefly distracted by how tall he was—I mean, they really just shoot up—and so missed the next few sentences. And then he was saying, "which is why we think a longer con is the best way of getting back. It avoids the meanness of a lot of these shorter-term pranks while still getting the point across."

"The point being, don't touch my phone?" I asked.

"Well we were thinking 'don't prank the director,' but also that," Lu said, finishing up the web of braids she'd been weaving into her hair.

"Love it," I said, belatedly realizing they hadn't actually said what "it" was. "What is 'it'?"

Pete looked down at me like maybe he'd already said as much. Lex handed me a piece of paper, smiling from ear to ear, a little too eager, I thought. Then again, she was Belen's younger sister. I could see how this vendetta might be personal in nature. I glanced down at the paper. A flyer, it turned out, advertising a performing arts fundraiser. It looked like it was part competition, part auction, and all cooperation with Mr. Sunderson, the demonic band director, Paul, and Mx. Dicky Kim, the art teacher.

"They *hate* working with band kids," Lex said, grinning.

"Um, *I* hate working with band…kids," I tried. Lu tsked.

"We aren't actually doing it. It's not like we know how to do a bakeoff." She paused, part of her brain actually working through the logistics. If there was anyone who could organize a cross-school bakeoff competition, it would be them. "No, just announce it, let them sweat it out for a few days. Bargain, a little. Then, when they're cracking, tell them that you'll ask the other directors to call it off if they promise never to mess with your personal devices ever again."

I frowned. It was an interesting idea. It was, of course, way too involved. I was pretty sure I wasn't legally allowed to "mess with students." I supposed this wasn't embezzling, though, which seemed to be the new standard for appropriate teacher comportment.

"But our department doesn't need any money," I said, shuffling over to my chair. The huddle moved with me. "Why would they believe that I'd signed us up for a fundraiser when we don't need any money?"

"That's why it's a joint fundraiser. It's believable that you'd have been roped into it by Mx. Kim."

They had a point. Dicky was my other work best friend. Mostly because obviously I love art teachers. A little bit because we share the same supply closet and you trap more bees with honey. A smidge bit because Dicky was a literal institution. They had been here for twenty-four years, this year, and knew everything there was to know about teaching kids, teaching parents, teaching administrators, teaching communities, teaching— well, you get the point. They insisted life was a series of "teachable moments" and "learning opportunities." They also showed up to work with blue hair, bead jewelry, print kimonos, and five gallons of maté. They never fought, never argued. They always got their way. I'm not sure I've ever heard a student say a bad thing about Mx. Kim.

"You know, this isn't a bad idea," I said, imagining how much goodwill I'd foster with Dicky if I got their department a few hundred dollars. Maybe they wouldn't "teach" me about how I didn't need nearly as much blue paint as I always seemed to think I did.

"Focus, Ms. Suré," Chris said, snapping his fingers. "That's the sort of energy that keeps you overextended and underpaid."

"Um, rude," I said. But, you know, spade, spade. "Fine. I think this will work, my perfect little goslings. Well, perfect goslings." Pete wasn't the only towering child. Lu was almost 6 feet and Nathaniel was built like a powerlifter. Mostly because he was a powerlifter. A state silver medalist two years in a row, in fact, go Diablos! This came in handy, as a lot of our equipment was very heavy. Anyway, there wasn't anything terribly "little" about these children, from a dimensions perspective.

"But I think it'll work best if *you* announce it at rehearsal, this evening."

Yes, dear Reader, you read that right: rehearsals begin the second week of school. And no,

I'm not the monster in this scenario. My students beg for rehearsals to start the first *day* of school. Thankfully, the California Interscholastic Federation limits summertime preparation to a single week, so I don't have to fight for my right to vegetate through July.

"Yes," Pete said, nodding once, glancing down at his notes—yes, he'd made notes for this presentation—which was around the time I realized this was an official presentation—"yes, Ms. Suré, I think you're right. They don't argue with us nearly so much as they argue with you."

"Um. *Rude.*" But again, spade, spade.

"Sweet," he said, flipping to the next page in his notebook. "So what did you say the budget for sound was again?" He knew exactly what the budget was, which was how I knew he'd found something fifty to a hundred dollars over budget and was about to use every big, technical word he knew to try and sell me on it.

And so it went.

Chapter Eleven

This is the story about how a fake fundraiser invented for the sake of teaching a half dozen teenagers a lesson about boundaries became a real fundraiser that involved half the school. It's not a very long story. It also, in hindsight, seems almost inevitable. I should have known better, of course. Lesson prep is hours to the minutes of in-class instruction. It only makes sense that a ten-minute lesson would cost me weeks and weeks of personal time that I already didn't have. This is why we do *proportional* responses, Pete. Anyway.

The sequence of events that led me to co-directing Clayton High's first ever "Great Diablo Bakeoff"—no, I didn't pick the name—is roughly as follows:

Monday evening went swimmingly. The tech crew announced the fundraiser to a roomful of students who thought participating in such an event was an actual circle of hell. I mean, truly. Hugo actually asked what he'd done to unleash such karmic punishment on himself. They looked to me, begging for their director to find a way out for them, how could I stand to work with Sunderson, wasn't he Satan Incarnate? I stood there, stoic, still, and let them grovel. Because I am an A+ teacher.

Unfortunately for me, Noel has choir second period, which meant that I needed to intercept Paul before school started that Tuesday to let him know that he might be hearing something about an interclass fundraiser throughout the day. He wasn't in his classroom, though, so I left the fake flyer on his desk with a sticky note that said "this is fake, I'm pranking my students, please back me up xoxoxo Bea."

I don't know what happened to that sticky note. Paul swears up and down it wasn't there when he found the flyer. I'm not sure I believe him. The fatal flaw of this plan, I've come to believe, was me forgetting how obsessed Paul was with the Great British Bakeoff.

Which was why Paul had gotten to Dicky first. I showed up, Tuesday afternoon, to let Dicky know of the "learning opportunity" I was giving my students only to discover that they were already planning their team's table for the competition. Because now the competition had teams and tables. I backed out of that room very slowly and began prepping my speech on why practical jokes are mean, why I'm very sorry, and why I'll never, ever do it again so long as you don't make me put on a fall fundraiser what part of "already on a thousand committees" did nobody understand.

Diana showed up Wednesday morning to congratulate me on my initiative. My students started getting into it, Thursday afternoon—they wanted to beat the flute section with a passion that was, frankly, disturbing—and Belen was asking if she should print an announcement in next Monday's school paper. I told her I'd let her know on Friday.

School ended, that Thursday, and I was twenty minutes into my newest "I am the worst of sinners, my dearest colleagues, and all I can do is beg grace and forgiveness, but this was never supposed to be a thing and for the love of god don't make me do it" speech when somebody knocked on my open door. I jumped—guilty conscience—and looked up, trying to remember if I'd somehow forgotten about an eighth period.

Hedi stood in the doorway and honestly everything I'd ever thought of thinking about flew out of my head. Context: I was ovulating. I didn't understand how a high school teacher could pull off a worsted woolen waistcoat but, well. There he was. I was pretty sure those were pansies printed across his bowtie, which I thought was both a little on the nose and ridiculously hot. Yep. I said it. Flower-print bowties are apparently my thing.

"Hey, Bea, I just wanted to say this looks like it could be really great," he was saying. It took me a second to realize he was speaking—hadn't made it past his neckwear—and a second longer to notice the bright orange piece of paper in his hand.

Oh, fuck all. Fuck absolutely all and one and one and all. Fuckity fuck fuck—

"Oh?" I asked, crossing and uncrossing my legs. Because that made sense.

"Yeah, I mean, the tickets alone would make a good bit of money, and the students would have to collaborate across clubs, which is always fun." I suddenly doubted he'd ever worked at a school before. "I'm not sure how much money bake sales ever make, but I'm sure it's more than nothing. This was really thoughtful of you. And Dicky was telling me your department doesn't even really need to do fundraisers."

"It was my tech students' idea," I mumbled, watching as Karma applied the sealant to my fate. Also, *Dicky*? Since when was Hedi on a first name basis with that heinous bitch?

"I was wondering if you might have space for another team?" he asked, looking up from the flyer. Why was his face so perfect? Why were his lips so kissable? Why was I cursed with *knowing* exactly how kissable those perfect lips were?

"Of course," I said. I had next to no idea what we were talking about, if I'm being honest, but assumed we'd eventually arrive at the same page.

"Thank you," he said, smiling. "I know it's technically just an arts fundraiser, but my students have been going to a lot of classes with Mx. Kim and are feeling very creative. That, and I think they'd really enjoy participating in the bakeoff. Also we need about two hundred dollars for classroom supplies that apparently weren't covered in this year's budget."

I was too hung up on the fact that he kept mentioning Mx. Heinous Bitch Kim to participate in any grounded conversation on the audacity of school districts to not provide basic teaching materials.

"Joey is obsessed with that British show, too. He's got about a dozen different treacle recipes memorized," Hedi was saying, glancing around my room. "Well, this is fun." He was staring at my wall of signed playbills. "I love *Some Like it Hot*." Of course he fucking did. "What is it with arts teachers and cozy vibes? I feel like I could just lay down and take a nap."

"Pretty sure that's not the room's fault."

He laughed, running his hand over his eyes.

"Well, there is that. But it's a very welcoming space. It's nice."

I almost made a joke about how very welcoming my spaces were, at present. Refrained, thankfully. Getting reported for harassment wasn't on today's to-do list.

"Yes, well," I began, trying my hardest not to think about the fact that I knew what he looked like mostly naked. "Inclusion matters."

"Couldn't agree more," he said, smiling, absentmindedly thumbing one of the buttons on his waistcoat. "Speaking of, I've got a Unified scrimmage to go coach. Apparently." He sighed. I raised a brow. He shrugged.

"Thank you again," he said, "my kids will be very excited." And then he was off. To a Unified scrimmage, apparently.

Which was how the fake bakeoff fundraiser became a real bakeoff fundraiser in less than five minutes. Keep your libidos in check, ladies. It'll cost you one month of co-organizing an event with the devil's butthole.

Chapter Twelve

"Kirk is not the devil's butthole," Paul sighed, throwing another balled-up piece of paper at me. He had terrible aim, though, made worse by the fact that he hadn't actually bothered to look before lobbing it in my general direction. A trail of half-assed projectiles lay between where I sat at his piano bench and where he reclined atop a riser, his eyes closed, half of his face covered by a cold, wet towel. He had had a long day, you see. His tenors were, apparently, being a bunch of "tetchy prima donnas." His words, not mine.

"Then *you* can remind him to fill out his portion of the spreadsheet," I said, staring at the piano. That little piece of slime was weaponizing his incompetence on entirely new scales. We're talking cold war levels of nuclear proliferation. Well, proliferation was a two-player game, and Kirk was about to figure out how hard I could Ronald Reagan his ass. I swear to Lilith, if he pretended like he didn't know how to access his Google Suite *one more time*—

"What would I get for my efforts?"" Paul asked, rubbing his temples through the towel.

I perked up. I hadn't thought I would actually get anywhere with him.

"What do you want?"

"I need a banner for Double, Double, Toil and Treble." He said it so casually, so smoothly, that I immediately wondered whether he'd somehow conspired with Kirk to get me into this corner. But no, never. Kirk might like Paul more—Paul had the whole "I'm a man" thing going for him—but Paul didn't like Kirk any more than I did. The man was the literal worst. Once, last year, an oboist's reed had cracked—who knew, right?—and cut her tongue open. She'd asked Kirk if she could go to the nurse's office. Kirk, in front of the entire orchestra, told her to stop acting like a girl and get back to it. She had asked him—keep in mind, she literally had blood dripping down her chin—what was wrong with acting like a girl—because, gen Alpha—and he'd said he wasn't allowed to say anything against "such and such" anymore—such and such being a literal slur for trans folks—so maybe she should just read between the lines like a good little girl or pack up. She very snarkily asked him to please make up his mind about whether or not she was supposed to act like a girl or not, packed up her things, and marched herself to the nurse's station. Very unfortunately, his behavior was reported to the then-VP, who, as you might imagine, did nothing. There were no "witnesses," he said, and then something like "in this generation, if it wasn't recorded, it didn't happen." Since then, half of the band students leave their phones recording through each period, just in case. Kirk seems to know, though. At least, he certainly wised up to what he should and shouldn't say to entire classes of self-appointed reporters.

The student quit band, joined choir halfway through the semester, and is currently in my Theatre 1 class. She's already made three comments about not realizing electives could be fun. It breaks my little 'ol heart, each time. Also, take that, Kirk.

"I can't just lend my techies out," I said, thinking about how they could make the best banner Paul had ever seen in under 15 minutes. "What's in it for them?"

Three years ago, my advanced tech students had set up a make-up booth on Halloween. Students brought their own make-up, told the techs what look they were going for, and, over the course of three hours, five hundred students were turned into corpses, animals, fairies, sparkling princesses, vampires, witches—both scary and sexy—and

141

about twelve drag queens, which was very fun, of course, but which also gave me major reflux. At least two of them did *not* have cool parents. One of the dads organizes the county's yearly quorum on "Bringing Back the Ban."

Anyway, five hundred students paid ten bucks each to get Cinderella'd by the generation raised on YouTube tutorials. They used the money to buy the department an industrial-grade banner printer second hand, because they are *absolute* nerds, and proceeded to get it tuned up by somebody's uncle who happened to know everything there was to know about printing mechanics. Because, at Clayton High, there's an uncle for everything. Since then, the tech students have printed banners for just about anything. Every time they need to buy something for it, they set up another booth, invent a reason for transforming oneself—you should have seen last year's Labor Day looks—and make a smooth grand off of the student body.

"No, no, *I* don't have to sweeten *their* pot," Paul said, pushing himself into a sitting position, "that's on *you*. *You're* sweetening *my* pot, remember?"

They *were* the entire reason I was adjacent to this mess in the first place. That, and they already worked with Paul to put on his yearly Halloween recital. They worked with anyone who used the PAC—Performing Arts Center—for anything. A little bit because nobody else knew how to run sound and light and a lot bit because they were incredibly territorial and hated the state of disrepair their little cave was left in, should somebody try to "figure it out themselves." I knew they'd say yes, if I told them Paul was asking for a banner. I also knew that, if I wasn't careful, I was going to release a half dozen highly skilled individuals into the world who had no notion of their market value and a propensity to say "yes" to unpaid labor situations. Which was, like, the entire premise of professional theatre, but. A teacher can dream.

"If you pay for the supplies out of the Choir budget," I said, nodding to myself, "I'll let them delay building sets for our fall play by a day and have them design and print it during class."

"Done," Paul said. Again, the word came so terribly quickly. I chewed on my lip. It was a new potential habit I was trying out. I sort of liked it. Sort of wondered whether I would ever accidentally bite a hole through anything. The jury was still out, is my point.

"I feel like I just sold Jesus for some silver," I said, sighing, brushing my fingers along the piano's keys.

"In this economy? Nobody would blame you."

I wondered if this was the type of thing I was supposed to confess before Mass. I began playing "Sugar Daddy" from *Hedwig and the Angry Inch*. It was a go-to for when I needed to clear my mind. I pulled its melody from the piano and let the calming affects of a Mitchell and Trask musical roll through me.

***

Paul delivered. I don't know what he did to get Kirk to admit that he knew how to use a damn computer but, there I was, days later, staring at a fully populated google spreadsheet. My eyes misted, a little. I mean, is there a more beautiful sight?

And then—

"That *fucker,*" I muttered. Belen and Claudia —the nearest two to me—looked up from the scripts they were highlighting. Their faces were mirrors of innocence. Claudia, because she actually *was* innocent, what in the world has so upset Ms. Suré as to inspire the use of foul language which she never—*never*—otherwise uses? Belen, because she wanted the tea and had this way of adopting an

144

increasingly neutral face the more she wanted a thing.

"What's wrong?" Claudia asked, her green highlighter stuck on the last word she had been marking. The ink bled into the page, slowly, inexorably, darker by the second.

"Nothing," I said, wondering how I still had a job. "How's the highlighting?"

"Ms. Suré," Belen said, capping her marker, the picture of solicitous feeling. "Is everything okay?" I refrained from rolling my eyes.

"Of course."

"But you don't sound okay," Claudia said, raising her right eyebrow. She was one of the gifted few who could do that. An invaluable talent, the autonomous eyebrow.

"What is it?" Belen asked again, hopping to her feet—oh, to be young—and wandering towards my desk. I decided redirecting was my best course of action.

"Band has submitted ten different teams for the Bakeoff."

"But I thought we were only allowed to have two teams per department?" Claudia asked, that liberated eyebrow going right back up again.

Sweet, summer child.

"Indeed."

"Oh, those *fuckers,*" Hugo shouted from where he'd been running lines in the shrine corner

"Hugo, I'm not saying 'language,' or anything, but you do realize that if anybody else hears you I'm going to have to write you up for language, right?"

"I'll just say it was in the script."

"That works too," I said.

"Ten teams gives them a major competitive advantage, Ms. Suré," Hugo went on, joining Belen at the desk.

"Indeed it does."

"Can you not just tell him it's not allowed?" Sophia asked. Because the entire advanced theater class had been thoroughly derailed, apparently, and I could, apparently, kiss good-bye any notions I'd had of them being productive for the last quarter hour of this class period.

"Ms. Suré doesn't like talking to Mr. Sunderson," Hugo explained.

"Why?" Sophia asked, her eyes wide, her brain thirsty for knowledge. Hugo opened his mouth. Shut it, after I gave him my best "don't you fucking dare" look.

"But that's not fair," Belen snapped, frowning as she studied the spreadsheet over my shoulder, "they're more likely to win, this way." I wondered if Katy Herkle chairing the flute's table

had anything to do with her sudden ire. I decided I
needed to take the high road.

"You can still crush them," I said, "one
table, ten tables. It's the theater, my darlings. The
underdogs always win."

"But then wouldn't that mean the art
students would win?" Angela asked, her voice
floating to us from where she was sketching designs
for this year's shrine.

I frowned, wondering what Mx. Kim's "Art
Club is Fun" kids had done to inspire such doubt..

"Why?" I asked, turning to face her. They'd
decided this year's shrine would be a "Fae Forest"
theme. They'd already lugged the box of fairy lights
down from where we kept them in the prop attic.

"Yeah," Hugo agreed, thinking. "Wouldn't
they be good at baking?" He took a chocolate from
my chocolate jar. "Aren't, like, half of them potters?
Isn't there a kiln out back?"

"And decorating, too," Noel added, miming
the act of icing a five-tiered cake. I don't think
anything was done in moderation in Noel's
household.

"I also have the feeling they'll be more
capable of following a recipe than any of you," I
added, trying to imagine Hugo measuring correctly
under pressure.

147

"Hey," Belen said, all but scowling, "I'm plenty good in the kitchen. Not in a weird way."

What was the weird way?

"I just meant that they need the money the most," Angela said, shading in who-knows-what. "They've got the least funding, right? And the biggest need for materials."

Oh. Right.

"Winning's not affecting how we're splitting the proceeds," I said. Otherwise I would be more actively sabotaging Mr. Sunderson's efforts to rig the scales. See what I did there. It's a pun. Scales, music teacher. Ha, ha.

"Oh?" Angela asked, finally looking up. She looked thoughtful. Because she more or less always looked thoughtful. A bit strange, and a little bit manic. La da da da dada da da—

"Wait," Sophia began, frowning, "so like... we don't actually have to crush anyone? But ... but then, why are we trying this hard?"

"Um, excuse," Hugo said, wheeling on Sophia, "Carnegie much? When did you start nursing at Capitalism's teat? We are *artists,* Sophia, we *love* subsidies *and* we love working our *asses* off for the sake of the craft or *are* you *suggesting* there's *some scenario where you wouldn't give Bowie your all? Hmm?* Because of, what? A little money?* We will *crush* them, Sophia, not because it is what we are paid to do, but because it is the *right. Thing. To. do.*" He had, by that point, leapt across the room, mounted a few chairs along the way, and stopped just beside the David Bowie poster, which he now turned to, murmuring, "forgive her, Lord, she knows not what she says." Angela actually clapped. Noel "here, here'd" and Belen told him to get his dirty boy cooties off of their bible.

There are some moments when I am so incredibly grateful parents don't know what we do in class. This was one of them. I was pretty sure Hugo's mother—the woman who had served me communion just last Sunday, I might add—wouldn't be terribly thrilled about her child's heretical inclinations.

"Ugh," Sophia muttered, trying not to look like she envied Hugo and every single thing about him, "whatever."

"Don't worry, Sophia," I said, "David Bowie did it for the money, too." And before you start judging me for encouraging the children to sell out, I'll remind you that my retirement plan almost entirely consists of at least seven of them getting rich and famous and/or going into corporate law and remembering old Ms. Suré when they're selecting charities to support with their piles and piles of cash. Okay, *now* you can judge me.

The bell rang and half of us jumped out of our skin. A tendency to hyperfixate and over caffeinate can really do that to a person.

"Okay, okay," I said, checking my pulse to make sure I wasn't actually in AFib, "I want us off-book by next Friday, people." There were murmurs of "already done" and "Sophia please only memorize your lines, this time" and one "do we have moss anywhere?" And then they were gone. I wondered why Angela needed moss. I wondered why she thought we would have already had it. I recalled that there was actually a half-used bag of it tucked under the garlands we'd used for *Midsummer Night's Dream,* two years ago. I made a mental note to get Angela's moss from the prop attic. I also made a mental note to find a magical pipe capable of luring a bunch of rats into Mr. Sunderson's office. I added a third mental note, when I remembered that I was supposed to go pants shopping with Lena, that weekend, and hadn't yet come up with an excuse to do literally anything but that. I briefly considered the benefits of writing one's "mental notes" list down. I ultimately ruled in favor of being in a constant state of "am I forgetting something?" It's gotten us this far.

Chapter Thirteen

Something crashed. It was a muted sound from somewhere "further down" RAG Hall. I didn't even really notice it until another something crashed a little more loudly. It was Monday once again—or was it Tuesday?— and I'd just been settling down to read that week's *The Queen's Will* during my free period. The third crash—it sort of sounded like metal buckets falling to the ground—had me rushing out the door and towards Mx. Kim's room, which was the likeliest candidate for the crashes, seeing as theirs was the only classroom in this hall with anybody in it, at present. Well, anyone that wasn't me.

I burst into their lavender-infused domain and barely avoided tripping over a pan of pink primer. That was the least confusing thing about the room I had just entered.

"Um…" I stuttered, blinking, trying to figure out what I was looking at.

"Did you need something?" Hedi asked, cool as a cucumber. Green as a cucumber, too. Somebody had dumped a bucket of paint over his head. That somebody stood just behind him, frozen, her eyes wide, her hands still clutching the bucket.

"Um... I just... I heard a noise," I said, scanning the classroom. Hedi's fourteen students were all working on what appeared to be a wall-sized mural. They'd pushed all of the tables to the edges of the classroom and rolled their butcher paper canvas across the room's center. Some students were laying on their stomachs, their chins propped in one hand, and painting little scenes along the border with the focus and precision of mechanical engineers. Two children—Kirsten and Joey, if I was remembering correctly—were walking a labyrinthine path along the mural's surface, stamping impressions of their bare, blue-painted feet as they carried out their quest. Bri and Amber were pasting buttons to a far corner. This corner was currently my favorite corner. Chloe was currently writing "more chromosomes, more better" across the bottom of the banner.

And, for reasons that were beginning to make sense—the half-finished set of green stripes somebody had painted through the middle, the abandoned roller, an empty green-stained paint pan in need of a refill—Cheyenne had been given a bucket of paint. I assumed there was a world where she had intended to dump said bucket of paint into the paint pan. I assumed Hedi had assumed as much, too. But Cheyenne is a little impulsive. Compulsive, too, and this whole bit about inhibitions. Anyway. I could practically see how she would have made the trip from the table, where the ruler she'd used to pry the lid open still lay. I saw how she would have walked towards the pan. How she would have passed Hedi, how he would have made for a much more interesting paint reservoir than that silly little pan, so far away. I could see it all, really, which became a problem. Because this was one of those situations where you really, really weren't supposed to laugh.

"I can see…" I breathed in through my nose, out through my mouth. I pinched the insides of my palms. I thought about dirty socks. "I can see now, of course, that you have everything well in hand."

"Very much so, yes," Hedi agreed, green paint dripping down the sides of his face, his entire back half fully coated in Behr's best. Cheyenne still hadn't moved. She was watching Hedi with the focus of one who has just realized a coiled snake lay between them and the place they needed to be. Her crime had produced some splashback, too, and green trickled down her hands and arms, slowly, wetly, guiltily. Her apron—because Mx. Kim made all of their students wear aprons—had a fine misting of Sea Foam.

"Yes," I repeated, blinking rapidly. I wanted to ask him how he felt about the situation. I had this niggling suspicion that now wasn't the time for an emotional check-in. "Well…carry on, I guess," I said, figuring I'd better skedoodle while I could still keep a straight face. Or before I began noticing how wetly Hedi's clothes were clinging to him, at present.

"Have a nice day, Ms. Suré," he said, bobbing his sticky green curls in my direction.

"You too, Mr. Dictine," I said, hurrying out. I was wiping my eyes before I'd even made it halfway down the hallway. I didn't go to my room, though, even though there were about fifty people I wanted to text about the scene that had just played out. No, I went through the stage door, climbed the ladder that led to the light and curtain rigs and, on the stage left side, the little half loft some tech teacher from Christmas Past had built. I'd had it evaluated for safety before braving the seemingly sturdy flooring, my first year. This had proved a difficult line to hold, as literally all of the props were stored in that space and as literally none of the school inspectors knew how to do anything in a timely fashion. It soared past standards, thankfully, and we've continued to use it as our own personal warehouse. Because, truly, it's the size of a small warehouse. I don't know how that storied tech teacher did it.

I walked past the "living room section" and, for the zillionth time, asked myself whose idea it had been to say yes when some mother had asked if we wanted the three different plaid couches she was planning on donating to the local Swiftly Thriftly. And no, we don't lug the larger pieces up the ladder, yes, we use the mobile platform the previous teacher bought when he thought he wasn't supposed to use scaffolding when rigging lights in schools anymore—as if there is a universe where students are supposed to be helping rebuild light rigs. I cut through the mismatched chair section and got to the three rows of shelves that constituted the back quadrant. Plastic bins lined the industrial-width shelfs. The previous teacher had also used bins. He hadn't, however, used the descriptive index card system I'd long ago instituted. He certainly hadn't tagged each box with a barcode sticker and created digital records detailing the contents of each box. Mostly because he probably didn't have a sister who thought barcode inventory systems were excellent birthday gifts but maybe a little bit because he, apparently, had been fine living in a state of hellish chaos. Once I'd been assured the attic was structurally sound, that first year, I'd come up here and spent three weekends in a row cleaning, culling, organizing, and, finally, inventorying. There had been dead mice, dead bugs, very much alive kittens —which is why Maya is now a cat lady, she's welcome—and about a UHaul's worth of stuff somebody acquired a decade ago that was no longer usable.

Point being, I was able to walk immediately to the bin I wanted, thank you very much. It was clearly labelled, for starters, and was always returned to its correct place. Because if there's anyone who loves a barcode inventory system more than Lena, it's my tech students. They guard our system with their dragonhearts and nary a freshman Dramatic is allowed anywhere near the bins.

I opened up Bin 3.34 and sorted through the leftover *Newsies* costumes until I found a pair of trousers that I was pretty sure would fit Hedi. I then picked out a white t-shirt, a waistcoat—the trousers demanded it—and a hat, for good measure. I noted what I'd taken in my BIS app—the students had been the ones to realize there was an app for the system—and placed the bin back before going merrily on my way.

I did all of this in about five minutes, which meant that by the time I was skipping back into Mx. Kim's room Hedi had only just finished talking to Cheyenne about why we shouldn't dump paint on others and what we should do instead, next time we feel the urge coming on. She didn't look terribly chastened, from where I stood in the doorway. I was pretty sure her only actual regret was that there was now no more green for her stripes. Hedi was only just taking the time to look down at the paint coagulating upon him as I leaned against the frame. I let him keep looking. I was doing the same, after all, and who was I to hold him to higher standards than I held myself? But then Kirsten waved at me with her glistening and still-very-blue foot. Hedi looked from her to the door and noticed me. He raised a brow, quirked a hip. It was a very "come at me" stance, if I'm being honest.

"Don't get me wrong," I said, "I love this look on you. Very 'understaffed chic.' But if it starts to get too cold, or if you decide you want to save your scalp from whatever they're putting into primer, these days, there's a private restroom in the PAC's dressing room. I can watch your students, if you want, and you can go see how much of your head fits into a sink built for fourteen-year-olds. I left a change of clothes in there, if those aren't salvageable."

He looked down at himself again, sighing. It had been a nice shirt, too. A cute little button-up covered in smiling suns.

"Are you sure?" He asked, glancing at his class.

"You don't trust me with your students?" I asked. He pursed his lips. Said nothing. I glared. Well, tried to glare. I was mostly just biting the smile off before it spread to my whole face.

"Rude," I muttered. "Suit yourself." I didn't bother turning to go, though. It's not like I was doing anything better.

"No, no," he said, walking towards me, his shoes squelching with every step. "Ms. Suré is going to be your aid for five minutes," he told his students, "I have to use the bathroom."

"Five minutes?" Joey asked, staring at his bright green watch.

"Five," Hedi confirmed. I dramatically flattened myself against the door frame as he passed through.

"Ha, ha," he said, rolling his eyes.

"Hey, this is a new shirt," I said. A comment which, of course, prompted him to reach out as if to touch me with his slimy, staining fingers. I jumped back before my adult lady brain could tell my panicking reptile brain that he wasn't actually going to leave handprints on my blouse.

He smirked. It did unfair things to his face. Just, unfair.

"Jumpy, jumpy," he tsked, his voice altogether too soft. And he was standing so close, too. Close enough for me to feel his body heat, anyway, and to smell the strangely pleasant mix of coconut oil and liquid plastic clinging to his skin. He looked down at me, then, in no apparent rush to continue moving through the doorway. All I could think about was how his eyes were practically black, in this lighting. That, and maybe I wouldn't mind his handprints on my blouse, after all.

"Do you really think me so vindictive?" he asked, staring at something. At me, I guess. I can't say anybody's ever stared at me like that, though.

"What happens if I say yes?" I breathed. I immediately cleared my throat, too, because "breathing" any reply in your place of employment whilst inches from the man you've already rejected is, in a word, mortifying. His face cracked into another grin. Literally cracked, to be clear. The Behr was semi-dry, by this point.

"Say the word and find out, Ms. Suré."

Honestly, I'm shocked I didn't commit three fireable offenses, then and there.

"No," I breathed again. I guess I hadn't cleared enough throat, that first go round.

"Mmm." He was so, so incredibly close. He reached out, then, and brushed a few loose hairs from my face. Brushed his fingers through my hair, too. I almost leaned into his touch. Would have, had he kept his hand there for a half a second longer.

"Wrong."

He withdrew, stepped into the hall, checked his watch, and went on his puckish way. His sudden absence left me cold and a whole bunch of other things that weren't appropriate to say or think while on school grounds.

Joey, of course, was the one who asked me why I had so very many green streaks in my hair. He was also the one who let me know when Mr. Dictine became officially late. He let me know this in thirty second intervals from the moment Hedi's five minutes was up. He let me know this fourteen times, all told. I, for my part, asked the class why their devil teacher hadn't been bringing them to theater class, didn't they want to be on the stage? Cheyenne said she very much did, thank you very much, and also that she would like to be Gabriella when we did High School Musical. I didn't have any plans of doing High School Musical, at present, but she made some excellent points and urged me to reconsider. I helped Kirsten wipe the blue off of her feet while Bri and Amber asked if we had better buttons in the theatre. I assured them we did— because screw Mx. Kim—and made yet another mental note to get better buttons. Because. screw. Mx. Kim.

Hedi returned twelve and a half minutes later looking like the dapperest dandy there ever was. He was still flecked all over with paint—sink baths can only do so much—but he no longer looked like he was auditioning for the Blue Group's verdant imprint.

"Thanks again," he said, pocketing his hands and trying to act like he didn't know how ridiculously handsome he looked, just then.

"Where's the hat?" I asked, frowning, pulling myself to my feet. I tip toed off of the mural, not wanting to smudge any of Cheyenne's stripes.

"They're against dress code?"

How dare he.

"But how will people know to come to you for their daily rags?" I complained. He rolled his eyes.

"See, part of me did suspect your motivations," he said, staring down at his clothes. "But then, they fit so well and I sort of stopped caring."

"How dare you," I said out loud, this time. "Suspect my motivations? Pah." I turned to Cheyenne. "You would never suspect my motivations, would you?" She shook her head with all the solemnity a fourteen-year-old could muster. Which is quite a lot, I'll have you know.

"I feel like this is a pot, kettle situation," Hedi mused, glancing from me to Cheyenne and back. I clutched at my heart, wounded to my core.

"The audacity of men," I sighed. I took my leave, then, because the bell was about to ring and I didn't want Nando in my room unsupervised.

"Adieu," I called behind me, waving farewell to Hedi's students.

"Adieu," they called after me.

Chapter Fourteen

I was beginning to wonder if maybe I had a problem. It's one thing to think colleagues are attractive. We're all human, after all, and legal adult humans have a way of attracting.

It's also one thing to develop a cutesy little crush on a colleague. Who hasn't, am I right?

It's another thing to spend an entire evening scheming up the best way to throw a party where everyone but him would cancel. Oops, guess it's dinner for two, tonight. Or, perhaps, an outing to the craft store that starts out so incredibly innocent—Bri wanted cool buttons, after all, and also why aren't any of your students in my classes—but then he sees you struggling to reach something on the top shelf. He steps in, reaches up, plucks the sparkling green buttons from their impossible-to-reach-unless-you're-at-least-average-height resting place. And then he's still just standing there, right behind you, his chest brushing against your back, and you could lean against him, if you wanted. So you do, just to see what it feels like. And it feels so, so good, and he laughs into your hair and lets his arm come to settle around your waist. He makes some joke about the buttons, because that's the snarkiest he can get—honestly, the man is too earnest—and just holds you there.

And then you're just at your kitchen table at 8 PM on a Wednesday, utterly alone, too tired to cook dinner and too overwhelmed to make a DoorDash choice. You've just spent the last fifteen minutes thinking about buttons instead of grading the eighty pop quizzes you convinced yourself your Theater One class needed to take.

I stared at the pop quizzes. I wondered if the students would care if I graded them pass/fail. Most of them would, I knew. I had told them they could get extra credit by drawing a playbill of a show they would write, direct, and produce, if given the opportunity. About half of them had gone all out. Several of their shows seemed promising, too. I sighed. Extra credit wouldn't make a difference, if I graded pass/fail. I pulled the first quiz from the stack and began to go over the responses. Five minutes later, I was camping in Yosemite with Hedi —don't ask me why, I had forgone fantasy logic in this one—and was watching him grill our veggie patties over the fire he'd made all by himself.

164

So, yes, I'd say I had a problem.

***

Open House is fine, I guess. I know most teachers have opinions about it, and all, but most teachers aren't theater teachers. My parents love me, for starters, and their children do, too. At least, they love me enough to sign up for another year of theatrical shenanigans. Because of course it doesn't occur to parents whose children are taking this as their mandatory elective to visit RAG Hall. Those parents are too busy frantically interrogating the freshman math teachers about homework assignments and sophomore English teachers about summer book lists—are you sure you want to be assigning that one, pretty sure the devil showed up at least twice? No, we don't get parents we don't know in RAG Hall on parent/guardian night. Mx. Kim actually brings nonalcoholic sangria and browned butter cookies to their room. Is it a bit much? Perhaps. But the only guardians showing up are the ones who have, over the course of two to four years, replaced most of their dishware with glazed bowls, plates, and cups from Mx. Kim's kiln. And that shit starts looking 40$-a-mug good, after about a year. Point being, Mx. Kim's parents and guardians love them, too.

And so it was that I was half a nonalcoholic sangria in and chatting happily with Belen's mother Pilar about the duo piece Belen and Hugo had begun rehearsing for this seasons' speech and debate competitions. I was asking about college applications and Pilar was asking about her daughter's emotional state—"does she seem angry, to you? Can you talk to her? She won't tell me what's wrong"—which I was sidestepping as best as I could. Mostly because I was pretty sure I knew what was going on, by this point in the semester, and wasn't about to out my student to her mother. That, and I had a pretty intense policy about when and why I would communicate to parents about their children's emotional distress, and Belen's current existential struggles did not come close to qualifying. I distracted Pilar with a story about Tia Rosa's gender reveal cake. By the time I got to the end, I had grown my audience to five mothers and an aunt, all of whom were cry-laughing and "Dios mio!"ing themselves silly.

Claudia's four-year-old brother was running around the edges of my classroom, two boas in hand and singing at the top of his lungs. He was "auditioning," he told me. His dad wouldn't stop apologizing. Everyone else wouldn't stop egging him on. He was just one of those ridiculously cute children. Hugo's dad came by, after a while, and started grilling me about last week's homily. I couldn't tell if he knew I had slept through most of it and wanted me to admit it or needed somebody to vent to about Father Collins, the new priest. This made sense to me, of course. I was Father Hoang's biggest fan and had to work really, really hard not to begrudge him his sabbatical.

A woman who I'd never seen poked her head in around seven PM. She was a redhead. I didn't have any redheaded students. She looked nervous. A little confused, too. I couldn't blame her. I assumed most of the other rooms hadn't looked like a miniature family reunion.

"Hello!" I called from where I stood halfway across the room. I thought better of yelling the rest of whatever conversation was about to ensue and hurried towards her. She was only one foot in, by that point. Her lack of commitment to entering this room would have been offensive had it not been so very comical.

"Hello," I said again, ushering her inside. "I'm Bea Suré. Welcome to Theater Arts!" I searched her face for similarities to any of my yet-claimed students—of which there were approximately fifty, to be clear, since, as previously mentioned, most caregivers of Theater One students didn't care about their child's mandatory arts elective.

"Hi," she said, stepping all of four inches inside the room. "Hi, I'm Greta. I—my daughter really wants to be in your class, and Dicky told me to come talk to you." I immediately relaxed a few degrees. If this woman was on a first name basis with Mx. Kim, she was probably fine.

"Who's your daughter?" I asked.

"Cheyenne?"

I suddenly felt very much like a cat who'd finally managed to break into the creamery. I hoped I didn't look too feral.

"Oh, *wonderful,*" I said, reappraising this woman, her violently red hair suddenly making more sense. "I would *love* to have her in my class. She's an *absolute* delight."

"What?" The woman actually looked confused. "I'm talking about Cheyenne Thompson?"

"No, I know exactly which Cheyenne we're talking about," I said, sticking my head out into the hallway to check and see if Dicky was, for some unknowable reason, strolling about instead of entertaining caregivers in their own classroom. They were not. "I would never scout talent away from another teacher, or anything," I went on, "but I think Cheyenne was made for the theater. No offense to Dicky."

"Oh, no, Dicky said Cheyenne could do both." Of course they did. "Probably. If Mr. Dictine can work it out, anyway. Which I'm sure he can, he's absolutely wonderful." She had this dreamy sort of look in her eyes, when she said it, that made me want to remind her that she was wearing a wedding band. Then again, I get it. It's not everyday your child dumps paint over a teacher's head and is dealt with in an empathetic, compassionate way.

"We're certainly glad to have him." I tried to make it sound like I hadn't just been clenching my teeth. "What can I do to help make this happen?" I would like to say it was a selfless request. A "wow I just love children so much, the more the merrier" request. And it sort of was. It sort of was also part of my newest entrapment scheme. If Cheyenne started coming to my class then Hedi would *also* have to come to my class—at least, once in a while—to make sure everything remained accessible. To make sure I knew how to adjust curriculum to fit into Cheyenne's IEP. Maybe he'd have to stay late, some days, and show me exactly how lesson plans worked. Maybe—

"Ms. Suré?" Greta was asking, her tone making it clear I had missed at least two sentences.

"Hmm?" I asked, trying not to think too much about the fact that I had just been thinking up

169

ways to use a student's IEP to score with her teacher.

"I said, I don't need anything from you except the 'yes' you just gave me. I just wanted to meet the woman Cheyenne hasn't stopped talking about and see if… if this could actually work. Hedi already said you were great with the kids—" obviously I mostly stopped listening after that— "but I wasn't so sure—art's been going so well, after all, and what are the odds two electives would work out, when she hasn't had any in over a year? No offense to Margaret, but, well, there's only so much one overworked teacher can do. But then Dicky told me it would work out, if I wanted it to, and that I should just come and chat with you. So here I am."

I began to ask her just what *exactly* Hedi had said before thinking that maybe, just maybe, that wouldn't be a great look.

"Well, I'm open to whatever Mr. Dictine thinks is best," was what eventually came out of my mouth. "And look forward to having Cheyenne in my classroom."

Greta looked around at the organized chaos. She still seemed nervous, I suppose, but there was a little bit of curiosity and—dare I say—hope peaking through.

"Well. She is too."

Poor Lena had to listen to me happy rant about my victory over students' souls for the entire twenty-three minute drive home.

Chapter Fifteen

It's always shocking to go to bed in late
August and wake up halfway through September.
There are some years where I blink and it's
Halloween. I don't know what it is about the
beginning-of-semester vortex, but it has a way of
eating the ninth month of every year. I'm not
complaining, of course. I've never really liked dark
blue.

We'd gone from "one week down" to "one
month down" in the span of a breath, it seemed. My
students had already competed in two speech and
debate competitions—Belen and Hugo had won in
Duo, last weekend, and Angela had gotten second
with her DI—and the fall's play, *Paganini*, was
almost completely blocked. My Theater One kids
were about to perform their first rounds of
monologues and if I'm being completely honest I'm
not entirely sure what my Advanced Tech students
were doing. It involved a lot of time in the sewing

room and a weird amount of internet searches about worsted woolens.

It was a Tuesday and it was past my lunchtime. I'd stayed after class to talk a fourteen-year-old off of a "no, your bangs look fine, don't listen to Samantha" ledge. They really did look fine, too. She had the face for it.

I waltzed into the Teacher's Lounge, hungry and unsuspecting, and didn't catch the look in Stacy's eyes fast enough to bail.

"Ms. Suré."

I wheeled around, saw Diana, and wondered what in the world it was that I could possibly have done. Well, that she would have heard about. I did accidentally say "fuck" in front of freshmen on Friday but I was pretty sure most of them hadn't been paying attention.

"Hello to you too," I said, wondering if I should just kiss my lunch half-hour goodbye.

"I thought I was very clear that I wanted all of you to do your best to be available as veteran partners to your mentorship program participants," she clipped off. Which was a feat, actually, because that wasn't the clippiest of sentences.

"Not entirely sure how that counts as a clear directive, but okay," I said, seeing fully where this was going. "Have I done something wrong, Diana?"

"You haven't met with your mentee. Not once. How am I supposed to get this program off the ground if my teachers won't even take it seriously?"

"That's never stopped you before," Paul chimed in. Diana's nostrils actually flared. She didn't acknowledge him, otherwise.

"Did Hedi snitch on me?" I asked, grinning, wondering if this was payback for teaching Cheyenne and Joey, my newest theater student, how to bite their thumbs at people.

"He did not. Well, sort of," Diana said, frowning, wondering, I suppose, why I wasn't also frowning. "I was processing reimbursement requests and noticed you hadn't made one."

"Oh, so you *didn't* forget," Paul chimed in. Again.

"She did," Yvonne said—hi, Yvonne!—"but somebody very helpfully reminded her." Paul gave Stacy the thumbs-up. Stacy shrugged, not even bothering to nonverbally deny it.

"I saw him this morning and asked why the two of you hadn't spent the money yet," Diana went on, ignoring her mutinying employees. "He said you hadn't been anywhere to spend it, yet."

"That doesn't mean we haven't been engaging in a mentorial relationship. Not all wisdom need be imparted in costly settings," I said,

174

unscrewing the cap of my thermos. I only had ten minutes left to eat this soup. If Diana wanted to hound me she would have to do so while I slurped. "You should be grateful, Diana. I'm saving the school district money."

"I would prefer that you didn't," she said. Which was probably the first time she'd ever advocated for spending more money in her entire time as a school principal.

"Very well. Your wish is my command. Your prerogative, my highest honor. The money will be spent. We will not spare a single dime. I'll pour manhattans down his throat, if that's what it takes."

Diana cursed a little. Muttered a little, too, before leaving us to our lunches, grumbling the whole way out about how none of us knew the meaning of taking a thing seriously.

"Stacy's plenty serious," Yvonne called after Diana, "which just cost you three hundred and sixty bucks, so—" but the door snicked shut, cutting us off from our boss's ears. Yvonne shrugged and went back to grading.

***

I was waiting outside my door when Hedi's class walked by on their way to their period with

Mx. Kim. I smiled. He smiled. Some of his students smiled. There was a whole lot of smiling.

"Anyone ever tell you snitches get stitches," I asked, still smiling. He rolled his eyes.

"I knew this was going to come back and bite me in the...bitables?" He tried, frowning, his students hanging on to his every word. "It didn't even occur to me to lie, if that makes you feel better."

"It does, but only because lying is wrong," I said, making direct eye contact with our teenaged audience. "Looks like I owe you an event wherein which thirty dollars can be spent, Mr. Dictine."

"An event? Is that what they're calling it, these days?"

There was a whole lot of eye contact, just then. A whole lot of Hedi daring me to say literally anything and a whole lot of me trying to remember why in the world we were dancing this dance. Why we weren't dancing the other one. The more fun one. The one that involved fewer clothes and him cooking dinner when I didn't have the energy. I had the vague sense it had something to do with me having a meltdown one night after a date that had gone mostly well and subsequently refusing to talk about it like a grown adult.

"Mom spent twenty-two dollars on one hour of bowling and three sodas yesterday," Joey added helpfully, "That's less than thirty dollars."

"Ooh, I love bowling," Hedi said, smiling, "thank you, Joey." I swore to all the gods there ever were and are and would be, if he suggested bowling, I was going to stab my eyes out. "We could go bowling, Ms. Suré."

"I'm free this evening."

"What a wonderful coincidence, I am too. Shall we go after school?"

"Works for me."

"Excellent. It's an event, then."

"It's an event."

* * *

Here's the thing about bowling: not to put too fine a point on it, but I hate it. I hate it so much. It's not even that I'm bad at it—though I am certainly that—or that I think the shoes are tacky—but I mean, come on. I just… I hate it. The balls are heavy, the floors are waxy, the scoring makes no sense. Turns are never long enough to get a conversation going. It's just a one- to two-hour activity where everything is constantly being interrupted by a screen telling you to stand up and throw a pair of balls around.

"I'll remind you," I said hours later, standing in the school parking lot and glancing at my phone's GPS, trying to figure out where the nearest bowling alley was. "We can do literally anything else."

"I'm afraid it's far too late for that," Hedi said, reading the map over my shoulder. "I've spent the last two hours mentally preparing for this activity. I'm physically incapable of changing gears now."

I scowled up at him.

"We could also just, oh, I don't know, go for a quiet beer?"

"But we've already done that," he said, his black eyes glittering in the falling sun, "And I don't recall it ending particularly well. Besides, the alley has beer. Now, pick a place and let's go. I haven't the time to spare." It took me a second to realize it was a pun. He waited the entire second, too. Grinned, once he saw that I'd gotten it, and waited for me to acknowledge his funny, funny joke.

Dear reader, I did not acknowledge his funny, funny joke. I was too busy reeling from the ad hominem attack he'd made on my quiet beer suggestion. I did, however, pick a place—the one equidistant from both our homes—and tell him to hop too. I may have even suggested that he'd better hope this place had some sort of salted and fried potato snack option, otherwise I'd strike. He didn't laugh, either. He did roll his eyes, though, and smile.

I thought about that smile for almost the entire way to the bowling hell. Sorry, alley. I spent the rest of the way wondering what the fuck my plan was with this guy. I wanted to be friends. I wanted to be more than friends. I did *not* want to be exes.

Furthermore, I wasn't entirely sure how he felt. We were friendly, of course, but I wasn't sure how long he had to know a person before he counted them as a capital-F friend. At the very least, he didn't actively hate me. I felt like most of our interactions had flirtatious undercurrents, too. Sometimes they weren't even that "under." But then, he *was* a scorpio.

But I didn't want to make his life harder. He had just moved across the country to a place that had once been home, which was rife enough. He'd made friends, in the past month—I was pretty sure that was an occupational hazard of his—but he still didn't have the sort of community he'd had in Boston. Yet, anyway. He was navigating a new job at a new school while trying to manage his mother's health, which was its own complicated mix of biological and emotional needs. He hadn't opened up too much about how that was going—yet—but he did take her the food I kept making. I'd initially been sending her pies and spiced brownies but then he'd said she was on some sort of anti-inflammatory diet, which I thought was fake until he explained it a few more times. Regardless, the past several dishes had been of the "no butter, no wheat, no sugar" variety. Which, not going to lie, is not my strong suit. He'd assured me she had liked the tortilla soup I'd made, but I was pretty sure I could make a boot casserole and he'd tell me it was delightful. Anyway. The soup hadn't been terrible, but the texture had been off. I'm not entirely sure why but I sort of think it might have had something to do with the three cups of mushrooms I added after reading that people with MS needed extra vitamin D.

All that to say, he had enough going on, at the moment, and adding my "will we, won't we" shenanigans to his "list of things requiring time and energy" seemed borderline criminal. Which was why, twenty minutes later, I walked into the bowling alley, fully resolved to be excellent friends and also to stop mentally undressing him every third minute.

This resolution lasted about forty-five seconds, which was the amount of time it took for me to spot him sitting at lane seven, bent over and tying his shoes, two beers and a basket of fries sitting beside him on the table. I watched him, for a moment, like an absolute creep. But honestly, since when does shoe-tying require that much forearm flexing? I reminded myself we weren't supposed to be lusting after him—see above—and that the provision of fried potatoes was not the same as a marriage proposal. Though, now that I think about it, I'm pretty sure I'd have more faith in a man who brought me potatoes than a man who brought me rocks.

"How fast do you *drive*?" I asked, seconds later, arriving at what was to be our lane for the next hour.

"I guessed you were an eight," he said, holding up another pair of shoes. I was, of course, and also a little concerned that he knew that. Like... why is that something a person would know? "And also, I drive the speed limit, thank you very much." That, and I took a wrong turn on Rose Avenue and had to circle a parking lot until my GPS updated with its new route.

I stared at the shoes. Stared at the beer. Stared at Hedi, as he plugged our names into the monitor so that we could begin our game. I ate a fry.

"What'd you get us?" I asked, studying the beer.

"Us? Who's this 'us?' Those are mine."

I smiled and put on the damn shoes.

It turns out bowling is not the actual worst. Especially when you tap out, halfway through, and make your bowling partner bowl for you as you stand beside him and eat bowling alley snacks.

"Ooooh, go us," I said, staring at the monitor as Hedi got me another strike. "We're so talented."

He rolled his eyes. Accepted a nacho for his efforts.

"So," I said, realizing, belatedly, that I hadn't gone over any of the things on Diana's checklist. I rummaged around in my hip pack until I found the sheet she'd handed me almost a month ago. "On a scale of 1-10, how welcoming are you finding Clayton High?"

Hedi paused, giant green ball in hand, to stare at me, confused. He saw the paper, which only lessened his confusion by about half a degree.

"Are you writing a report?" he asked, throwing his ball. It looked promising. I waited until I saw it knock every pin down before going back to my twice-folded paper.

"No," I said, showing him the page, "I'm dotting a scale." Indeed, Diana had created eleven fields, all ranging from one to ten. "I guess there's space for explanation under each one," I mused, "so feel free to expound, as the mood strikes." I looked up at him. "How has your first month been?" His

182

gaze slid down to a spot near my right shoe. For a second I thought something had gone seriously wrong. Then I thought maybe I'd dropped a jalapeño on the ground. I finally realized the man was actually taking the question seriously and thinking his way through an honest, useful answer.

"It's been different," he finally said. "I like the teachers, here. They're very supportive. Margaret's great. She seems about a day away from a breakdown at any given moment, but—wait, no. I shouldn't say that." He looked at the paper. "Don't write that down." Y'all, I didn't even have a pen on me.

"I would never," I said, hand to chest, wondering what sweet summer child this was that couldn't even say one true fact about his colleague. "Pretty sure the mentor-mentee relationship follows 'confessional seal' rules. Whatever you say here, stays here." I tapped my forehead. "So, you know. Spill all the tea. I'm Bounty strong."

"Anybody ever tell you not to mix your metaphors," he said, throwing his next ball.

"I feel like we aren't done talking about your first month at Clayton High," I said, trailing after him as he went to collect another ball.

"What else am I supposed to say? What would be useful information to share?" He asked, frowning, still thinking. "What's this for, again?"

I rolled my eyes.

"This form doesn't need you to be useful, Hedi. It's just a conversation starter. It's creating a script for emotional check-ins. I think Diana wants us to become work friends so that you have somebody to go to with problems you don't feel qualify as 'principal problems.' Because a lot of teachers quit over things that they didn't talk to anybody about. Or something." Wow, maybe I was more of a shill than I thought I was.

"Oh." He took the beer I handed him. Took a sip, gave it back. Bowled a strike. "Well, that's nice. I don't really think I'll be quitting any time soon. I may be new to the school, but this is my eighth year teaching."

"So I'll mark you down as 'not a flight risk,'" I said.

"Is that an actual categ—oh, ha, ha."

I took a sip from my beer. Or was it his beer? I'd sort of gotten them mixed up, ten minutes ago.

"How're the relationships going?" Well, that wasn't what I had meant to say. Not at all. He threw a spare, that time, before turning to give me the dictionary definition of "sardonic glare."

"Diana wants to know!" I squeaked.

"I find it hard to believe that Diana's allowed to ask questions about my love life."

I wagged somebody's beer cup at him.

"Um, first of all, I didn't say anything about romance and, second, it's perfectly normal to check in on a person's care community."

"Just like it's perfectly normal to call it a 'care community.'"

"Somebody hasn't kept up with their CTEs," I said, finishing off his beer. "So, relationships? This sudden defensive energy makes me think they aren't going so well." I was just seeing if he had an inner bear I could poke, by this point.

"Beatrice Josefina Suré," he said, glancing up at the monitor. "If you want to know something specific, you're going to have to ask for it specifically."

I couldn't help but think he wasn't referring to my curiosity about his care community. I decided to put a massive pin in that one and focus on what really mattered, here.

"The hell do you know my middle name?"

"You've mentioned it before?"

"When did I—" oh, right. We had filled out a "what would your millennial bakery be named" quiz on Buzzfeed and middle names had been part of the equation. This was somewhat of an awkward memory, though, because the quiz had been taken after "we'd gone to his" but before "we'd lost our bra." Oops. "Never mind." He looked about as

185

awkward as I felt, just then, which made me think he hadn't actually meant to resuscitate certain historical details.

"I've made friends," he blurted, so obviously in a bid to change the topic that I actually did laugh, "just, to be clear."

"Ugh. Who are these bitches."

"Well, you, I'd like to think."

The literal cockles of my literal heart superheated. He didn't even seem to notice. He was still talking about his friend-making endeavors.

"Anita's lovely. Dicky, too, but you already know that."

I'm not so sure that that was something I knew, thank you very much.

"My neighbors are the types of people who think being a single adult is the same as being on hospice, so that's fun. They keep inviting me over for dinner. Buying me things. Bringing me cookies. I walked outside the other morning and Cheryll had left a bouquet on the porch. She'd picked the flowers from her own garden and arranged them with her own hands."

"Well, that sounds positively whimsical," I said, thinking about how much I wanted a wife who would fill our house with flowers she'd grown herself. "What sort of flowers?"

"I'm not sure," Hedi said, his mouth flirting with the idea of a smile, "I can't say I've ever really tried to learn flowers' names."

"How rude."

"Indeed. I'll be better in the future." He threw another strike, which somehow ended the game. I thought we'd been shortchanged on time until I checked my watch and saw that an hour had indeed passed.

"Hey look," I said, grinning at the monitor, "I won! Way to go, me!"

"You really earned it."

We sat down and began the business of shoe removal. Weirdly enough, I wasn't quite ready to take the shoes off. I didn't think I'd left myself much space to request we play another game, though.

"I would ask you to dinner," Hedi said, taking the words from my mouth. Well, sort of. I would have used a different verb tense. "But I don't want you to think I'm...oh, I don't know."

I looked up, realizing this was probably a "requires eye contact" sort of conversation.

"I like you, but not like... I'm not trying to get in your pants, is what I'm saying, and I know the way we met doesn't exactly... oh, I don't know." He sighed, scrubbing his hands through his hair. "God. I thought I'd mapped out a perfectly

187

professional way of addressing the elephant in the room. I was going for eloquence and the best I could do was 'don't worry, your panties are safe.' Which is, of course, inappropriate, I shouldn't be talking about a colleague's panties." He buried his head in his hands and left it there. "God."

I was a little bummed to learn my panties were safe, of course, but mostly I was amused that he'd said "panties."

"I like you to, Hedi," I said, very much aware of the multiplicity of meanings contained in that single, silly phrase. "And I know. What you're trying to say, I mean. You've seen my boobs, I've seen your comic book collection. And now we work together. And, gasp, get along. And I don't think our shit timing and regrettable use of a dating app should preclude an actual friendship. Regardless of what I may or may not have very aggressively stated at eleven PM on a Thursday. Which, to be very clear, is two hours past my bedtime."

He studied me through his fingers.

"Not a good enough reason to say 'boobs,'" he muttered. Which was funny. I hadn't really taken him for a mutterer. But I suppose everyone is allowed a little fit of petulance, now and again.

"You just mentioned my panties, like, ten times."

"Kind of like how you just beat me at bowling," he agreed, finally dropping his hands. He seemed less embarrassed, though, which was good, because I was fully gauging how embarrassed I should be from his reactions and it had gotten a little sticky there, for a moment.

"Exactly." I finished lacing up my shoes. "Does this mean…are we good?"

"I am if you are."

"I'm great.'

"Perfect."

"We can be friendly and not worry about the other person thinking we're trying to jump them in the hallway." A bold-faced lie, but he obviously didn't need to know that.

"And we can pursue an actual friendship outside of school without worrying that the other person will misread our intentions as romantic in nature," I went on.

"An excellent idea. I wished I'd thought of it myself."

"Ha, ha." I looked up at him, wishing that he would stop agreeing with everything I was saying.

"It was a zine collection," he said, standing. I rose, too, and tried not to feel the sadness sinking into my stomach.

"What?"

"They aren't comic books. They're zines."

189

I refrained from making any comments about him being a stereotype or how low the lighting had been or how I'd been a little distracted by the fact that his lips had been all over me when I'd noticed the twenty or so magazines neatly ordered on one of his immaculate bookcases. "Sorry I didn't take a second look, you'd been doing something with your tongue, just then, that precluded conscious thought" didn't really seem like a thing I was supposed to say out loud after the conversation we'd just had.

"You. Are an absolute nerd," was what I finally managed. He quirked an eyebrow. Smirked, then. Opened his mouth to say something else—to change the topic, one could only hope—when his phone dinged. He checked it, chewed on his lip a few times.

"I really was going to invite you to dinner," he said, typing out a reply before pocketing his phone. "I've got to go. My mom just fell and my sister's worried she might have hit her head."

"Oh dear god," I said, "do you need—can I? Is there anything I can do?"

He shook his head.

"No, no, my sister says she's probably fine. She just wants me to stay up with her. Make sure there's no concussion or anything."

"Of course," I said, my eyes misting. I had a terrible habit of sympathy crying. "You are released, then. This was fun."

"It was," he said, smiling tightly. I started to go for a hug—habit—before realizing this was maybe one of those relationships where I shouldn't just be physically affectionate all the time. Not until emotional boundaries had been settled, anyway. I paused, arms half up, and must have looked as awkward as I felt. The asshole actually smirked. Hugged me, too, and tried to act like he wasn't panicking about his mother, just then. And then he was gone.

I looked around the bowling alley and told myself not to weep over his mother's tumble. I was easily distracted by other thoughts, of course, selfish creature that I am. I waited for our new friendship pact to register with my libido. It did not. I kept waiting to stop thinking about every single place our bodies had met, during that brief embrace. I did not. I trudged out of the alley, defeated and deflated and wondering how in the world I was supposed to be friends with this jerkwad.

I called Lena on the way home. I was going to tell her all about it, too, but she was crying when she picked up and that sort of derailed my thoughts. One of her clients had died, apparently, and she couldn't stop thinking about the headache the man had had, the morning prior, when he had come in to discuss a contract he'd wanted her advice on.

Chapter Sixteen

The funny thing about planning school wide fundraisers is that eventually you have to actually do the thing.

"I'm just…so confused," I said, that first Friday of October. Maya patted my shoulder, the bastion of moral support that she was.

"It'll be okay," she said, staring at the eight tables ringing the stage, each decorated… well, differently, is one way to put it.

"But… they know they have to use the surfaces for food prep, right?" I asked, wondering if nobody had listened to my Tech students as they gave the various contestants the run down of how this event would be technically executed. Belen, of course, had shepherded our team to greatness. They had gone with a spooky vibe—mostly because it was the hallowed month of October and there were no other vibes to be had, at present, but also a little bit because they are seventeen- and eighteen-year-old drama students—and their station looked like the table version of "We Have Always Lived in the Castle." So, mason jars full of random objects, sugar bowls labelled "XXX," and a black-lace table cloth that looked like a shawl, from some angles, and a shroud, from others. And, most importantly, a neat middle surface area that had been covered in a very large, very sanitizable cutting board that would double as a general "countertop" area.

Dicky's students had hung their table with handmade wind chimes. All of their cutlery was ceramic, too, and they had painted a backdrop for themselves that was one of those impressionist blue-on-white "maybe it's a sky, maybe an ocean, maybe an inner monologue." It actually brought tears to my eyes. I had already asked Dicky what they were planning on doing with it, after, because I had an empty wall in my house that needed some more oceanic inner monologues. They said they'd have to ask their students.

The choir kids' two tables looked like a Pride parade. Rainbows, everywhere, and vomits of glitter. There was tulle bunched across every conceivable square inch of surface area which made me wonder if they actually knew how food prep worked. I supposed they could mix cookie dough in the valleys of their omnichromatic fabric.

The home economic class got a table, too, because we had to use their classroom's ovens. Their table was perfect, of course. Measuring cups set just so, four different types of cutting boards, knives carefully stored for optimal safety. Fourteen clean and folded dish towels ready to meet every conceivable drying and wiping need.

The chemistry teachers, also possessed of sets of ovens, had agreed to participate. They did not volunteer any of their students, though. Something about the sophomore classes lab reports not suggesting much latent baking talent. I wasn't entirely sure we were allowed to say that about entire classes. Then again, none of my Theater One students had been allowed anywhere near the stage props. I just didn't trust fourteen-year-olds with so many donated knives. I didn't even know what the teams planned on cutting, if I'm being completely honest. Then again, they didn't either. The "Challenge Committee"—the set of teachers responsible for planning the three rounds of competition—had been selected by Diana, who believed that the teachers putting the event on— Paul, Dicky, myself, and Satan—were not entirely impartial and could not, apparently, be trusted to come up with challenges that wouldn't stack the odds in our students' favor.

Which led me to the next two tables. Yes, two—Paul had come through for a second time and convinced Mr. Sunderson he couldn't have a dozen entrants, the stage wasn't that big and nobody would sit through four hours of teenagers trying to figure out what a beet was. The band students' tables... well, we'll just say that, much like their director, they weren't terribly inspired.

Hedi's students hadn't messed around. They had color coded every kitchen instrument—reds for quarters, blues for halves, yellows for wholes—and had asked the tech students to help them alter the table's height so as to better accommodate Julienne, who used a wheelchair and couldn't be bothered with craning. They had printed out visual interpretations of common measurements, rolled in a cooler full of gatorade—needs must—and hung all of the aprons they'd been dying with Mx. Kim in a neat, ready-to-go line.

A ninth table sat in the center of the stage. It was stacked with eight sets of ingredients and covered over with a giant purple tablecloth. The urge to peak was so, so, so terribly overwhelming. I looped my arm through Maya's and clutched both hands together, reminding myself to stay strong.

"I just hate him so much," Maya said, staring at the band kids' table. "And half of Newspaper is *in* band. And I love them. How could somebody so terrible be surrounded by children so wonderful and just... stay so terrible?"

"I couldn't have said it better myself." Not even I was sure if I'd meant that sarcastically. I checked my watch as Lex ran up to us. She was in the stage manager's classic black shirt/black pant combo, replete with a headset and clipboard.

"Doors open in two hours, Ms. Suré," she said, glancing at her phone. "Call time was ten minutes ago and seven of the teams have checked in. We'll give the last team about five minutes to show up before making them forfeit." Which let me know the missing team was probably populated with flutists. Lex would have tried a lot harder to find any other team, but the flutists ... well, she had dated one of them, last year, until said flutist cheated on her with a mathlete. Their breakup had taken about two weeks of class time to emotionally process. Well, "emotionally process." There were a few days of tears and then about a weeklong revenge plot that got disturbingly specific. They didn't do it, to be clear—there are limits to what I, a state-mandated reporter, can and cannot allow—but I definitely know who to go to if I need to plan the mental and spiritual destruction of a person. Barbara —the flutist—didn't know how close she'd come to emotional annihilation.

"Works for me," I said, checking my watch again. "I'm going to check on the bakery booths."

"Oh, same," Maya said, shuffling after me as I hopped off of the stage and made my way down an aisle to the doors at the back of the theater. I sort of abandoned Maya, halfway there—"two hours before curtain" me cannot accommodate her shambling pace—but it's not like she was going to get lost.

I burst into the atrium and was met with organized and (mostly) deliciously fragrant chaos. Usually this space was where people bought tickets and formed the queue to enter the theater for whatever show was on. Which, I guess, was its function today, too. But today every single inch of wall was lined with tables full of things for a bake sale. Most of my collaborating teachers thought we'd make more money off of the ticket sales. But most of my collaborating teachers didn't understand how heinously competitive some parents could get when their reputation as a "good cook" was on the line. Only a few arts and performing arts students from each class would be on the stage, tonight, but all of the students had been asked to participate in the Bakeoff Sale. Paul had even had the nasty idea of turning it into a competition. He had set up a table where people could cast their votes for the best treat. Which meant that thirty of our most manic caregivers had railroaded their children, taken creative control of their child's submission—because they were submissions, now—and were currently ten seconds away from a riot over whose polvorones de canale were the very best.

I had complete faith that every last dessert would be sold.

I did a lap of the booths and did not laugh despite the fact that some of the contrasts were comedy gold. I passed two girls from Choir One who hadn't even bothered to plate the ghost-shaped sugar cookies they'd clearly just bought from the store. Beside them, a dad was setting out his tiered cupcakes—who tiers cupcakes?—that he'd covered in black sugar-glass and made look like gothic cathedrals. Because "October," he'd said. Three moms were arguing over where to plug in their deep fryer—because "it's a sin to eat a sopapilla any other way than fresh"—which I decided I'd let Paul deal with. They were his moms, after all, and there were only so many times I felt like explaining to a person that school regulations did not permit a deep fryer out in the open. I realized Paul didn't know this, though, doubled back, and took it upon myself to shepherd them into the concession stand's kitchen. It's not like I didn't want them to succeed. They'd brought three jars of dips for their fried dough and one of them was cheesecake-inspired.

Chris buzzed me on the headset and told me I was needed in the blackbox. I did one last scan of the Bakeoff Sale, hurried over to where Maya was sampling product, and deputized her to "oversee this." I made a vague gesture with my hand but she knew, more or less, what I meant. I felt a little bit guilty about entrapping her like that, but this job had sugary perks. Not like that time she'd asked me to run the water station with a bunch of basketball dads at the yearly athlete carnival. I shivered at the memory. Congratulated myself, too, on being the superior friend.

I jogged to the blackbox—if you don't know what that is, just google it, I can't think of an explanation that will take less than five hundred words and I don't want to repeat the prop attic incident—and realized, upon entering, that I should have been sprinting. No fewer than five students were screaming at each other. No, scratch that, four students and one teacher. I was not best pleased to see that one of the screaming students was Claudia but was a little bit better pleased to see that Dicky's students made up the rest of the delegation. They tended to be on the right side of history.

I ran between the students and Mr. Sunderson—the adult screamer—before he could suspend anyone. That was around the time I noticed some of Hedi's students were crying in a corner, and that Hedi was doing his best to keep his entire class from having a total meltdown. Which explained why the only other teacher in the room hadn't been doing his teacherly duty of deescalating whatever the hell was going on between Kirk and the other students.

Claudia was yelling in Spanish, thankfully, so Kirk wasn't aware that she was telling him in explicit detail what Hell would be like, when he arrived. Kirk was going on about disrespect, which was about as much as I could understand in the two seconds it took to get from the door to the three feet of space between him and children.

"Hush," I said to the students. They stopped shouting immediately. One of the senior art student's was actually panting, she was so mad.

I wheeled on Kirk, filtered out the first eight things I wanted to say, and landed on the least abrasive question I was capable of, in that moment."

"What in the world is going on?"

He looked like maybe he was going to punch something.

"What's going—Bea, I don't know what sort of hippy dippy classroom you run," he spat, his eyes wide and white, "but students usually aren't allowed to scream at teachers."

I nodded. Of course not. Silly me.

"Right, well, we need to carry on with places, Kirk. We can circle back—"

"Your students aren't going anywhere *near* that stage, after the stunt they just pulled."

"Kirk, please just—"

"God, Beatrice, the fucking *audacity,* it's like you think rules don't apply to you.*"*

I blinked. Heard a little static, too. It was mostly the com going off in my ear. It was a little bit the rage overwhelming my every ounce of being.

"Thank you for your help, Kirk," I managed, "but I can take it from here. Paul needs your help in the parking lot."

"Where the *hell* do you get off—"

"That is inappropriate speech for school, Mr. Sunderson, and I'll be happy to involve Diana in a conversation about how you shouldn't ask colleagues about their sexual encounters in front of students. Paul put you on traffic duty, which is where you're needed."

"Your students will be in detention for the month, Beatrice, when I get through—"

"Pretty sure that's not true, Kirk."

He was spitting mad. A foot taller than me, too, and seventy pounds bigger. He was every bully I'd ever known and every bigot I'd ever cursed. He looked within five seconds of a stroke, too, which wasn't something I would wish on my worst enemy.

I didn't look away. I didn't blink, didn't breathe. Just stood there, puffing out my chest like some Garland Damned bird of prey, and stared him down.

He left cursing. He turned on his heel and stormed out, looking at no one and slamming the door as hard as he possibly could. After, everything was so intensely still. Silent, too, but for Joey and Kirsten's sniffles and Hedi's quiet encouragement.

Chris was by my side in less than a second. Everyone watched him. He didn't seem to notice.

"Sorry, boss, I would have tried to handle the situation but you told me to call you whenever teachers are the problem."

"Exactly right," I said, shaking, suddenly, the adrenaline abandoning me all at once. Dicky sprinted into the room, just then, their rainbow shawl whipping behind their shoulders. They looked like a gay fury. Like the Queer Avenging Angel, out for the blood of bigots. I wondered which of their students had texted them.

"What the fuck happened," they asked, scanning the room, trying to figure out what had transpired.

"I don't—" but my throat closed up, just then, and I had to take a moment.

"Give us the room," Dicky said to no one in particular. Chris took that as a personal directive.

"Let's practice stations, people," he said, snapping his fingers and leading the way out of the room. People followed him without a word.

"Not you," I said, staring at Claudia. The other three art students understood that instruction to include them, as well. A minute later and it was just Dicky, me, the screamers, Hedi, and his entire class. He was still crouched in front of Joey and Chloe, who couldn't quite get their tears under control. He was alternating between instructions on breathing and assuring them that they were perfect and wonderful and that bad men would always be around, but that was okay, because we always had each other. We always had the power to chose to sit and stand together. To love ourselves and one another, no matter what. Cheyenne was hugging Chloe close and echoing every fourth word Hedi said which was, of course, around the time I started crying.

"What happened?" Dicky asked, turning to their senior, Alex. Alex looked like maybe she hadn't completely ruled murder out.

"Mr. Sunderson came in, looking for who knows what, and wasn't watching where he was going. He stepped on Chloe's sign. The one she just finished making to hang from their table. Joey got upset and asked him to apologize. Mr. Sunderson didn't. Instead, he yelled at them and..." she leaned in and whispered so quietly I could barely hear, "he told them that if they couldn't keep up they needed to get out of the way."

I looked forward to my yearlong campaign to get him fired.

"Es eso incluso legal?" Claudia spat.

"Mi querida," I said, remembering, last second, that I couldn't just go around telling students that their teachers were breaking the law. "You can't yell at teachers."

"*maldito infie—*"

"Not because you shouldn't, Claudia, but because it isn't safe. He's bigger than you and has more power. You come get me. You always come get me. I will yell for you."

"They were yelling at him?" Dicky asked, their eyes closed, their breathing slow and intentional.

"Pretty loudly, yes," I muttered. Dicky said something in Korean that I was pretty sure meant "fuck every blade of grass in and out of this world."

"I'm not sorry," Alex said, standing straighter. "He wasn't backing off. Joey started crying and he didn't back off, not even when Mr. Dictine told him to. And then he yelled at Mr. Dictine, too, and some of the other kids started crying, and… and I'm not sorry, is all I'm saying." I know it wasn't an appropriate reaction, or anything, but I did actually smile at Alex's words.

"Hey," I said, turning to Dicky, "maybe we really will get him fired, this year." They, too, were attempting to bite back a grin. It was a very angry grin, to be clear, and they, too, had gone a little misty-eyed.

But this was a tomorrow issue. The show had to go on.

"Go to your stations," I said, "and do not engage with Mr. Sunderson, if you see him. You're probably going to be asked to give a report tomorrow morning. In the meantime, try to make sure band doesn't win the motherfucking competition."

They saluted us, first, then Hedi's students, before making their way out to the stage.

I finally gave my full attention to Joey, Chloe, and their classmates. Bits of me began to crack.

"Ms. Suré," Chloe sniffled, "I want to go home."

I watched her, wondering whether or not this was one of those "get them back on the horse" situations. I beckoned her over, after a moment of deliberation. She walked slowly, scrubbing at her eyes, her blond hair covered in glitter. Her twentieth birthday party had been last Friday and half of her classmates had gifted her body glitter and shimmer eye shadow.

I leaned in conspiratorially. Kept leaning—she was all of four foot eight inches—and pitched my voice into my best stage whisper, making sure that the entire class could hear.

"Would you do it for twenty bucks?" I asked, reaching into my wallet, "I'll throw in an ice cream Sunday bar, this Friday. Dicky and my's treat. Your whole class can come, too, if you're feeling generous."

"She'll do it!" Julienne hollered from where he sat in the corner. "She'll do it, Bea!"

Glad to see Julienne and I were on a first name basis.

"Will there be sprinkles?" Cheyenne asked, hurrying over to stand by Chloe. Chloe glanced from her to me, nodding.

"Yes, we want sprinkles," Chloe said, "and the secret sauce." She meant my mother's caramel sauce. I'd brought it to an ARD meeting, four years ago, and the woman had never forgotten.

"That can be arranged," I said, nodding, flipping to a clean page on my clipboard and taking notes. "Are there any other requests?" I asked Hedi's class. And one by one, I got them. It was going to be a strange Sunday bar, to say the least—Donnie was very insistent on his Flaming Hot

Cheetos—but "weird ice cream social" was certainly better than watching one asshole rip the joy from a class of kids who had been practicing for this very competition an hour each school day for the past thirty-eight days.

"Joey?" I asked. He was the only one who had yet to give me his order. "Do you think Chloe should compete?" Dicky had finally located a box of tissues. They handed it to the boy, who desperately needed one or ten. He wiped at his nose for a while before Hedi intervened, taking another tissue from Dicky and cleaning Joey's face for him. And then Joey nodded.

"Sh-sh-she should," he said. "B-b-but, Bea —" wow "—she won't do it for anything less than thirty-five."

Chapter Seventeen

Brewing lawsuit aside, the Great Clayton Bakeoff went better than anybody except the children had expected. It was a fully full house—as in, Maya had to turn people away twenty entire minutes before the show started—and every last scrap of bake sale was sold. An auditorium stuffed to its fire-safety-regulations limit with people sticky from fourteen different combinations of butter, sugar, flour, and cinnamon roared as the curtains rose at seven, sharp. The teams sat and stood in front of their tables as Hugo, who'd volunteered to serve as the night's MC, explained the rules to the audience. And then he told his self-appointed assistant, Noel, to cue the timer. A timer counting down from thirty minutes was projected onto the back curtain of the theater. He told the bakers to on their mark, get set, and go. On go, he whipped the purple cloth off of the center table, revealing eight palates of random ingredients.

I craned my neck from where I stood in the theater's wings, dying to know what the "committee" had selected. The students descended on the table before I could peak, but it didn't matter. Hugo described the ingredients to the audience. Halal marshmallows, vegan butter, no-stir peanut butter, three types of pretzels, and blackberry jam.

"Ooh, and that's the good brand, too," Dicky said from where they stood beside me. "I use that on my brie spreads."

"The jam?"

They nodded. Put their arm around me, too, which was very infuriating because I very much needed a hug, just then, and hated it that Dicky was so obnoxiously good at being a human. I leaned into the embrace.

"We're going to have to follow-up with Hedi," I muttered into their shoulder.

"What?" Chris asked over the headset.

"Shit. Nothing, Chris." I fumbled with the pack until I'd put myself on mute.

"Yep," Dicky agreed, patting my back. "And his students, too. I got a little more out of Alex and it just… well, it just wasn't good, Bea."

Not even a little.

"Am I having a stroke or is somebody burning toast?" Dicky asked. "Does the theater department have toaster ovens, now?"

"We borrowed bunsen burners from the chemistry classrooms."

"Is that… you know what, never mind," said the person whose classroom's kiln hadn't been technically legal when they'd first installed it.

The first thirty minutes came and went amidst a mess of organized chaos. Children actually yelled at each other, which made for pretty good theater, and the audience shouted out suggestions and cheered on their friends and students and children. Some of the suggestions were louder and more aggressive than others, which made me think I'd underestimated how invested caregivers were in their children's competitive baking careers

The buzzer went off. Well, "buzzer." Noel had rigged it to start playing Louisa's song from *Encanto*. All of the competitors' hands shot up into the air. I took as many pictures as I could and hoped Lu, the one with the actual camera who'd been actually tasked with taking photos of tonight's event, was doing the same.

"My, my, a heated first round!" Hugo crooned into the microphone, wearing every inch of his sparkling green blazer. "I don't know about you, Noel, but that's the last time I write off fluff pieces as insubstantial." I could hear Maya laughing from wherever she was sitting on the front row. She had a very distinct laugh, of course, and also happened to be the only one who thought the joke was funny.

"Contestants!" Hugo shouted, undeterred by the peasants, "approach the judges!"

And so eight students ever-so-carefully walked their plated marshmallow situations to the front of the stage, where three teachers sat with their feet dangling into the orchestra pit. Stacy looked excited, as usual. Anita looked scared. I cackled, suddenly realizing she was the vegan reason the students had been given fake butter and bougie marshmallows. Ms. Faye looked like it was so far past her bedtime that she would say yes to whomever got her out of there the quickest.

There would be three rounds, with three teams getting eliminated the first two rounds and the last round being a 1 v 1 challenge. I was shocked that the home economics team lost in the first round. I was also shocked that they had chopped and crushed and spooned and mixed and presented the judges with a giant ball of marshmallow-pretzel-jam-butter. Stacy was the only one who even pretended to eat it.

Joey presented the judges with—I shit you not—nougat drizzled with blackberry sauce with pretzels on the side for dipping. Dicky's kids were the only ones who came anywhere near tying with them, that first round, and it was only because of presentation. They'd gotten their little scalpels out and used the peanut butter and jam to fresco a surprisingly moving beach scene onto their plate, replete with marshmallow clouds, a buttery sun, and pretzel beechwood. My students did third best, fair and square. They made a crushed pretzel pie crust—the cause of the burnt toast smell—filled it with peanut butter and jam, and topped it with marshmallow fluff. I don't think it tasted very good but it looked holiday-ready.

The band table with Katy Herkle and Lex's ex got booted, too, which I certainly did not smile about. Not at all. One of Paul's tables also, very unfortunately, did not make it. They weren't upset, though. The senior Womens' Choir representatives had sort of begun to fold, under pressure, and, after breaking their bunsen burner—oops—they decided to just sit back, eat marshmallows, chat with their Mens' Choir peers, and wait for the time to run out.

Stacy, Anita, and Trudy hammed it up so much. The women were naturals. The crowd went wild, every time they took a bite of this or that, and yelled out what they thought the rankings should be. Plenty of people were literally on their feet. And then the victors were named, the losers dismissed, and my intro tech students descended upon the stage, little black-clad silhouettes bussing and resetting and cleaning until everything was ready for round two. The second table of ingredients was rolled out, its contents obscured by a blue tablecloth. Hugo told his five remaining teams to get to their marks.

"I'm going to take a lap," I said, looking across the stage to the other side, where Hedi was standing in the wings behind his students. Two pairs of noise-cancelling headphones dangled from one arm. Some of his students were sporting sets already, bright green and purple muffs standing out against their bandanna'd heads. He was there to help and supervise, just in case they needed assistance, but the one time he'd tried to lift a hand —they had wanted a quarter cup of the butter but couldn't figure out how to level it—he'd gotten yelled at by the entire team. "Don't mess with our jeuje, Mr. Dictine," Cheyenne had hollered. "You gotta let us fly, Grasshopper," Julienne had agreed. Which he'd said loud enough to get picked up on a mic, funnily enough, and which was now what half the crowd was chanting. "Fly! Fly! Fly!" And "Go, Grasshoppers!" Which wasn't exactly what had been said, of course, but the meaning was clear enough.

The booted teams stood in the orchestra pit and rooted their classmates on. Except, actually, some were also heckling their classmates. I couldn't believe some of the things coming out of the choir students' mouths. One minute, they're anti-competition. The next, they're convinced a person should know how to flambé a brownie mix over a tiny open flame.

I circled backstage until I came to stage left's wing. I walked to the edge of the curtain, listening to Pete ask Chris about the lighting spots. One of the tables had been pushed off of its mark and Pete wanted to know whether crew members should go move it back or if he should move the light. I let them talk it through, tried not to get weepy over my babies growing up too fast, and switched my attention to the stage and crowd before me.

I cursed whichever asshat had decided to include powdered sugar in these ingredient palates. We were going to be cleaning for days. Then again, it did make for good theater. Puffs of white accented movements as students ran around, whisking this, opening that, measuring who-knows-what. Students got covered in powdered sugar and cocoa powder as they wiped their hands on their aprons and pushed their hair back. Why hadn't I thought of hair nets? Two teams sprinted off the stage, pans of goo in their hands, as they went to put them in the already heated Home Ec ovens. Hugo, meanwhile, was interviewing the teams who had already lost. They giggled their way through sob stories about how much this had meant to them, about how they'd just been doing it to make their cousins proud, what was there for them, now? They didn't know how they'd show their face in the choir room again. Paul hollered from somewhere that they'd better not even try, he couldn't bear the shame. I snorted. Hedi jumped, then, and turned around, clearly not having realized somebody was lurking behind him.

"Oh," he said, rubbing at his chest, stepping backwards until we were level, "I didn't hear you."

"Your children are machines," I said. "Joey wasn't kidding when he said he'd seen every episode of the Great British Bakeoff three times through."

"Oh, yeah. Not at all. I mean, Joey doesn't joke around. Literally." He smiled, his arms tight across his chest, his eyes glued to his students.

"I know," I said, "nothing quite like watching your kiddos compete. And perform, I guess. Getting to that point where everything is completely out of your hands. There's not a thing you can do but watch and cheer."

"Oh my gosh, it's *awful*," he groaned, deflating, a little.

"I prefer the term 'inspiring,'" I mused, patting his rigid bicep. As a gesture of comfort, of course.

"Is that not what I said?" he asked, giving me the cutest little sideways grin that I'd never realized I'd needed in my life until that exact moment.

"They sure are resilient," I said, watching them work together to make browned butter truffles. Because that's something high schoolers know how to do, now. There was a literal spiced orange dipping sauce on the side.

"Well," Hedi said, frowning, his arms unflexing—sorry, I meant uncrossing—briefly as he unconsciously took a step forward. But no, Chloe got the jar of cinnamon open, and all was well. "I mean, they are, of course, but you're the one who saved that moment. I was going to let them get a bunch of snacks from the bake sale and have a movie night in the classroom until their families were ready to pick them up."

"Oh." Well, that would've been fun, too. "Well, I wanted to see them crush their enemies into dust, Hedi. Call me selfish."

"Mmhmm. That's exactly what I think of, when I think of you." His words were too low and soft when he said it. I really just don't know what a girl's supposed to think when a man whips out his bedroom voice and sarcastically compliments her for being sort of decent and sort of overly committed to the healing affects of theater.

I stepped closer, my arm brushing against his. Not to flirt, of course. I didn't want to say what I was about to say loudly, is all, which meant that I needed to be physically proximate. Is all.

"Are you okay?" I murmured, "I think that might be the worst thing I've ever seen in my six years of teaching. And our vice principal embezzled forty thousand dollars from students, last year."

Hedi didn't say anything. I realized he might not have known about the vice principal thing and, for a second, wondered if it had been my place to tell him. I turned to him, about to clarify, and discovered my actual mistake.

Hedi's eyes were full of tears. He stared straight ahead, every muscle in his face straining to keep from crumpling into sadness. I kicked myself for being so crass. I mean, I'd had a full adrenaline response to Kirk's outburst and had broken down after only thirty seconds of experiencing that inanity. He'd been there the whole time, been the only body between his panicking students and a clinically heinous man.

"Dicky just let me wallow in their arms for a full minute," I said, "shall I pay it forward?"

He laughed once. A few tears got knocked loose, in the process. He wiped at them, sighing shakily.

"You're so weird," he said. "Normal people just ask if I want a hug."

"Sorry, but are you trying to weaponize normality against me? Mr. 'On Wednesdays We Wear Rainbow Suspenders?'" He grinned, more tears falling from his eyes.

"What could she possibly mean?" he said, pulling out a daisy-embroidered handkerchief to pat at his face. I almost choked. I did wrap my arms around his waist and pull him into a side hug. I kept it very professional, of course—is there any hug more professional than the side hug?—and didn't think any wayward thoughts when he rested his temple against my head. Not a single one.

"It was awful, Bea."

"I know."

Louisa started singing about surface pressure, ending the second round. Forty-four pairs of hands shot into the air.

"I didn't realize people like him still had jobs in education."

"I know."

"I just..." but what else was there to say?

"I know, Hedi. But think about it this way: our students may have encountered a bully, but nobody around them normalized his behavior. Nobody in that room was made to believe that his words were true. That's something, at least. That, and there's about fifty witnesses to the report I'll be filing the moment this thing wraps up and maybe, just maybe, I'll finally get his ass fired."

Hedi pulled away—very upsetting, I know—to stare down at me.

"You were being serious about that?"

"I'm sorry… do you think this is a lawless state?"

"I… huh."

I quirked a brow. Well, quirked both brows. I'm no Claudia, after all. My forehead is not comprised of autonomous entities.

"Besides, the school district's attorney goes to Mass with my mother."

"Of course she does."

"Right? Terribly convenient. Now, feel free to go back to crying on my shoulder. I'm not sure you got it all out."

He laughed again. More than once, this time, and without any accompanying tear streams. He pocketed his handkerchief.

"As ever, your sincerity is overwhelming," he said. I smiled.

"I get that a lot."

The next panel of judges—three of the most cherished subs Clayton High has ever known—were tasting their way through five of the most creative combinations of banana, powdered sugar, cocoa, orange juice, and cayenne I'd ever seen. Which was made all the funnier by the fact that Mrs. Malley couldn't tolerate black pepper on the coldest of days.

To the crowd's absolute delight, the finalists were Paul's Boys Choir and Hedi's Grasshoppers. I smiled, patted Hedi's bicep—again, a totally professional gesture of encouragement and solidarity—before hurrying to the back of the auditorium, where Pete, Nathaniel, and Chris sat in the sound booth. They'd been trying to mitigate a minor emergency for five minutes before finally calling it in. We spent the next ten minutes getting the stage right mic back online. By then, the third round was underway. The crowd was on their feet, shouting, cheering, rooting for their teams. The orchestra pit full of losers was going wild, too, hollering, drumming their hands against the lip of the stage, calling out encouragements and unsolicited advice as the remaining sixteen competitors turned tempeh, kiwi, pickled carrots, baguettes, brown sugar, and soy sauce into something edible. Hugo shouted into the mic, narrating the onstage drama with the speed and enthusiasm of a sports commentator.

By the time "Surface Pressure" was going off for the third time, I could barely hear the music over the roar of the crowd. It took the contestants a second, too. And then one of the choir kids heard it, threw his hands in the air, and jumped away from his plate with such vigor that he almost overturned the bruschetta he'd spent the last five minutes putting together.

A hush fell over the crowd as the two teams approached the bench—because we'd finally brought a bench to the stage for the judges, I hadn't quite thought through how uncomfortable it was going to be for teachers to sit directly on the stage—and laid out their offerings. Diana was one of the judges, this round, as was our superintendent, Marcia Fernandez. The third judge was the local weatherman, because our students are weird as hell and treat every extracurricular activity as an excuse to beg Don Cloudy to come to school grounds. I don't know why they're so obsessed, if I'm being honest, but there are some art students who haven't missed a meteorology report in the three years since Mr. Cloudy took over the weather station.

The finalists clung to one another as the judges narrativized their tasting experiences. One of the choir boys actually started weeping when Mr. Cloudy said the slice of tempeh-kiwi-carrot roulade was rolled as well as any tornado he'd ever spotted.

Like I said, they're absolute freaks.

Diana took a bite of Team Grasshoppers' Bahn Mi and made a noise that was not at all school appropriate. Which reminded me of how incredibly hungry I was, just then. The auditorium was full of the smells of cooking, by that point, and not entirely in a good way—the tuba section had flared out magnificently, in that last round, having burnt enough anise to wake the dead.

The judges continued evaluating and I continued reminding myself to breathe. Standing in the sound booth with my students, I was pretty sure every single one of us was on the brink of a cardiac event. Which, friends, is why you shouldn't model "caffeine addiction" to teenagers.

"Okay, judges," Hugo finally chirped, vibrating with energy, "what is your final decision? Who is the winner of the first annual Great Clayton Bakeoff?" *First* annual? What the hell, Hugo?

Don Cloudy reached out a hand for the microphone, more than happy to lend his celebrity status to the pronouncement we'd all been waiting for.

"After much deliberation over some truly delightful, inspired dishes, we have decided that this year's winner is," he paused—because of course he fucking paused—"Team Grasshopper!"

The crowd went absolutely wild.

Which, dear reader, is how you turn a fake fundraiser into an annual, community-wide event.

Chapter Eighteen

Kirk was not fired. He was sent to mandatory weekly therapy. The comment I made to the teacher's union rep who delivered this news to me almost got *me* signed up for mandatory weekly therapy.

Thankfully, the rep had scheduled our meeting Monday morning before school. The moment he left I was able to scream into my hands for twenty seconds before immediately distracting myself with that morning's installation of *The Queen's Will*, which had somehow gone from "aw, that's cute, so proud of my adorable little students" to "where the fuck is the next chapter" overnight. I tried to play it cool. We all did. But, I'm going to be honest, Monday lunches in the teacher's lounge might as well have been a neighborhood bookstore during the midnight release of [your favorite fandom here]. Some teachers had begun bribing Maya for advanced copies of the Monday morning paper. Which was why her students had begun coming in early, Monday mornings, and printing the papers before immediately distributing them throughout the school. They'd started printing three times as many copies, too, which had sent Maya down a "are school papers allowed to solicit corporate sponsors" rabbit hole for two solid hours.

I don't know how they did it. One Monday, the queen and the hawk man were exchanging flat dialogue about curses and warlocks. The next, they're tumbling down staircases together, banging into each other, panting, slick with sweat, landing in spent heaps. So, to answer that question, no, they hadn't just been reading D.H. Lawrence "for school." Maya and I had actually turned those installments into a drinking game. Every time we were bludgeoned over the head with a not-anywhere-near subtle euphemism for sex, we had to down eight ounces of water. First person who had to call an aid to watch their class because they couldn't hold their bladder until passing period was the world's biggest loser.

And then, one day, Oliver—the crowd-sourced name of the man hawk—was kneeling before the queen with a sort of innocence and openness that was described so perfectly, with a love that was described so honestly... I don't know. For all we can rail against teenagers for not knowing a thing about romance, some of them sure can write the stuff. Anyway, the man hawk knelt before the queen, smiled a secret little smile, and told her that he would love her for as long as he drew breath. He said it quietly, too. Not crassly, not dramatically. There was no vibrato, as in the way of public declarations. No, he said it as an oath is whispered to the gods.

I mean, who writes like that?

High schoolers, apparently.

Anyway, Queen and Oliver had to figure out a way to get out of the enchanted tower, which required them to trick the warlock, which was around the time their authors discovered the "cliffhanger." Two weeks in a row had them barely escaping from the warlock's clutches, and always with a "she could only pray that man couldn't hear her beating heart—join us next week for the latest installment of *The Queen's Will!*" Which, quite frankly, made me want to pull my hair out. The main characters' romantic tension continued to be subtly woven into the narrative. They hadn't fallen down a single step, last installment. No, it was just stolen kisses, sweet hugs, and gentle promises to persevere.

And then—and *then*—last week they had gotten out of the tower. Finally. *Finally.* And so this week's much awaited piece began with the queen sweeping across the meadow, mind reeling, not believing she was free. Tears filled her eyes, old sorrows lifted, new sorrows crashed in, et cetera et cetera. I'd read all that before the meeting with the asshole from the union. I scanned to where I'd left off, an hour earlier.

And then a golden thread, so small and delicate as to be almost imperceptible, wrapped itself around her wrist. She frowned, not understanding what was happening, and watched as the thread unspooled through the air. As it wrapped around Oliver's wrist, too. She held her arm up, confused. She pulled at it, trying to tug herself free. She could not.

"What is this?" She asked her man hawk. He, for his part, looked stunned. Panicked, too. But worst of all, deeply, terribly resigned. She did not weep. She did not yell. She simply waited.

"You promised me a favor," he said. "When we were in yon tower. You asked me to get you out. I asked what you what you would give for freedom. You said a favor, any favor." He held up his arm, gesturing to the to thread between them. "I didn't realize... I don't always know how the old fae ways work, Queen. I would never have asked for this."

"What favor?" She breathed, her world collapsing down around her. She'd been stoic for fifty years. She'd put up with an evil warlock for

228

fifty years. She'd lived, knowing everyone she knew and loved was growing old and dying, for fifty years.

This, however, was too much.

"There is an ancient magic in the wills of queens like you. Those whose resolve renders them immortal, I mean. I left my home, years ago, searching for one such queen. For you. I need your help. My kingdom sleeps under a dark curse, and none but you—one like you, anyway—can wake it."

The queen fell to her knees. All was silent, but for the roaring in her own ears.

"You... tricked me," she whispered.

"No, I didn't mean for this—"

"I loved you, and you tricked me. You used my loneliness, my desperation, for... for this?" She pulled at the thread, then, harsh and cruel. "I would have followed you anywhere, Oliver. I would have done anything you asked. Was... was any of it real?"

Oliver stepped forward, face pale and panicking, "no, my love, it's not like that, I didn't —"

"Don't touch me," she spat, wrenching out of his grip, "don't you dare touch me."

Tears streamed from Oliver's face, then, but the queen could not see them. She had hardened her

heart to him, right there and then, and could not
bare to look upon his trickster face.
   Join us next week to see what will come of
our quarreling heroes!
   "What. The actual. Fuck." Was I...was I
crying? Though, to be fair to myself, it had been a
trying morning.
   My classroom door burst open, just then,
which had me yelping, jumping, and scrubbing at
my face in no particular order. Paul stood in the
doorway, the school's paper clutched in his hand,
his mouth more or less on the ground.
   "I know," I said. "I. Know."
   "This is..."
   "I know."
   "But—"
   "She doesn't even know—"
   "Did he trick her, though? Was it all a ruse?"
   "No, it is *true. Love.*"
   "But how would she know? She was all
alone in a tower for so long, after all, and probably
would have loved the first person she saw who
wasn't whatshisname, and—"
   "*True. Love. Dammit.*"
   I said it so much more aggressively than I
had meant to. Paul's hands shot up in placating
surrender.
   "Okay, okay, you want love, we get it."

I rolled my eyes.

"I'm not sure how that's what I said, but okay."

Paul smiled at me. Winked, too.

"Oh, darling dearest, you don't have to say it."

"What could you possibly mean by that?"

"I mean nothing, my lady."

"You can't just quote Hamlet at me and think that's enough of an explanation."

Paul skipped fully into the room, then, and poured himself a cup of coffee before plopping down on a beanbag.

"I'm not saying anything," he quite literally said, "But that new essential academics teacher is very, very hot."

"And?"

"And someone saw you hugging it out at the bakeoff. Report."

I stared him down.

"I hug you all the time. If that's giving you the wrong idea, I can stop. I understand why you would fall for me, but you're not really my type. Now, shoo."

"She wounds," he said, clutching his chest and making not a single move to leave. "And you're no fun. Hedi, on the other hand—"

"Oh, dear *god,*" I muttered. "Don't you have a class to prep or something?"

"I have a free period, first thing, and also, methinks the lady doth protest too much. We talk about dating all the time. You talked me through my entire breakup, last spring. Because, you know, we *are* friends." His smile grew positively wicked. I almost took a picture for my class. It's nice to have a model for the rarer, usually-not-seen-in-the-wild expressions. "I feel like this current impassioned denial is indicative of one thing, my darling, and one thing only. You've got a crush. You've got it bad."

I wanted to tell him no, Paul, Hedi and I chatted it out and decided we weren't going to crush on each other. Like adults. But that would require too much backstory.

"Oh, come on," he said, reading meaning into my silence—I don't know what, to be clear, and usually didn't like the ways his brain worked, anyway—"there's nothing wrong with crushing on a teacher. Nothing wrong with dating one, either. We're all adults, here."

"In numbers only."

He scoffed.

"Ugh. You are NO FUN, Bea. Some of us are clinically single. We have to live vicariously through those of our peers who have actual

232

prospects. You're saying you aren't even a *little* bit invested in knowing what kissing him feels like?"

Oh, but if only I didn't know. My life would be that much easier, right about now.

"Paul, you're going to have to sew your vicarious oats elsewhere. He isn't interested in anything."

"So you've already talked about it."

"What? No, that's not what I—I just meant, neither of us would be interested, anyway."

"You might need to practice that one in front of a mirror."

I pinched the bridge of my nose. I'm not sure what the nose-pinch was actually supposed to accomplish, but I've found that performative self-collection helps calm my racing heart.

"Jokes aside, Bea, I do like him. That's all I meant." He had stood, at some point, and walked over to my desk. "Now I feel like a dick for not remembering, but I take it the meeting didn't go well?" He was looking down at the folder I'd been given by the rep.

"I mean. No? Not as bad as 'we aren't doing anything, stop being sensitive.' He's got to go to therapy for twelve months. Which, actually, I'm not allowed to tell anyone, so. You didn't hear it from me." Only the people who had lodged formal complaints were allowed to know about the district's remedial courses of action.

"Of course not."

"I'm sorry, Bea."

"Me too." Me fucking too.

Chapter Nineteen

"Bitch, I'd do the same for you." Always an excellent way to request a favor, truly.

"Maya," I ground out, wondering why nobody ever cared about the fall play rehearsal schedule. Probably because almost nobody ever remembered we did a fall play until the November performances rolled around. Each year. Because, to be clear, we did a fall play. Each. Year. "Maya, I have three hour rehearsals every evening, this week, and a four-hour rehearsal on Saturday. When am I supposed to throw you a dinner party?"

"First of all, I don't like your tone," she said, snatching the bag of chocolate-covered almonds from my hands, "second of all, snacks are for winners only. This," she gestured at me, "this is not the attitude of a winner, Bea." I stared at the bag of chocolate, my body filling with sudden and soul-crushing sadness. I sighed. I really drew it out, too.

"Third of all," Maya went on, inured to my sorrow, frigid bitch that she was, "I've thought the problem through from every angle and Bea, you're the only one who can help me solve it. You, my best friend in the whole world, are the sole arbiter of my happiness. Does that mean nothing to you?"

"Chocolate," I moaned, flopping backwards as much as I dared in her ergonomic chair.

"Bea. I need you to focus. You can have the candy once you tell me what I want to hear."

"Your mother has always loved you and definitely did not immediately donate the sweater you gave her, last Christmas."

"I take it back. No candy for you."

I straightened in the chair, grinning, studying her face.

"Some people pay big bucks for comedy," I said, tapping my fingers along the arms of the chair. "Okay. Let me get this straight. You want to spend more time with Abeni"—the Nigerian-Canadian golden retriever from Harvard—"but couldn't possibly just, I don't know, ask him. So you need help manufacturing an afterschool setting wherein which you would both be present. Casually. Naturally. So you want me to host a dinner party."

"Because you already owe Stacy one, and Anita's already brought it up a few times."

The woman *did* keep bringing it up. I couldn't figure out what stakes Anita had in coming back over to my house for a "thank you for cooking a hundred cupcakes with me until after midnight" dinner. My apartment wasn't that cool.

"And it would be super normal for you to also invite some of the other first year teachers. The ones you already know. Which includes Hedi, who is good friends with Abeni, which means it would make sense for him to say as much to you and for you to extend an invitation. Boom, dinner party. Perfectly casual."

I stared.

"You do hear yourself, right?"

"I really don't see why you're refusing to see my side of things, Bea. I thought you loved me. And it's not like it'd be the weirdest reason either of us has had for a dinner party."

Well, she did have me, there.

"So I'm throwing a dinner party on the one day I have off in the next three weeks, inviting Stacy, Anita, Hedi, and Abeni. I call you over for reinforcements, because I need help... cooking?" This, of course, was the least believable part and would have given the whole thing away to a person at all familiar with Maya. The woman didn't know soda from powder, is all I'm saying. "Maybe we should invite a few more new teachers. Just so it doesn't seem so… exclusive?"

"No. If you go any bigger, you have to invite them all. Do you want to cook for a fourteen-person dinner party?"

Right, right. Because I was the only one who would actually *be* cooking. And it's not like I could potluck the thing. "Thank you, Stacy and Anita, and by the way could you bring a casserole?"

"You know, I bet Hedi's a great cook. You could always ask him over early. I bet he'd *love* to help." She didn't even try to veil her meaning. I rolled my eyes.

"For a writing teacher, you're terrible at subtlety."

"Um, it's newspaper, first of all. Clear, concise writing is key, thank you very much."

"Did you have a second of all, or…?"

"Accept this as inevitable, Bea. This is happening. Send the text."

I gazed at the chocolate, my one, true desire. She held out her hand. "I'll make an exchange. The almonds for your phone."

I didn't even think about it. Because, of course, the only biblical character I have ever actually related to was Esau.

She sent a group text to Stacy and Anita, first. Then, one to Hedi and Dicky—because I

238

panicked, at the last second, and didn't want to
make it look like I was trying to entrap him or
anything—saying I was feeding the others for being
so kind and helpful and thought I should probably
include them on that list, too. Not how I would have
said it, but Maya wasn't really accepting feedback,
at this moment in time. And then I was taking the
phone back, because Maya was going to choke at
the last hurdle.

"Trust me, he'll play it perfectly cool," I
said, typing out a text to Hedi, "and, you know,
actually do the thing, too. If we're relying on me to
casually run into a teacher I only see every other
day for a length of time that is long enough for me
to casually mention and casually invite him to a
dinner party—well, let's just say it'll be Friday,
before that happens, and he'll probably have
Sunday plans by then."

I sent the text. *Hedi, this is a ruse. You can't
ask me why but I need you to invite Abeni to this
dinner party.*

His response was delightfully swift. *For
illegal or immoral purposes? I won't abet any of
you or Maya's criminal activities.*

I cackled out loud.

"What? What did he say?"

"Oh, nothing much. But he's onto you."

She groaned.

"Truly," I agreed, typing out a response, "is there anything more mortifying than a crush?"

Purposes upstanding. He won't regret coming. Unless he can't palate peppers, in which case, do we even care.

And then, *that was a joke, of course I care, to be very clear there will be options for all spice tolerances, over.*

Over?

Oh, ha.

I'm not sure we are morally obligated to accommodate the palates of weak people. I am unsurprised, however, that your compassion extends to even them. I will help you entrap this man. Over and out.

"What is he *saying*—god, Bea, you are *literally* giggling."

"I am not," I giggled, looking up from the phone. "Do what now?" Maya rolled her eyes, snatched my phone, read the texts until she was satisfied, tried to scroll up in our messages to see what else we'd texted about in the past week. Dicky had unwittingly served as my fairy godparent, in that regard. They'd started having Hedi and me over for maté before school on Wednesdays, ostensibly to discuss how Hedi's students were doing in the RAG Hall, if there were any needs that weren't being met, et cetera. Mostly we just talked, though.

Dicky had made a group text to communicate these maté plans. Put us both in it. Boom. I had his number. Had involved Maya in the seven hour turmoil possessing said number had spawned. Do I text him? Can I? What about? Should I? Friends text friends, right? Is this too thirsty? ("No, Bea, texting your students' teacher about making scripts accessible is not thirsty").

And then, of course, he'd been the one to text first. *Does this mean I don't have to email you every time I wan to go bowling?*

What the fuck was I supposed to do with *that?*

Anyway, that was *so* ten days ago. I grabbed my phone back before Maya could get too deep in the weeds of our messages. They were all perfectly innocent, of course. School appropriate to a fault. Sigh.

"I can't believe you have the audacity to mock me for a dinner party scheme," she said. I didn't know what she could possibly mean by that. "You know what? I'm not even going to count this as a favor owed, Bea. We're doing each other a solid. This is mutually beneficial."

Which, of course, led to a fifteen minute tangent about where the hell her students were going with *The Queen's Will.* Not even she knew. They'd begun making her wait until they sent their

241

stories to print. She got, at best, an hour head start. Enough time to censor them if they stepped out of line, they assured her.

"I've never felt so thoroughly betrayed," she said, sighing. "Here I was, thinking they needed me. Wanted me. Nope. I was just a means to an end. The keys to the printer. The proletariat will rise up, Bea, and when they do, pray that you aren't too bougie to be on the wrong side of history."

I really didn't know what to say to that. For a few seconds, anyway, and then, "oh, are they reading Marx for Mr. Holson, right now?"

"They won't shut up about the means of production, Bea, I'm losing my mind."

I cackled, standing, clutching the chocolate to my chest before she could snatch it away again. I had more than earned this bag.

"You know what they say. One minute, it's *Lady Chatterly's Lover,* the next, the youths are manifesting communism. Maybe there's something to this whole book banning thing, after all."

I was shocked I made it back to my own classroom without being struck by lightening.

Chapter Twenty

This is just a friendly neighborhood reminder to all of my people-pleasing enneagram-two older-sister first-child socialized-as-a-woman people out there: "no" is a complete sentence.

"No I will not host a dinner party two weeks before a show" is also a complete sentence.

"No I will not deep clean my entire apartment, plan and execute a themed cocktail, and cook a vegan, peanut-free spread for six other adult humans after waking up at the asscrack of dawn because Lena has begun to insist on the eight AM Sunday mass" is not only a complete sentence but also possibly a run-on, or, at the very least, bad grammar.

Unfortunately, the completeness of a sentence has almost no bearing on whether or not said people-pleaser will hear what is being said. Which is why, et cetera et cetera. Here we go again.

And thus it began: the dinner scene. A staple across genres. I can not count the number of dinners I have directed, over the years. The number of times we've wondered whether the sandalwood or cherrywood table would serve the drama better, the number of chairs we have lugged up and down from the prop attic. The number of times Noel has thrown dishes and stalked off of the stage. The number of times Hugo has jumped up on a table to belt his solo (so actually I can count that one, it's twice). How many climaxes take place over a fruit salad and omelette? How many emotional breakthroughs happen whilst a person sips on their welch's grape juice "wine?"

All that to say, it was time for another dinner party. And, scene.

I don't know why I'd insisted on a dish that relied on caramelized onions for its base. I don't know why I'd insisted on stuffing individual ramekins instead of just making one big pan of enchiladas. I don't know why I'd insisted on *roasting* the green chiles instead of just buying roasted green chiles. Besides, you know, the flavor being fourteen times bigger and better. I do know why I forgot to wash my hands after dicing jalapeños but before wiping my eyes. Someone had knocked at the door. No one ever knocked. I answered, confused, and chatted with a nice

Mormon on mission for five minutes. Went back to the kitchen, chopped my eight—yes, eight—onions. Began crying, of course, and wiped at my eyes. And then the tears really came. Which was around the time I started smelling smoke. I ripped open the oven, got a face full of aerosolized capsaicin, and rescued my charring green chili babies from their inferno.

Which was why I was coughing, crying, and snotting in a kitchen full of smoke when Maya arrived, moments later, hands full of five times the amount of cilantro I'd asked her to bring.

"What the—" but then she was coughing, too, because capsaicin.

The next hour felt like a war zone. That's all I'll say about that.

Sixty minutes later, Dicky was welcomed into a clean house that smelled of baking apples and frying cinnamon. The table was set for dinner, the counter was laden with a charcuterie board, two dips, and a mural of veggies and chips that Maya had spent way too much time plating. The punch bowl was full of oranges, herbs, and gin. A carafe of sparkling water and berries sat beside it, just in case people didn't like the taste of orange-inflected paint thinner. The crystal was out, of course, as well as my little jar of edible glitter, should anybody want to sparkle on the inside and out.

Dicky walked in, hugged me, and asked where to put the plate of mini plum tarts they'd "whipped up, thought it might be a fun little treat." I refrained from suggesting the bushes. It wasn't Dicky's fault their tarts were going to effortlessly upstage everything I'd just sold my soul to get done in time. That, and I was ethically opposed to killing dessert.

"Here's good," I said, putting the obnoxiously beautiful tarts atop an empty section of counter space. I should have seen it coming. Dicky never showed up empty handed, after all, and they knew how much I loved fruit desserts. The absolute fucking nerve.

Abeni showed up next, fifteen minutes early, which surprised me. Dicky, I expected—they're terrible with directions and have developed the habit of intensely overshooting so that they're never late. Abeni, on the other hand... I mean, who arrives fifteen minutes early to a party? It served our purposes perfectly, though. I welcomed the six-foot-three Canadian transplant into my two-bedroom apartment and tried not to immediately make eighteen jokes at Maya's expense. But honestly, I could feel her salivating from the living room.

"These are for you," he said, making an obscene amount of smiley eye contact as he handed me a bouquet of daffodils.

"Go make yourself comfortable," I said, grabbing Dicky before they could do the same, "And have Maya put these in a vase for us, please." Wow, I was an amazing wingwoman. He wasn't ten seconds in the door and I already had him giving her flowers.

"I forgot we were supposed to be getting them together," Dicky whispered once Abeni had turned out of the entryway's little hall and into the room beyond. I winked.

"And also thanking Stacy and Anita for helping me bake a trillion cupcakes," I added, patting their shoulder, "don't forget about the cupcakes."

"Ah, yes. For the celebration of the unborn child's genitalia."

"And that's why *you* weren't my first call."

Dicky laughed.

"There's a time for sharing space with others and a time for creating space for oneself, Bea. Besides, if I don't restate the company line, here and there, my nonbinary card might get revoked. And I'm just too old for that."

"You're only…forty," I tried, completely oblivious to their age.

"Yes, and a friend told me the other day that his daughter considers herself a 'late in life lesbian' because she didn't start dating women until she was twenty-two. Twenty. Two."

"Well, you know what they say about queer years," I said. Hedi, of course, chose that moment to walk in. He didn't even knock.

"Ooh, what did I miss?" he asked, smiling, handing me a bottle of wine and a warm, towel-wrapped loaf of what turned out to be sourdough, still hot from the oven. I refrained from making any of the more obvious jokes.

"Bea was just about to tell me what they say about queer years," Dicky said, taking the loaf from me and unfolding the towel. Hedi had sculpted a bunch of flowers across the surface. Because, of course. "This is *beautiful,* dear. Oh, it turned out so well."

A raging green monster erupted somewhere between my esophagus and large intestine. It felt like where I imagined my gallbladder was.

"Well?" Hedi asked, waving off Dicky's praise as he watched me, waiting, his black eyes crinkling into a premature smile. His undivided attention did wonders towards calming my little green gallbladder monster.

"I was just going to say that queer years compound faster than dog years. A statement that would have been funny, had you been here for the bit about late-in-life lesbians. Which you weren't.

248

So don't feel obligated to laugh." He smirked, which was way worse. My hormones weren't over his smirk, yet, and my poor little heart didn't know what to do when he threw one my way.

"Bea, I would never insult you with a pity laugh. Shoes off or on?" Hedi asked, glancing down at my and Dicky's bare feet. He kicked his loafers off. I was very disappointed his socks were nothing more or less than a coral plaid. "Now, I gave Abeni the wrong time so that he would arrive early. Is he here yet? Are they getting QT?"

I had to scrape my jaw off of the tile.

"That was on pur—you sly *dog*." And then, "ugh, brilliant. Chef's kiss."

"This isn't amateur hour, Bea. I refuse to be implicated in a poorly-executed crime."

I sighed. Thought about Dicky's tarts. Thought about how I should have gotten all three colors of bell peppers for what now was so obviously a lackluster vegetable spread. Thought about taking myself out to the bushes.

"Not to say that this isn't already perfectly executed," he hurriedly added, pulling something out of my hair.

A jalapeño seed.

He bit his lip. "I do love a good fashion statement. This took guts." He waited for us to get the joke. I wondered how much of his life was spent waiting for people to get his jokes.

I almost started crying. Dicky, however, whooped once the pun clicked.

"Oh, dear," they said, wiping their eyes, "oh, I'm going to have to use that one. I feel a seed jewelry-making session coming on. Oh, Tony is going to love this. Took guts. Oh, that's too funny."

Hedi smiled. Pulled another seed from my hair, too. "I would demand the tour, of course, but I suppose we should stay put and optimize Maya's time. Anita will be here soon."

He checked his watch. I checked my self, having just spent a very serious five seconds contemplating kicking everybody out of my home so that I could give him "the tour."

"I'm surprised Anita's not here yet, actually," Hedi went on, "she was very excited."

I frowned.

"Why?"

Dicky raised an eyebrow.

"Wait… that came out wrong." I really couldn't figure out how, though.

"This is her first semester teaching," Dicky said, fully donning their Teachable Moment voice, "last spring *she* was the student, finishing up her bachelors and teacher's certification and wondering where life was about to take her. She's two months

250

into about three major life transitions, right now. New job, new city, new home. All new class preps, too. Not a lot of free time, and a whole lot of second thoughts. If you remember."

I shivered. I did remember. Dicky went on:

"Having a dinner party to look forward to, every now and then, can really help break time down into manageable chunks. Something to look forward to in what otherwise would be a series of early mornings, late nights, and existential dread."

"That," Hedi said, glancing out of the long, narrow window beside my door, "and, you know, maybe she enjoys spending time with you. Just a thought." He opened the door. Stacy waltzed in, tray of stuffed broiled tomatoes in hand. She smiled when she saw us all standing there.

"Why are we hiding in the entryway?" she asked, stepping out of her bright purple crocs.

"Stacy," I said, trying not to sound exasperated, "this party is *for* you, you *were told* not to *under any circumstances* bring *anything* except *yourself*."

"Was I?" she asked, the picture of innocence. Dicky popped a stuffed tomato into their mouth.

"Oh, dear," they said, swallowing, "divine, Stacy, divine."

Anita arrived before anything could escalate into a proper Tomato Incident.

***

Everybody had a great time, besides the fact that a few things went very, very wrong. The first wrong thing was that Anita did actually have almost no tolerance for spicy food, which ruled out the molé ramekins, two of the three dips, and the corn chowder side. She had a delicious meal of broiled tomato smeared across fresh sourdough bread, veggie sticks, lemon hummus, and plum tarts.

The last wrong thing was that Abeni was, in point of fact, a homosexual.

The middle wrong things involved me and Maya demolishing everybody else in a game of charades. Why would that be wrong, you might ask? I couldn't tell you. Dicky said something about as being "hyper-competitive nightmares," but I have come to accept them as an unreliable witness.

We had dessert in the living room—dinner party 101, spread the courses across both time *and* space—which certain guests took as an open invitation to snoop. It's the risk I took, inviting coworkers over for dinner, and I was pretty sure I'd triple checked every nook and cranny for sex toys and heroine needles. Have I ever even thought about doing heroine? Absolutely not. Do I store my sex toys in the living room? Never. Did that stop my brain from telling me that Anita was going to find butt plugs beside my copy of *Bunny?* Not even a little. Do I even own butt plugs? You see where this is going.

Hedi was openly heckling me about my Cat Sebastian "shrine," as he immediately started calling it. I held my head high. I know art when I see it. Abeni perked up, halfway through the conversation, his hand hovering over my copy of *Untamed.*

"I love Cat Sebastian," he said, wandering over. "Do you have *Hither, Page?* I actually bought that one. My library never carried it."

I've never avoided eye contact with a person more than I did with Hedi, then and there. Maya, straight kitten that she was, had no idea what tragedy was fast approaching.

"I do," I said, remembering all of the times he had complimented my bi-flag earrings and rainbow socks. Funnily enough, the memories felt a little different, all of a sudden.

"I loved the one with the highwaymen but I always come back to *Hither Page,"* he went on, taking the copy from my bookshelf. "I didn't know how to come out to my parents. The not knowing was overwhelming, for a season. And then my

253

mother was visiting and saw this book on my shelf. She started reading it. She's always been curious about what I read, you know. Obviously reading gay books doesn't make you gay. My mother doesn't know that, though. And so, well, Cat saved me the trouble of telling her. Saved me from putting it off, too. My mother was excited, of all things. Apparently, she had begun to worry that she had raised a son with no game. She was thrilled to discover that 'lack of charm and charisma' was not the reason I wasn't bringing girls home."

This presented yet another one of those life moments where you absolutely cannot laugh.

I stared, my brain spitting forth nothing but static noise. Not a great look, by the way, when your coworker is trying to relate to you about the unifying power of Cat Sebastian. And also coming out to parents.

Hedi was no help at all and Dicky was too busy coughing into their mocktail glass to do a single diddly of good. I couldn't bring myself to look at Maya. Thank the goddess for Stacy.

"Books can be so helpful when we can't find our own words," she said, smiling, "I'm glad it worked out for you! I know those conversations can be so difficult." Abeni gave her a very polite smile in return.

"Thank you, Stacy."

"But like, *gay*, gay?" I blurted, losing every card I'd ever cultivated. I couldn't remember the last time I'd so entirely overlooked a member of the community. Abeni raised his left eyebrow. He, too, had fully autonomous brows. I was struck with envy before I remembered that I was supposed to be focusing on this man's homosexuality. You know, like a normal person.

"…um, yes?" He said it like a question, like he wasn't entirely sure he hadn't just fully misjudged the safety of this space.

"Dude, same," I said, my palms sweating, my vision tunneling, my lungs threatening to collapse in on themselves, "well, sort of. Bi, you know? Or pan. No transphobia here." Because that wasn't a weird thing to say. But nervous babblers will nervously babble.

Hedi spewed the drink of water he'd just taken. He excused himself and disappeared down a hallway that I belatedly realized he thought lead to a bathroom. It did not. He reappeared, seconds later, and tried to pretend like he hadn't just seriously considered waiting it out in the coat closet.

"I know you are," Abeni said, frowning. "Bi, I mean, not transphobic. Though I wouldn't have thought that, anyway. We had an entire fifteen minute conversation about attending LA Pride."

"We certainly did," I said, "I just don't like to assume people remember everything I say, you know? I talk so much." How was I supposed to know he wasn't just an ally? The man wore his shirts all the way buttoned, people, and the *straightest* ties you've *ever* seen.

"That's wonderful," Dicky finally managed, "I love adding more queer folks to our ranks. When I first began working at Clayton High twenty some-odd years ago, I was the only out and proud teacher."

"I can't even imagine," Abeni said, smiling —genuinely, this time—and looking just a little relieved that our resident wisened elder had retaken the conversation.

"There's the timer," I said, jumping up, rushing to the kitchen. There *were* two pies in the oven—because Anita also hadn't come empty handed—but their timer wouldn't go off for another ten minutes. That being said, I wasn't entirely sure I could survive the daggers Maya was staring into the side of my face for the next ten minutes, and also there's only so long one can keep one's hysterical laughter at bay. I escaped through the kitchen's screen door and stepped out onto the stoop, giggling, crying, peeing a little, and wondering if Abeni was going to avoid me for the rest of the school year.

"Whoops," a voice came from beside me. Hedi's, of course.

"I'll say," I wheezed, leaning agains the glass, "dear god."

"Dios mio, de hecho."

Reader, if a sexy man has never whispered sweet Spanish nothings to you on a back stoop under a waning moon, I highly recommend making different life choices.

The door slid open a third time in so many seconds. Maya slipped out, her eyes wide, her fingers looking like she'd regretted giving up the smoking habit she'd never had.

"Sorry to break up the not fling you're definitely not having," she said, closing the door behind her, "but I was running the risk of spontaneously combusting, in there, and thought you probably needed help with whatever it is the fake timer was for."

"Maya, I am so sorry—"

"We are never. Mentioning this. Ever."

Oh, that certainly wasn't a true statement.

"I didn't even think to ask him if—"

"Never, Hedi. Never, ever."

We stood there in silence for all of ten seconds. And then I was laughing again. Hedi joined in half a heartbeat later. Maya just stood there and took it. And then,

"I can't believe Paul hasn't said anything," she muttered.

Which, of course, sobered me right up. I turned to her, eyes suddenly wide. She frowned, then gasped, realizing our mistake.

"Fuck." Fucking fuck fuck. "Fuck."

"What?" Hedi asked, looking from her to me and back.

"We forgot to invite Paul," we both groaned.

"He's going to kill us," Maya breathed, palming her forehead.

And he just about did, reader. He just about did.

Chapter Twenty-One

I hate to say it, I really do. But here's the thing: not all plays are created equal. Just like not all graduating senior classes send you into a spiraling depression.

Paganini had been fun, don't get me wrong. My students rocked it. They hit all their moments and looked amazing doing so, thanks to the Tech students' wardrobe endeavors.

That being said, the Monday after the last Sunday show when I and my advanced theater students were striking the set, cleaning the props, and returning everything to their proper places in the BIS, I was not filled with post-show blues. I was filled with "well, that was a job well done, thank god I get to go to sleep on time tonight" satisfaction.

The students felt differently. They frequently do. Some were even teary-eyed as they stared out at the stage, so recently filled with the lives and stories of the people they'd spent months creating. My poor little babies were feeling the emptiness that comes after, the voids in their souls that had, just hours prior, been overflowing with other peoples' dreams and desires. And, like, so much adrenaline.

Such is the way of high school theater, I suppose. After one long, caffeine-fueled weekend of performance highs, it's all over. The curtain closes. The show is done. The script is placed back on the shelf. Students are no longer lovers and mothers and heroes and nemeses. They are classmates. They are friends, no more, no less.

I helped for a solid fifteen minutes before my body gave out. Every single square inch of me was either exhausted, sore, or exhausted and sore. I couldn't take another second of moving ramps around until I'd had three proper meals and twelve hours of sleep. I slid off the stage, sat in the first row of seats, took two Aleves, contemplated taking a nap, and told students to sing if they needed me.

Hugo joined me, minutes later, sighing, swallowing down his sobs. Belen sat down on my other side, seconds after that. She wasn't crying, per se. She wasn't not. Angela plopped down beside Hugo, hugging him, her eyes swollen.

"Stop it," I said, my own eyes misting up, "stop it, it's only October, Hugo, you can't already be—"

"It was our last fall play—"

"Hugo I swear to Bowie if you don't keep it together, I'm gonna—"

"—and then we're graduating, Ms. Suré, and leaving, and—"

And then there were four people crying in the front row of an empty auditorium. Which is why I always block two days for post-show cleanup.

***

Halloween isn't so much a holiday in the RAG Hall as it is a way of life. A month-long religious observance culminating in a day of festivity and ritual and, before you accuse us of sacrificing small animals to pagan gods, no, the red puddle on the floor is just grape juice.

Halloween fell on a Thursday, that year. Our students spent the entire week trying to tweak their costumes into something that would pass our less-than-rigorously enforced dress code. The bits that didn't stand a chance—hats, mostly, but also some trains that would never make it down the stairs during a passing period—got stored in my room, where they patiently waited until after school, when the party started.

Dicky had been throwing RAG parties for years. It was a fairly typical "give teenagers a safe space to do safe things on a night when people could otherwise get up to no good" teacher move, on their part, but it was also super fun and the students were mostly oblivious to the fact that they were being managed.

Anyone from the school was welcome, and there was a sizable choir and newspaper contingent. Paul, Maya, and I tended to have a post-party party and, years ago, they'd made a habit of waiting around for me at school. Their students had caught on and, in so doing, discovered that if they came by RAG Hall on their way out the tech students would do their costume makeup. And so two became four.

Dicky and my students spent Thursday's class period turning our rooms into hauntings, the hallway into a half-dozen trick-or-treat stations and tables for Dia de Los Muertos, and the PAC into a space capable of hosting a dance party, should the night turn thus.

This year, my students were fae obsessed. Their shrine, which had overtaken an entire corner of my classroom, was a puckish woodland paradise. They had covered the plant stands in moss and ivy and nailed two sections of plywood trellises into a corner "v." The live rose plants they'd woven into the trellises weren't all thriving, unfortunately, but the students invoked the Fallen Roses with a weird amount of reverence and specificity and I was

262

beginning to think they'd decided that a graveyard of flower corpses better matched the shrine's aesthetic, anyway. They'd wrapped the stands' legs in fairy lights and hung the platforms with dozens of crystal-filled twine hammocks. Atop one moss-covered plant stand stood a cast-iron cauldron that Claudia had found at Goodwill for eight dollars. Each of my students placed a handwritten wish into the cauldron at the beginning of class on Mondays and each Friday they lit the wishes on fire (don't worry, we did this outside). In May, they planned on giving everyone little glass vials for bottling up a school year's worth of wish ashes. Talismans, Angela told everyone, for bringing hope and good fortune in the years to come. Because everyone knows children's wishes are the strongest of them all.

Yes, my students are a bunch of little freaks. Moving on.

They had decided to turn our classroom's haunting into an extension of this year's shrine which, in turn, was an extension of their weekly *The Queen's Will* column. It was the quietest I've ever been, during a Halloween decorating party, as I let them talk amongst themselves, plan, and, hope among hopes, drop plot spoilers. Queen and Oliver were stuck in a bog, currently, and it was absolute torture. The two were doing their best to ignore one another after Queen said several very mean things about fairies. Oliver, of course, continued to struggle with his love, which the queen no longer believed in. Should he confess it anew? Remain silent? He could no more let it go than he could release his own soul—I was pretty sure Belen had personally penned that particular line—but he did not want his love to be her problem. Not when she was bound to him through the promise of a favor owed.

Those little fuckers were steel traps, too. They covered the walls with brown and green butcher paper they'd crinkled and torn to look like trees, all the while letting not a single detail slip. They pinned up riddles and placed burlap sacks of mystery tokens around the room and refused to give up a single hint about where their silly little story was going. Which wasn't entirely true: they turned an entire corner into the backroom of a witch's woodsy cottage and I was too irked to realize that that probably meant a witch was showing up in the next few weeks.

The tech students spent their period finishing what their acting peers had started. Lex and Lu, also in Newspaper, had apparently been conspiring with Hugo and Belen for days about what the aesthetic needed to "accomplish"—their words, not mine. Their aesthetic apparently needed to accomplish a lowlit rave. They stationed three fog machines at equidistant points around the room, anchored blue and purple floorlights in the corners, and hung a banner proclaiming "Nimmy's Boils and Brews" above the cottage.

"I'm confused," Hedi said during my free period, that day. He, Dicky, and I were overseeing his students as they finished painting their masks in Dicky's art room. "Is this a Halloween party or a book launch?"

He made an excellent point.

"I've got this theory," I said, sipping on my coffee, watching Joey dust his will'of'the'wisps mask with gold, "about why high schoolers make such beautiful art. Like, peak beautiful. And with weird levels of consistency, I mean."

"Is this the thing about seniors?" Dicky asked. I rolled my eyes.

"Spoilers, much?" I huffed. Dicky had the decency to look chagrinned. Hedi smiled. Rested his hand on my shoulder, made a bunch of eye contact.

"I'm listening," he said.

I, of course, completely forgot what I had been saying.

"About the art?" Dicky prompted, politely pretending like they weren't seeing what was right before their eyes.

"Right, right. Well, each year, we extra curricular teachers get combinations of students who consistently raise the bar. Dicky's art students make more ambitious sculptures. My students produce better and better performances. Paul's students win state, then nationals, with bigger and more technically difficult pieces. Band...something nice here, I suppose, but who knows. I've never had a 'dud' year. Not yet, anyway. And they keep showing up in other ways—the state of my classroom, right now, would be a case in point—that surpasses paid professionals. I guess I don't know what profession does haunted house classroom makeovers, but you get my point.

"Once I noticed it, I thought it was weird. I didn't like the idea of people actually peaking in their teenage years, but I wondered why it would be that eighteen-year-olds show up so much and so hard. I don't know a troupe of adults who could put on a better *Twelfth Night.* But then, that's it, isn't it? Each year, some of our students are seniors. Seniors, who constantly invoke their immanent departure, who are keenly aware of the liminal space their entire year occupies. Who want to go out with a bang, each time, and who pour everything they have into their 'lasts.' When else, besides your last year of high school, were you so self-conscious about the end of an era? When else in life is there a transition like high school graduation? You see it coming for over a decade. For so many, it marks moving away from the life you've always known. The family, the friends, and onto the next chapter. I'm not saying we don't all constantly transition and change. I'm saying I can't think of anything else that has the same *culture* of change built around it. And so each year has two or three seniors, constantly calling people to do not better, but *best,* because this is their last ever chance." I drank more coffee, wondering where in the day I found the time to soliloquize about seniors.

"I'm not moving away," Chloe said, painting eyelashes just above her mermaid's eyeholes. "I'm staying with Mom."

"I stayed with my mom, too," I said, smiling. I refrained from making the joke about how I still would have been there—we had such fun —had she not decided she was being smothered. I thought it was a funny joke but I also didn't want Chloe to think there was a world where her mother might make her move out.

"Such a wonderful lady," Dicky said, smiling. "How is Alexa?"

"She's perfect, as always," I said, smiling, "Lena and I are staying with her over the weekend."

"Dia de los Muertos?" Hedi asked.

"Si," I said, waggling my eyebrows.

"Do you observe the day?" Dicky asked Hedi. He nodded.

"Really?" I asked, surprised. From what I'd gathered, he'd run as fast as he could from religion as soon as he was able. Besides weddings and funerals, I was pretty sure he hadn't been to church since he was eighteen.

Hedi gave me a "what about me has suggested to you that I don't value this aspect of our shared culture? Just because I don't like priests doesn't mean I don't want to remember those who have passed" look. Or something like that.

"Yes," was what he said out loud. "It was always our favorite, growing up, and that never really changed. My mom's been making candy all week."

"How lovely," Dicky said, hurrying forward to help Julienne, who'd dropped his paintbrush on the ground.

"We tried to make mazapán last year," I said, grinning at the memory, "We found renegade patches of powdered sugar for months. Had to replace Mom's blender, too."

"But you're so good at baking?" Hedi asked, writing Cheyenne's name on her Elphaba mask when she came to him, marker in hand.

"You've never cooked with Lena. That woman is a nightmare."

"I'd like to see that," Hedi said, smiling at who-knows-what. "For some reason, I find it hard to believe."

"Ugh, he wounds," I said, clutching my chest. "A foul Claudio, to doubt a lady's words."

He looked up from Cheyenne's mask, smirking.

"Lady?"

Um. Rude.

"I'm just saying," he went on, writing Chloe's name on her mask, next, "I have it on some authority that you actually *have* spoken with people at your window."

I think I blacked out for a second.

"A *proper* saying!" I managed, barely refraining from telling him I would eat his heart in a marketplace. That felt a little too violent for school.

He looked up from Chloe's mermaid's face. Winked. Went back to signing.

I had to walk away.

Chapter Twenty-Two

What none of us teachers realized was that
our students had friends outside of RAG Hall—not
our fault, they never talk about them—and also that
our students had been telling these so-called
"friends" about this year's Halloween Hall. More
specifically, about the ways they'd decorated our
classroom to match their *The Queen's Will* vibe.
More more specifically, about how they'd woven
hints about upcoming plot lines into the room's
design.

Apropos of nothing, I've begun to suspect
some of these fuckers would be millionaires by
thirty.

They came, dear reader, in droves.

***

By some act of God, nobody broke
anything. We did send out SOS texts, thirty minutes

after school, asking for teachers without plans to hang back and help chaperone. About ten remained, thankfully, and eight more returned with their children, thinking it would be fun for their kids to get their make-up done by my students before "going out on the town," as it were. Our students' parents showed up, too. With platters of food, which should have surprised no one. Belen's mother put a samosa in my hand before I could try to pretend like I'd eaten dinner already.

It was a delicious samosa. It was also a weird samosa. I'm not sure why it wasn't an empanada, if I'm being honest, except I suppose she'd used curry spices in her bean and veggie filling. That, and she had given me mango chutney for dipping. Which was more or less mango salsa, which had me googling "what is chutney" for two entire minutes.

I sat on top of a table we'd put at the end of the hall. I watched as dozens of children milled in and out of the hauntings and the PAC, where a dance party had one hundred percent commenced. Parents and teachers sat at the tables we'd placed up and down the hallway, handing out candy to teachers' children and food to their children. I had no idea what was going on in my classroom. Belen and Hugo had created some sort of game—the bags with the mystery tokens weren't just decor, apparently—and what felt like half the school had shown up intent on playing. Something about trying to figure out what "the favor" was.

I desperately hoped nobody had come to school with a virus, today. I can't remember the last time I've been in a situation where the word "fumigate" crossed my mind with such regularity.

"They're so frickin' cute," Cheyenne said. I looked up from the spreadsheet I'd been updating—Lena was on her way to the store and wanted to know what spices I already had for the pastries we were making tomorrow—to look at the three-year-old twins skipping around their dad's legs. They were dressed as little gargoyles, which was, indeed, "frickin' cute."

"A little young for Hunchback of Notre Dame?" I asked Mr. Holson as his children pulled him towards our table. Cheyenne let them pick their own candy out of our bowl.

"It is never too early for Hugo," he countered, grabbing one of his daughter's hands when she tried to dump the entire bowl into her bucket. The other one took that as an opportunity to make a break for it. Our fearless English Literature teacher sighed, scooped up the candy dumper, and hurried after his defecting child.

I turned to Cheyenne, who was grinning behind her green half-mask. We'd found her a witch's hat and cloak in the prop attic an hour earlier. The hat sat crooked over her noise-reducing headphones, which was, in a word, adorable. I would never say that out loud, of course. High school students hate being told that they are adorable. I don't know why.

"I like that movie," she said, "I was Esmeralda when I was seven."

"Oh my gosh, same," I said, high-fiving her. "Well, not seven. I was nine."

"Did you have a tambourine?"

"Ugh. No. My sister was *also* Esmeralda that year and she got all of the tambourine privileges. But I got to carry the goat."

"You had a *goat?* An actual *goat?* "

Oh, did I. Which was why we were scrolling through two-decades-old photos of me and Lena when Hedi walked up, minutes later, each hand holding a napkin-wrapped curry empanada.

"Mr. Dictine, what are you supposed to be?" Cheyenne asked, looking him up and down. He was wearing what he'd been wearing all day. So, an orange polo covered in tiny black cats, black jeans, and a black-and-white spiderweb-print tie.

"A high school teacher," he said, "boo."

She squealed, laughing, then made space for him between her and me on the table.

"Very scary," I said, smiling. "The stuff of nightmares, truly."

"Why are you looking at pictures of goats," he asked, setting the empanada-samosas down on his lap.

"It's Djali," I said, putting as much "duh" into the words as possible.

"We were both Esmeralda when we were kids," Cheyenne said, looking for all the world like she intended on stealing one of Hedi's empanada-samosas. "Were you ever Esmeralda, Mr. Dictine?"

"I was," he said, scrolling through the pictures. He got eight whole swipes in before I remembered it was my phone and the photos were of me. I snatched it back, harrumphing. "I didn't have a goat, though. Very jealous, Ms. Suré."

"Yes, well, we can't all be me," I said. Cheyenne grabbed an empanada-samosa and ran. Her mother intercepted her, halfway down the hall, and looked around, trying to figure out why her daughter was cackling like the wicked witch of the west. We waved. She waved back.

"What did you do with the goat?" Hedi asked, tearing his remaining pastry in two. Steam billowed out. How were they still so hot? "After Halloween, I mean."

"He was my Papa's," I said, "we just took him back to the farm, that next day. He was a happy goat. Lived a happy life." I sighed, remembering all the times I'd bottle-fed Djali. "He never got sent to the butchers, either. He acted too much like a dog. My grandfather couldn't bare the thought of killing a dog."

Hedi tried to blow on his would-be dinner. He was smiling too much, though, for the wind stream to be any use.

"Have you been to your room, yet?" he asked. I shook my head. I didn't want to know what damage was being done. I was going to drop a few lysol bombs before going in, tomorrow morning.

"You should. They've made some sort of choose-your-own adventure scavenger hunt. It's so clever. They're not giving any spoilers away while still letting people feel like they're participating in the story-making process. Very inclusive of them. 10/10 on pedagogy."

"Yes, well. They're excellent students." I tried to make it sound dismissive and huffy but I accidentally started tearing up, halfway through.

"There, there," he said, patting my shoulder. And the funny thing is that he meant it. Who says "there, there" and means it?

"Do you think they're going to get back together?"

"Who?" I didn't know of any recent teenager breakups but I assumed he wasn't talking about Mr. Peterson's divorce, because, yikes.

"Oliver and the queen."

"Oh. Right." That made so much more sense. "Surely? They wouldn't drag us along for months only for the characters not to end up together."

"You don't think?"

"That would be *heinous*," I said, rummaging through the candy bowl.

"Oh?"

"Don't 'oh' me. This is a *romance*, Hedi. The people demand it."

"I feel like a lot of the older love ballads didn't have happy endings, though. And who's to say, by the end of the drama, that them getting back together *would* be happy?"

I gave up my candy search to scowl at him.

"How dare you. Oliver and the Queen were *created* to be together, Hedi. You think Belen is going to deny her creations their *literal* reason for existence? You would leave them to their world, alone, bereft of the purpose they were *made* for? To do what? Hmm? Travel? Get a job? 'Find themselves?' How *dare* you, Hedi Dictine. I never would have suspected such levels of MC abuse from *you*."

He chewed on his samosa-empanada for what felt like an inordinate length of time, maintaining eye contact all the while. Finally, he swallowed. And then,

"You're saying you wouldn't be satisfied with a lovers-to-enemies-to-friends arc?"

For some strange, nigh unknowable reason, I wasn't entirely sure that we were still talking about *The Queen's Will*. He was making so much eye contact.

"I mean... enemies is such a strong word," I said, holding out the bowl for Ms. Faye's little nephew, who was dressed as the cutest little dolphin you ever did see.

"The queen literally just tried to leave Oliver tied to a tree in a werewolf-infested bog."

Okay so maybe we were talking about *The Queen's Will*. I looked away and did my best to mentally redress him. The shirt was difficult to get back on, but I persevered.

"Oh, like you've never left a friend tied up before," I muttered, wondering why Maya was rushing towards me. Well, Maya's version of rushing.

"Well, yes," Hedi mused, "but I got consent, first."

I almost excused myself. I was sure there was a cold shower somewhere in the vicinity. An emergency eyewash station would do, in a pinch.

"Bea," Maya wheezed, colliding into my knees, "Bea, what's your Spotify password?"

It took three whole breaths for me to drag my brain out of the gutter and into this conversation.

"Pardon?" I managed.

"Your spotify—"

"No, I heard you. Why?"

"No reason."

"Maya."

"Well, Pete was using mine for the dance party, but I'm not ad-free. And I don't think the students need to hear about how they could armor up with Nexplonon every three songs. I know we aren't an abstinence-only state, but I feel like this much product placement is pushing it."

Excellent points, of course. I wrote the password down and she was off. I glared at Hedi.

"What?" He asked, the picture of innocence.

"You..." words failed, of course, because "you can't just go around making me want to jump you" was one of those "not his problem" sorts of things.

"Me, what?" His black eyes were inches from my own. When had he gotten so close? His body heat was in range, his eyelashes, distinguishable.

"You...um..." what had we been talking about? His lips were too distracting. I had completely lost my train of thought.

"Bea?" That fucker had the nerve to *murmur,* people. He was fighting *dirty.*

"I... am going to go find more candy," I managed, stumbling to my feet, thrusting the bowl into his hands. He quirked that stupid, semi-autonomous brow.

"There's plenty of candy, Bea."

There were also plenty of reasons to avoid propositioning your co-worker in front of half the school, but you didn't see me going on about it.

"Right, but, not enough?" I managed, hurrying away before he could say anything more about bogs and consent and his unnecessarily gorgeous eyelashes.

I ducked into the first room I passed. The blackbox which, thankfully, was nothing more or less than the place my tech theater students had set up their make-up booth. A dozen kids were still standing around, waiting for their turn, but most of the traffic had abated by this point in the evening.

Lex looked up from where she was turning an eight-year-old into a dragon. She raised an eyebrow—an "is everything okay?" look if ever there was one. I gave her a thumbs-up and stood in a corner until my executive functioning could wrest control from my hammering heart.

***

My tech students made a thousand dollars, that night. I was beginning to wonder if somebody needed to be reporting this as income, somewhere.

We sent out the "last call" around 8 PM—they're high schoolers, after all—and began cleaning, fifteen minutes after, which was a surefire way to end a party. Even the stragglers were gone by 8:30, desirous, as they were, to avoid clean-up duty.

Maya and Paul abandoned me at 8, off to begin setting up Paul's apartment for our after-party. I was glad he had let us back into his good graces. He had pretended like he wasn't going to invite us to our Annual Hallowbalooza for an entire seven days.

Dicky and I were running around triaging RAG Hall, doing only what was absolutely necessary to lock up in good conscience. Which was a pretty low bar, on Halloween night. We both firmly believed that our students should clean their own messes, for starters, and also Halloween was our favorite holiday and we were morally opposed to spending more of its precious time than was absolutely necessary on cleaning classrooms.

I circled the auditorium three times, unplugging various things and making sure all food and drink had been properly disposed of—I had a rat-free record, after all, which was not something that could be said for the school's former theater teachers—and locked up. And then I was rushing to my own room, glad to see somebody had already unplugged the fog machines and hoping that there weren't too many abandoned water bottles. Our singular cardboard "Lost and Found" box was two Stanley Cups away from capacity.

I tried not to panic when I entered my room. Not because it had been trashed—I think—but because it was going to take two entire days to deconstruct. Which would have been fine, under most circumstances—if you're going to do a thing, do it thoroughly—but we did need to start going through scripts for the spring musical. It usually took us a week to finalize the choice, after all, and two weeks to cast it, which needed to be done by the third week in November so that we could post the cast by the Tuesday before Thanksgiving break. Paul and I had discovered, years prior, that it was better to post the cast list as students left for a three-day holiday. It was much easier to deal with five-day-old disappointment than minutes-old rage.

Anyway, restoring this room to its previous version was going to take at least two days. I stopped, mid-stride, and stared at the quarter-cottage occupying a third of the room. It wasn't terrible. Worse, it was growing on me. I wondered whether or not it was realistic to think a partial witch hut could be integrated into a year's worth of theater class.

Which was when I noticed Hedi sitting at my desk and reading who-knows-what. No no, it was my copy of *We Have Always Lived in the Castle*.

I was very proud of myself. I only screamed a very little.

He almost jumped out of his skin, though, having been unprepared for unprompted shrieking.

"Sorry, sorry," I said, clutching at my chest. "I didn't see you there." Was I too young to see a cardiologist? At what age did people have to start worrying about being scared to death?

"Sorry about that," he said, looking like maybe he wasn't so sure he wasn't being attacked by a bear. "I came in to help clean up and got distracted. I've been meaning to read this for ages."

"Of course," I said, "it's a great book." And then, "god, you're such a snoop."

He grinned, denying nothing. I rolled my eyes.

"You're lucky you're cute," I muttered, circling my room and trying to pretend like my skin wasn't suddenly entirely too tight and hot and itchy and—

"Oh?"

"Shut up."

He laughed. It was a very self-satisfied laugh. And then, wonder of wonders, he went back to reading.

"So you didn't actually come to help clean?" I asked, picking up the first of many candy wrappers.

"I really thought about it," he said, glancing up from the book, "but then there was so *much* mess, and I'm only endlessly selfless until about 8 PM."

Fair.

"I do love a good oxymoron," I said, hoping that whatever had just popped in my back wasn't important.

"Pretty sure we don't use that word anymore."

I chuckled. I gave up on picking the wrappers up individually and wandered over to the supplies closet. I deputized Bob the Broom and together we began a much more efficient sweep of my classroom.

"I've always wondered what being haunted would feel like," I said, refusing to look anywhere near his general direction. "It's not so bad."

It took him a moment. And then,

"Bea, I'm pretty sure I could come up with better ways of poltergeisting you than quietly reading in your classroom on a Thursday evening."

I told myself not to ask, not to turn around, not to wonder why that sounded like a promise of pain and pleasure.

"Oh?" I asked, turning around, wondering away. I made a mental note to ask my nurse practitioner whether "I think it'd be sexy if my crush haunted me" counted as a mental illness.

He hadn't even looked up from his book.

"I mean, you'd certainly never sleep again."

That fucker.

"Cruel man," I muttered, staring at Bob, waiting for my brain to come back online.

"Like I said," Hedi said, turning the page, "I pumpkin at eight."

"No no, you *poltergeist* at eight," I said, slowly getting myself back into a sweeping rhythm, "focus, Hedi. Commit to the mixed metaphor."

He laughed, putting the book down.

"Sorry," he said, leaning back in my chair, stretching his arms up and out. I avoided ogling his biceps by the skin of my chinny-chin-chin.

"Did you need something, Hedi?" I asked, dumping a dustpan's worth of candy wrappers and paper scraps into the trashcan. "Besides a quiet place to read, apparently?"

"Fine, fine," he said, running his fingers through his hair, "you caught me. I have an ulterior motive."

You know you're ovulating when "ulterior" sounds like a filthy, filthy word.

"I wanted to make sure you were okay. You ran off, earlier, and I couldn't find you. Which made me think you were in the bathroom, which made me think you'd gotten sick, and Dicky said they hadn't seen you, either, and I thought about sending a student into the bathrooms to check but then I thought you might not like that much attention, especially if you *were* sick, and—" he cut off, not feeling the need to compete with my laughter.

"But I see now that all is well," he finished, crossing his arms.

"You are too sweet," I said, wiping my eyes and wondering why I sounded like a southern aunty, all of a sudden. "I appreciate the concern, really, I —" but I was too busy giggling to finish the thought. Obviously it wasn't *that* funny, but you have to remember that I was a little tightly wound, at the moment, and tightly-wound me is prone to hysterical giggles.

"Now that I've personally verified that you are indeed alive," he said, rolling his eyes, "I guess I'll leave you to it."

He did not leave me to it. He straightened desks and picked up garbage.

"Are you going to Paul's?" I asked after a moment. He shook his head.

"My sister and I are hanging out with our mom," he said. "She was excited we'd all be together, this year. We're making an ofrenda for our dad."

I smiled.

"That'll be nice," I said. The words came out quieter than I'd intended. But then, he had me thinking of my own father, and how my sister, mother, and I would be doing the same exact thing, later that night. "You don't stay up until midnight?"

"Mom can't make it past ten." He checked his watch. "Speaking of." He looked up, smiled. "I guess I'd better get going. You really have some great students, Bea. This was incredible."

"They really are." I looked around, took in the remains of our evening. "Thank you."

"For what?"

I went through the list of things I could thank him for, if I so chose. Landed on the one that was least likely to embarrass me. Or lead to a declaration of undying, everlasting love.

"For coming. For coming back, too. I didn't mean to worry you."

"Oh. Ha." He stood, pulling his backpack on over his shoulders. "No, spiraling has become one of my brain's favorite pastimes. My sister was five minutes late to dinner, a few nights ago, and that was all the time it took to convince myself she was dead in a ditch somewhere." He sighed. "I used to be the composed sibling. The calm child. Now look at me, Bea. An utter wreck."

"For sure," I said, scanning him head to toe. A few times. Just to be safe. "An absolute disaster."

He frowned. It was a thoughtful frown. Small, too, barely touching the corners of his eyes. He watched me, for a moment, with his small, thoughtful frown, his black eyes flashing blue in the low lighting of the floor lamps.

"What?" I asked, feeling overly exposed. And not in the good way.

"I... nothing," he said, running his fingers through his hair. I wondered how many times he did that, per day. "I just..."

I was struck with the thought that there was a universe where he didn't realize I wanted him. Where he thought we'd—"we'd"— drawn that neat little boundary, all those weeks ago, and were both abiding by it with steadfast vigor. This thought made me realize that openly ogling him might have been a confusing experience, to say the least, and might, perhaps, have caused him to question a few assumptions he'd been holding.

I sort of panicked, sort of disassociated, sort of wondered if there was a universe where I could play my cards right enough to get laid. Which made me realize that it was high time to extract myself from this particular encounter, libido be damned.

"Are you okay?" I asked, hoping that I was half as good at gaslighting as Paul. "What's wrong?"

Hedi's need to avoid making other people feel his feelings kicked in, of course, and he was back to his tight smiles in no time.

"Nothing," he said, blinking, "I just… am just tired, is all."

"Do you want a roady?" I asked, walking over to my coffee pot and mentally kicking myself. We were trying to get him *out*, Bea, not have him stay for a cuppa.

"No, I'd better not," he said, "I don't have quite your tolerance. I'd be up all night."

He said it like it was a bad thing.

"Okay, okay," I said, putting the empty pot back on the cold burner. He didn't make a move to go, though, which had me more seriously analyzing the pros and cons of jumping his bones, as it were.

But, no. We'd already tried to hook-up, once. I'd ruined it for both of us. Next time I had him—and I was increasingly thinking of it as a "next time" and not an "if"—it wasn't going to be because of some whim.

"Good night, Hedi," I said, smiling up at him. "Tell your mom and sister I say hi." The poor man looked a little lost, if I'm being honest. I told myself not to enjoy it. Too much.

"Good night," he said, his arms half rising before stalling in the air as he second-guessed himself. I smiled, refrained from making a comment about poetic justice, and hugged him good-bye. I was mature enough not to linger. Mostly. And he was respectful enough not to let me. Mostly. And then he was hurrying out of the room and I was completely and utterly alone.

I collapsed into my chair, every fiber of my being on fire. I set a timer for five minutes. Thought of nothing except cold showers and dirty socks for the entire three hundred seconds. Took breaths, in and out, and waited for the panicking butterflies to leech from my bloodstream.

The timer went off, eventually, and I found it in myself to leave.

It was one thing to pine after a person who was trying to keep a professional boundary. It was another thing to pine after a person who thought you were the one trying to keep the professional boundary. I called Lena on my way to Paul's. She stopped me, ten seconds into my incoherent babbling, and made me wait for her to set up an emotions log. I got the notification that she'd shared a google document with me five seconds after she told me to "carry on, then, I'm just going to take notes so that we can keep track of your feelings."

I burst into hysterical laughter. Lena often recycled her psychiatrist's tactics, when interacting with her intimates. I sometimes wondered if we shouldn't all be financially contributing to her therapy sessions.

Chapter Twenty-Three

"You did what?" I asked my dearest, darlingest mother. We'd been up into the wee hours of the morning, that day, making bread, setting up an ofrenda for our family, and swapping stories. My abuela had come, too, as had Tia Rosa. If it had been up to those hags, we wouldn't have gotten any sleep at all.

I'd woken up at 5:30 so that I could drive home, change, and get to school on time. I was barely conscious, that whole day, and left as soon as the bell rang, knowing that my mother had about a thousand things planned, that evening, and that we needed to start five minutes ago if I wanted to get any sleep, that night.

"I invited Carmen to dinner," my mother said, not looking up from the masa she was kneading into dough.

"Do you even *know* Carmen?" I groaned, knowing I had Lena to blame for the chaos that was about to ensue.

"Of course I do. Her cousin is in my rosary group."

I considered kicking something. I wasn't wearing shoes, though, and didn't like my toes' chances against the wall.

"Doesn't she have, oh, I don't know, her *own* family to be with, right now?" I asked, knowing the answer before my dearest mother said it.

"Of course. I invited them, too."

"Well. Nothing like an entrapment dinner with one's parents to really set the mood."

"What did I miss?" Lena asked, rushing in, hanging her briefcase on the peg and disrobing as quickly as she could. And by that I mean "suit blazer off, kitchen apron on." She was ten minutes late and very clearly hadn't wasted a second of that time being calm about it.

"Alguien traicionó a Bea," Rosa said, tsk-asking the air. Lena frowned.

"What? Who?"

"Tu, mi querida," I said, flinging a dish towel at her. "You're on wash duty."

"But—"

"No buts. Judas' don't get buts."

The rest of dinner prep was nigh unbearable. The bit after that was even worse. I don't know what Lena told my mother or what my mother, in turn, told those crones, but all of them were pretty convinced I needed to "freshen up" before "company" arrived. I didn't know what that meant, exactly. I washed my face. Patted at my hair. Turned the sink on and off, just in case Lena was listening at the door. I put my mom's green sweater on. She never let me wear it—something about how I didn't know the meaning of the word "borrow"—but I felt like I had the upper hand, in this situation.

The doorbell rang. Every woman in that house refused to answer it. I gave them all death glares, implored them to behave, then hurried to answer the door.

They were all copies of one another. Hedi's mom was the shortest by inches. She was thin, wiry, dark as a chestnut, and wrapped in the brightest green shawl I think I've ever seen. Her curly black hair had been pulled into a loose bun. Her daughter, Penelope, was a little taller, a little softer, and a little darker. She wore a black smock dress. Hedi was Hedi, of course, and, while his mom and sister were smiling politely, he was giving me a look that made it hilariously clear that he had had no idea whose house he was going to and that, furthermore, he had certainly not expected to know anyone there.

"What the——" he bit off the words before his mother could chastise him for cursing. "Bea?"

I put my hands up.

"My mother didn't tell me we were having company until thirty minutes ago," I said, realizing I could have texted him. I guess it didn't occur to me that *his* mom wouldn't have said anything. And the look on his face was so delightfully shocked. I wouldn't have wanted to spoil that for myself.

"Oh? Should we come back another time?" his sister asked, every inch the exhausted nursing student.

"Sorry, sorry," I said, opening the door, "that's not what I——Hedi and I work together, and I just——"

"Oh, you are so beautiful!" his mother exclaimed in that accent that let some people get away with saying anything. Like, for example, "hello complete stranger, you are a beautiful Angelo and your soul sings to me." A favorite of my father's, God rest his soul. We were never sure how literal he was being. Whether he meant the person was an *angel*, angel, or that the person resembled a sculpture by his favorite artist, Michelangelo, or that they were a native of Los Angeles. Did he actually mean sing? Or soul, for that matter? He wasn't a poetical man, in Spanish, but he was always going on about essences calling out to each other when he had to speak in English.

Carmen took my face in her hands and kissed my forehead. "And so kind! I have never been better fed. I keep hearing such wonderful things about you, and now we meet. This home— que bonita! And your mother is such a wonderful woman."

Hedi looked like maybe he needed to take a lap. I refrained from asking his mother how long she'd been conspiring with Lena.

"Come in, come in," I said, ushering them inside. Carmen took her daughter's arm and let Penelope lead her into the home. Hedi stalled at the threshold, trying to rally from the whiplash.

"What… how do our mothers know each other?"

"I'm not entirely sure that they do, Hedi," I said, sighing. Sighing again, once I took him in. He was just so ridiculously adorable. He'd put on a deep blue button-up, an argyle sweater vest, and trousers for a dinner party he'd known nothing about an hour ago (if his timeline was anything like my own) but that his mother had asked him to come to. And that he'd dressed up for, for his mother's sake. Like an absolute gentleman. "You look very nice." He looked down at his outfit as if he'd already forgotten what he was wearing.

"Oh. Thank you." He looked me up and down. I tried to read meaning into the glance, tried to determine whether it was lingering, flirtatious, or just politely curious. I couldn't tell.

"I like you in green," he said, smiling. I wondered if it was reasonable to only ever wear green ever again.

"Thank you. It was my mom's." Yes, "was." If you think that schemer was getting this sweater back, you are absolutely mistaken. I think it's called a "child tax."

"Well, she has excellent taste. Clearly." He peaked inside.

"Shall we?" I asked, hoping he would say no and offer to make love in the bushes instead.

"I suppose." He didn't make a move to go in, though. I tried not to snicker. Mostly because my snickers generally came out as snorts, which was not very cute and I was currently trying to seduce a man.

"Did you have a good evening, last night?" I asked. "Once you got home, I mean?"

He nodded.

"It was really sweet," he said. "I… I didn't always think about everything I was missing by living in Boston. It's…different, somehow, being able to remember my dad with people who share

296

my memories. He felt more real. Being with people who still love him made him more real."

I nodded and, completely explicably, went a little misty-eyed. He took a step forward, a gentle smile tugging at his lips, but didn't quite know what to do. Once the sniffle escaped, he decided on "tentative hug" and wrapped me in one of the softest, sweetest, most uncertain little embraces you ever did see. Did I lean into his arms a little too much? Perhaps. Did he pull away? Not even a little. Did this make me consider crying more often in front of him in the hopes of eliciting more physical comforts? I'll let you decide.

"How was your evening?" he asked, not quite bringing himself to let go.

"'Evening?' Ha!" I scoffed into his shoulder. "Those freaks kept us up until two in the morning." He laughed. Squeezed me, released. I almost followed him as he stepped back. Instead, I stepped inside the house and beckoned him in. "Come on. We don't want anyone to get any ideas."

"We don't?"

Well, if that wasn't a panty-dropping statement. I cleared my throat. Cleared it again.

"I...um," was what I managed. He smirked.

"Very eloquent, Bea." He stepped into my mother's house and put zero effort into avoiding brushing past me.

What proceeded was one of the tastiest meals I've ever had with some of the least discreet women I've ever met. Who knew weaponized candor would pair so well with braised carrots.

Penelope took all of two seconds to warm up to my family. She hadn't been frosty when walking in, per se. Just tired and confused as to why her mother had dragged them across town to a random dinner. Lena got a hold of her, seconds in, and whispered who-knows-what into her ear. Metaphorically. Lena isn't much of a whisperer. Regardless, Penelope entered the party tired and confused and by the time Hedi and I were joining everyone, two minutes later, she was wide-eyed, less confused, and grinning. It was one of the scarier grins I've ever seen. It felt a little vindictive. It gave me the distinct impression that Hedi was one of those sorts of people who didn't tell his sister everything. Or anything, really. I assumed it was a family trait, given the fact that she and her brother had been lured here under false pretenses. Carmen, clearly, didn't feel the need to clue them into *her* machinations. I bet *they* didn't have a group chat within which they discussed their daily BMs. What a bunch of losers.

My mother and Carmen were new best friends within two minutes and were loudly critiquing "children these days" and their "inability to chose happiness" within five. Tia Rosa and Abuela had plenty to say, where children looking for love in all the wrong places was concerned, and everyone was complaining about not having more in-laws before we even had dinner on the table.

Hedi, innocent dove that he was, had had no way of anticipating any of this. He'd been expecting an evening at his mother's friend's house. It never would have occurred to him that some families don't know the meaning of the word "boundary." It clearly hadn't crossed his mind that I would have confided anything to Lena who, in turn, would have conspired with my mother who, in turn, would have asked a mutual friend for Carmen's number and boldly called, that morning, to hatch a scheme. I will say, though, that not realizing how willing of a co-conspirator his mother would be is fully on him.

He was staring from Lena to his mom to Penelope to my mom and back, his food untouched, as he slowly worked out that this dinner was a set-up. And then he was staring at me, frowning, undoubtedly trying to determine what could possibly have happened to *provoke* a set-up dinner.

Halfway through dessert, Rosa asked Hedi if he'd be a dear and get the horchata out of the icebox. He stood without a second thought and was halfway to nowhere before he realized he didn't know where the icebox was.

"Está en el garaje. Bea puede mostrarte," my abuela said.

"He can find the garage—"

"No me amas?" she asked, eyes wide and full of feigned hurt. I stood up and hurried after Hedi, giving my cackling sister the middle finger as I did so.

We walked through the kitchen, down a hallway, and into the garage before either of us said anything. I closed the door behind us, flicked the light on, and prepared myself for an interrogation. Thankfully, Hedi was too distracted by the fact that our garage was doubling as my mother's art studio to turn on me. He stared at the five-by-five canvas she was currently working on, curious. "Is that a honeycomb?"

"Don't ask." I scurried to the icebox and briefly considered doing a few shots of the tequila my mother kept in the freezer.

"Bea?"

"She's into bees, right now, what can I say?"

"Bea."

I sighed, shutting the freezer door and turning to face him. He was giving me his best attempt at a sardonic stare. He was too earnest, though. His face didn't quite stick the landing.

"So this is a fun dinner."

"Super duper."

"They seem to be full of ideas already," he said, rephrasing my words from earlier. He sat down on the worktable, entrenching, ready to talk this one out. "I don't suppose you know where they got their ideas *from*?"

"Not a clue," I said, clearing my throat and otherwise looking guilty as sin.

"You told somebody about our date, didn't you."

"I didn't tell *somebody*," I tried, wagging a finger through the air as if I ever wagged fingers through air. "I told *Lena*."

"You told your sister about the date?"

"To my credit," I went on, "I told her about it right after it happened. It's not like I thought we'd ever see each other again."

He stared, his brain probably doing that thing some brains do when they realize some other brains are members of larger committees of brains for whom there is no such thing as a private brain thought.

"What... what did you say about it?"

"Dios mio, Hedi," I said, rolling my eyes, trying not to panic. "Don't worry about it."

He was visibly working through some things. He sat there, staring and silent, for almost an entire minute. And then, "but... but what did you say about it?"

I stared back, my lips locked. He looked away, then.

"So it *was* something I did," he said quietly. "I thought ... I guess I just believed you when you said it had been an off night. I should have known better?"

I didn't realize he was capable of hurting me until that exact moment. He wasn't done, though. "What did you tell Lena? That some sad sop seemed fun enough? But you couldn't leave fast enough, once he started kissing you?"

That, of course, was exactly the sort of fear that I had never realized he might have. Because, as you will recall, he was an excellent kisser.

I laughed, shocked, before I could stop myself. Clapped my hand over my mouth, too, because he seemed very sad, all of a sudden, and laughter was not the appropriate response. He looked back to me, his expression shuttering. His sudden withdrawal was a slap to the face. I hurried forward, reaching towards him as if to grab his emotional retreat.

"I'm sorry, I'm sorry," I said, "I just... you've clearly never made out with yourself, if that's what you think happened." He wouldn't meet my eyes. I stood there in front of him and realized we should have had this conversation months ago. "I meant what I said, Hedi. I didn't want a hookup. I

302

still don't. And it wasn't fair to leave you like that. Like, not fair at all. Like, what I did still haunts me. Like, so much. Like, I may or may not have chatted about it with a few different priests. And all I can do is apologize, Hedi, because I am so, so sorry. And you were so wonderful, and sweet, and compassionate. And understanding, it seemed, and I guess I should have realized my actions threw you more than you let on."

"You think?" He still hadn't looked up at me.

"Hedi," I said, reaching forward, taking his face in my hands, pulling his gaze up to meet mine, "Hedi, I... it wasn't the kissing. It certainly wasn't the fooling around." My face flushed all over again.

"Why did you leave?" His voice was so quiet, so small, as his eyes bore into mine. I tried not to flinch from the honesty they demanded.

"I ... I don't know. I just... I couldn't believe I was thirty-one and hooking up with another stranger." Sigh. "I just... I suddenly felt so terribly old. And tired, Hedi. And the date had been so fun, and you were—are—so *perfect*, dammit. And I know I'm the one who suggested we go back to yours. And I know I'm the one who came on to you. And I... well, I thought I'd ruined it. I'd taken what could have been a wonderful first date and turned it into nothing more than a quick romp. And

I was ashamed, and frustrated, and… and tired, Hedi. I just… I'm too old for it. And then I went off on you, instead of thinking for two seconds about what I was actually feeling, and ran out before my mortification could catch up with me. I called Lena on my way home, that night, because I felt a little bit like a heinous bitch. And was panicking, because you had been so lovely and I couldn't believe I had so royally fucked up. I immediately regretted leaving and had no way of telling you that. It's not like I thought I could reach back out. I didn't think you would trust a word I said. God. I've never broken down like that, Hedi. At least, not to a stranger on a first date. I called her on the way home, yes, but not to say anything bad about *you*. What bad thing would there even be to say?"

His expression wavered between irritation, relief, and curiosity.

"You could have told me as much," he finally said, "just saying. You could have put a man out of his misery."

"I didn't realize you were miserable." I brushed his hair back. It was too intimate, I knew, but so was standing between a man's legs in your mother's garage. "I thought we were having a good time."

"Up until you got me naked and decided to bounce," he muttered, leaning into my touch, his eyes closing.

"I meant *since* then, Hedi. I meant that I thought we've been having a good time at school."

"Oh. Right." His hands had come to rest on the sides of my thighs, just above where our legs were already touching. "I suppose most of that hasn't been miserable."

"Glad to hear."

"What was that about me being... what did you say? The best kisser you've ever encountered?" But before I could so much as laugh he was opening his eyes, frowning and distracted. "Wait, if that's old news, what is *this* dinner about?"

"Haven't the slightest." I was thinking too much about the physical and ethical logistics of straddling him on my mother's art table to give his question much thought.

"Bea," he said.

"Hmm?" I was pretty sure the table could take our weight.

He squeezed the backs of my legs which, of course, earned him a few seconds of eye contact.

"What?"

"I just feel like I don't have your undivided attention, right now."

"I mean, parts of you certainly do."

"Why the sudden invitation to dinner? What happened?"

"Nothing." But his face was too close, his eyes too perfect, his hands too ridiculously near my derrière, to bother pretending like we both didn't know exactly where this was going. "I called Lena on my way home last night, too."

"Oh? What did you say?"

"What do you think?" My heart was throttling my throat, just then. I couldn't breathe, couldn't blink, couldn't think.

"No, no," he murmured, his eyes dropping to my lips, "that's what keeps getting me into trouble, Bea. I don't know what you're thinking."

I didn't see why that had to be my problem.

"Fine," I said, letting my hands come to rest on his shoulders, "fine, Hedi. We talked about you. And it would seem that our conversation gave her some ideas. Ideas about my need for a wingwoman, apparently. Ideas that she shared with my mother, apparently, who, in turn, shared them with my grandmother and aunt. And with your mother. Apparently."

His gaze made its way back up to mine. And he stared, and stared, and stared, and I began to wonder what he saw, when he looked at me.

"Does that mean Rosa doesn't actually want horchata?" he finally asked.

"Hedi, I'm not even sure there *is* horchata."

I leaned in before he could get it in his head that we needed to bring my great-aunt a possibly nonexistent beverage. I stopped, though, when our faces were inches apart, and waited, letting him decide whether or not to close the distance.

His eyelids flickered as his gaze roved across my face. It was a little languid. A lot lazy, too. A teensy smirk tilted his lips up, after a moment, which was around the time I realized he was toying with me. I huffed. Began to straighten.

"So sorry, I didn't mean to—"

But then his lips were on mine, and he was pulling me into him, and my entire existence was nothing more than the places where our bodies met.

The kissing was not how I remembered it. I don't know if it's because my memory could never have done him this much justice or because I liked him so much more, two months later. Regardless, we went from zero to one hundred in all of five seconds.

Fun fact: the table could indeed take our weight.

Funner fact: my aunt Rosa did *actually* want the horchata.

Lena was loudly "struggling" to get the door open for a full ten seconds before she was sticking her head in and asking if we'd "died or something."

We were more or less disentangled, by that point. More or less put together, too, minus a few unbuttoned places, here and there. Quick enough to fix, of course, and, after I'd rebuckled Hedi's belt, we were good to go. Moments later, and the three of us were reentering the dining room, horchata and tequila in hand.

The rest of the evening happened. That's pretty much all I can say about it. I have almost no memory of it. I did, at several points, nearly announce to the room that Hedi and I needed to go bang at his place, ta ta for now. Every time I got close to doing that, though, I noticed that Hedi seemed to be having a genuinely good time. I noticed, after a few more moments, that this was because his mother was having a genuinely good time. I wondered how many times were good for her, these days. And so I stayed, and he stayed, and the evening happened. Everyone seemed a little too smug about it, too. I couldn't bring myself to care, though. I was too ridiculously happy.

Chapter Twenty-Four

I slept like the dead. Which is to say, not at all, that night. The dead were very much awake, just then, and ready to play.

I tried to go to bed at a reasonable hour—we'd barely slept, the night before—but my body wasn't having it. And so I slipped out from the bed Lena and I shared when we stayed at our mother's, wandered downstairs, and crashed the card party my abuela and her sister were having. Because what else is there to do at 2 AM? They dealt me in, poured me what very unfortunately appeared to be straight mezcal, and required not a word. They had poured out four more snifters and set them on the shrine we'd made for our dead. My grandfather, my father. Tia Rosa's daughter, Starla, who had been born too soon. Their parents and siblings and friends. There were a lot of people, actually—these women were ancient—and I wasn't quite sure how they thought four shots was going to cut it.

They told stories as they played. I listened, and thought, and tried not to get taken for everything I was worth. But honestly, who bets money on Five Crowns?

Their words washed over me, softer than any lullaby, lilting, loving. My mind wandered every which way as we sat in that space between asleep and awake, as we settled into the quiet moments between midnight and dawn. We remembered, together, and we smiled. We cried, too, and we laughed. And we loved. I imagined being their age, on nights like tonight, and wondered at what carrying all of that love and loss felt like. The price of loving was steep, in this life. But one we all pay, over and over and over, because what was life without love?

These thoughts are exactly why I try not to stay up too late. They are certainly why I don't drink straight mezcal. I turn into Ewan McGregor's character from *Moulin Rouge* faster than Nicole Kidman can sing "diamonds."

***

The day-after text: a modern hellscape, truly, filled with landmines and toxic fumes and one very patient vulture, circling, watching, waiting for death.

I'd fallen asleep on the couch some time around five. I woke up, some time around ten, to the sounds of my mother cooking and my sister singing and my grandmother stirring two sweet'n'lows into her coffee. I did not move, though. No, I whipped out my phone, hoping to find messages from Hedi.

There were none.

I didn't panic—why would I panic—I didn't have anything to panic about, did I?—but I did draft a text. "Good morning!" Deleted it immediately. "Hope you slept well!" Don't be desperate. Delete. "Why am I struggling so much with this text?" Delete, delete, delete. "Why haven't you written eighty-seven odes to my body, yet?" Maybe.

Thirty minutes later and I was deep into the "morning after text" wikihow page. This, of course, was not a great place to be, as it reminded me that we were not dating. We weren't going on dates, either. Not only were we not dating or going on dates—twenty-first century semantics for the win—but, I was realizing, I had no idea what his dating goals *were.* Did he even *want* to be in a relationship? Long-term or short? Was he planning on staying in this area or moving away, once his mother was better? Dear Judy Garland, was he even *monogamous?*

This was around the time that I realized, passionate and very much two-sided kiss aside, that I had no idea what he wanted. I had never asked.

There's nothing quite like the panic that comes crashing in after one is vulnerable with another human being. I was going back over everything that was said. Everything that wasn't said, too. I was turning every memory of last night —of the last three months—over and over and over again and arriving at the very logical conclusion that he probably hated my stinking guts.

This was the state Lena found me in when she came looking for me a half hour later. She glanced from me to my phone and back. Pried the phone from my fingers, scrolled through my search history. Frowned. I opened up the messages for her, then, which clued her a little more into the devolution that was happening before her eyes.

"Okay, well, let's get you some food," she said, patting my head, "and maybe just take it easy, today. Nothing wrong with a post-brunch nap, am I right?"

"But... but I should text him, right? Or... or should I wait? Should I... what should I?" Sometimes complete sentences are hard.

"How about we go with a nice little 'good morning, I hope you're well?'"

"THIS ISN'T AMATEUR HOUR—"

"And, sent," Lena interrupted, handing my phone back to me. I stared at the screen, thunderstruck. Stared some more, once the little dots appeared. Laughed out loud, when I saw the reply.

Did your sister just send that?

How could you possibly have known.

I'm not sure you've ever wished me well, Bea.

Ouch.

That, and your dots have been dotting for the past hour. I assumed somebody decided to intervene.

WHY DIDN'T YOU??

All's fair, Bea. Besides, it was bringing me too much joy.

Cruel man.

It is a weekend.

I wondered what that had to do with anything.

"I think he means he's off the clock and can be as mean as he wants."

I jumped out of my skin. I'd forgotten Lena was there, if I'm being completely honest, and had not been expecting her to be perched above me like a cat, perusing our conversation at her leisure.

"Right," I mumbled after four or five deep, calming breaths. I tried to angle the phone so that she couldn't see the screen from where she sat on the arm of the couch. She angled it right back.

"You and Penelope seemed to get along, last night," I said, "what did you think of her?"

"We can talk about her later," Lena said, her tone impatient. It reminded me of every time I'd ever come between her and the cartoon she'd been watching, growing up. I rolled my eyes and went back to the phone chat.

Do you have plans tomorrow?
Tomorrow?
"*Tomorrow*?" Lena asked, huffing.
I had a hot date with 43 student worksheets. Do you have a counterproposal?

"Bea, Bea, Bea," Lena tsked, "a little early to be using the word 'proposal,' don't you think?"

Is Lena still there?

...

"No! Don't tell him! That's weird."
"Yeah, *that's* what's weird about it."
In that case, I'll say "panettone."
I do love bread. Counterproposal accepted.
Such excellent news.

I wondered how I was supposed to make it until tomorrow. *Anybody ever tell you you're way snarkier in writing?*
Focus, Bea.
On what?

We haven't finished making plans.

I thought we were going to have wild animal sex and then you were going to feed me panettone.

"*Bea.*"

I was too busy giggling to heed poor Lena. His dots dotted away. Disappeared, for a few seconds. Dotted some more. I was a little too satisfied with myself. It seemed unhealthy. And then,

I'm free any time after twelve.

And then,

Come hungry.

And then,

And when you get here we can talk about how maybe you share too much with your sweet sister.

"Um, I should think not," Lena said before I could say more or less exactly that. I was still smiling as I typed in my reply.

I'll be there at 12:00:01, utterly parched, and you should be grateful. We wouldn't have these fun Sunday plans if not for me sharing too much with my sweet sister.

I said hungry, not thirsty.

Oh.

Ha, ha.

Perfect.

I'll cede your point on Lena—hi, Lena—and say thank you, too. His dots dotted a few more seconds. *Penelope's been informing Mom and I all morning that we've got to have more open lines of communication. I guess I'm just reacting to how your family's apparent openness is affecting my family's equilibrium. I had no idea Penelope was so starved for familial information.*

We could always add her to the group chat.

Dios Mio, Bea. And then, *wait but I want to be added to your group chat.*

Better hope you make a good panettone.

"You can't add Penelope to the family group chat. She's a nurse. Half of Mother's links are at-home remedies."

"I'm sure it's nothing she hasn't heard before."

I'll pour my soul into it.

I refrained from texting anything like "are you sure you're not free until tomorrow, you coy bastard?" Didn't want to seem too desperate.

Scratch that—I had no problem seeming desperate. I didn't want him to cancel any plans he'd deigned important enough to keep at the beginning of this conversation. And I certainly didn't want him to have to tell me no.

Have a good day, Bea. I miss you. I'll see you tomorrow.

I twisted away from my sister abruptly, feeling weirdly protective of his sweetness. Lena rolled her eyes, hopped off the couch, and took a little bow.

"My work here is done, anyway," she said, heading off to the kitchen. "As is breakfast. Hop to, Bea, Tia Rosa won't wait forever."

"Coming," I said, distracted.

I miss you too, Hedi. I'm glad you came to dinner last night.

It took a lot of will power to keep from telling him I wanted to hear from him every hour—for in a minute, there are many days—but I persevered,

Thank you, was what I managed.

If all I have to do to win your gratitude is eat your mother's cooking, Bea, then I'd say I'm set.

I smiled. Sighed, too, and tried not to burst out of my skin.

Okay I really do have to go, now. Enjoy time with your family! Tell them I said hi.

As if.

Chapter Twenty-Five

Many days per minute, indeed. Time crawled by, that Saturday. I napped. I watched soaps with my aunt. I ate. I went on about four manic walks. I napped some more.

My mother asked me eighteen times what I was going to wear to my date and it took all of my will power to keep from saying something along the lines of "a raincoat and nothing else," " sweatpants, do you think that's cute enough?" Or "is it a date if we never say anything?" I let her make us all do face masks and happily accepted the eyeshadow palate she'd gotten a few weeks ago—"rose gold looks good on you, maybe wear that paisley dress I got you for Christmas."

More family came over, that evening, and we had a potluck and a game night and Lena and I absolutely crushed at codenames. Lena kicked me out of bed, some time around midnight, telling me she was going to tie me down if I didn't stop tossing every which way. I absconded to the couch, thought about texting Hedi for the next hour, and fell asleep sometime around who-knows-when.

I went back to my apartment early, the next morning. The pre-date rituals had grown embarrassingly intricate, in the past decade, and I didn't really need my darling family to observe my every breath.

First, I danced around for thirty minutes. This step is crucial, as it fulfills the "maybe do a workout?" requirement without killing all joy. Second, I donned my bathrobe and wandered the apartment as I came up with today's grooming game plan. To shave or not to shave? How much were we going to pluck? Makeup or no? Should we let the hair air dry or should we blow it into limp submission? In what order did these things need to happen for optimal appearance?

I was dotting the rose oil behind my squeaky-clean ears when the first text hit my phone.

We're going to need to raincheck, Bea. I'm so sorry.

I was surprised I didn't immediately burst into tears. I'd been in that danger zone between excited and manic for too many consecutive hours, by that point, and it was shocking that I didn't just immediately combust.

I waited for more explanation but nothing came.

Of course! Is everything okay?

Nothing, for a few moments.

I think it's going to be okay.

That didn't bode well.

My mom woke up and couldn't see anything, this morning. We just got her checked into the hospital.

My stomach bottomed out.

Which hospital?

Chino Valley Medical Center.

Are visitors allowed? Or wanted?

There was nothing for a few minutes. I did start crying, then, but mostly because I was freaking out about Carmen. Fully ninety-eight percent, I'd say.

You are.

And then,

but maybe hold off on telling anyone else? From school, I mean. We aren't quite ready for that much support.

He was so much nicer than me. I would have just said outright I wasn't emotionally up for Dicky's crystals or Maya's prayer circles. I read the room, though, and decided he might not be in a joking mood. Or a "make fun of Dicky" mood. They were, most unfortunately, fast friends. And

Hedi didn't make fun of friends. An admirable quality, truly, though it did force me to dial up my filter.

Of course. I'm on my way. Do you want me to bring you anything?

We're good, thank you.

And then,

Actually, yes.

I never realized that a "things to bring to a friend while their mother is in the hospital" list could be adorable. This one was. It was also utterly inadequate. All he'd asked for was a packet of Kleenex's with aloe in it—his mother was particular, for which he profusely apologized—fluffy blankets, if I had any—as if he hadn't seen the hip-height basket of blankets when he'd been over—and vapor rub. So, naturally I showed up an hour later toting six boxes of kleenexes, eyedrops, a duffel bag full of blankets, fuzzy socks, games, and a backpack stuffed with healthy-ish snacks for his mom that I'd picked up from the market and a shitton of chocolate and peanut butter for him and his sister. Oh, and the unopened, industrial-sized tub of vapor rub my grandmother had given me and Lena for Christmas two years ago.

I had to stop at two different nurses' stations for directions. The second time, the nice man just up and walked me to the correct room. I stood in front of the door, my body a weird mix of nerves, and waited. I told my cardiovascular system to get its shit together, just because we were about to see the man we'd been thinking about nonstop for the past forty-eight hours didn't mean we weren't still at a hospital.

"Were you going to knock, or…?"

I yelped. Turned, saw Hedi, his hands full of cups of ice.

"You really shouldn't just sneak up on people like that," I huffed, thinking that today might be the day to begin seriously considering a reduction in my coffee intake. He looked utterly exhausted. Hot, of course—I mean, gray sweatpants might as well be men's lingerie—but utterly exhausted.

"Were you planning on going in? Or were you going to pitch camp at the door?" he asked, smiling, taking stock of the bags I was carrying. "You are… ridiculous. Did you know that?"

"You'll thank me at midnight," I sniffed, "when your toes are almost frozen off and you're in dire need of a nibble."

"I'll thank you now," he said. I waited, thinking he was going to add something else to the statement. He didn't. And so we just stood there, him looking dead on his feet, me, carrying half a pantry's worth of chickpea puffs and seed crackers.

"So, about that door," he finally said, the corner of his mouth quirking up.

"Oh, shit. Sorry," I said, belatedly realizing I was blocking his entry. I knocked a few times before letting myself in.

"Hedi, who—oh hi, Bea," Penelope said, looking up from the textbook she'd been reading.

"Bea?" his mom asked.

She...well, she looked like she had been hospitalized, earlier that morning. She was small and pale and wide-eyed. Hedi had said she hadn't been able to see, that morning. I wondered if any of her vision had come back, since then. I wondered if it would.

"Hello, Carmen. I brought you some blankets."

"Eres una santa, Bea," she said, holding out her hand. I put my bags down and walked over, taking her hand.

"Como te sientes?" I asked. Like a stupid person. She laughed, clasping my hand with both of hers.

"Como el caballo de la muerte," she said. I frowned, confused.

"Like she's been ridden to death's door," Penelope clarified. "I have no idea where she got that from, so don't ask."

323

Hedi came over to his mother's other side and tucked her under two of the blankets I'd brought. Carmen felt at it with shaky fingers.

"Que linda," she cooed, clutching the material. "Thank you, Bea."

"Yes, well. I take blankets very seriously." Needless to say, I felt very stupid.

I don't really know what one is supposed to say to a woman who woke up without working eyes or hands or feet. I didn't let the not knowing stop me, though. Penelope stepped out, for a few hours, as I kept her mother and brother company. I don't know what we talked about. Everything, it seemed, and nothing at all. We spent an entire five minutes, sometime around three, that afternoon, trying to determine whether or not sherpa was synthetic. Did we have three working phones between us? Yes, yes we did. Did it occur to any of us to do an internet search? Not even a little.

A nurse came in at four and gave Carmen some sort of infusion. Carmen fell asleep, minutes later. Silence descended. My ears rang.

Hedi stared at his mom, for a few seconds. He sank back in the hospital chair, moments later. Everything was so terribly quiet, all of a sudden. I nodded towards the door before standing. He stood as well and followed me out.

We didn't speak, outside, but at least it wasn't so unbearably still. We sat on a little bench, halfway down the hall. Hedi sighed, leaning forward, and rested his face in his hands. HIs shoulders began to shake.

It took me a weird amount of time to realize he was crying.

"Oh, Hedi," I whispered, wrapping my arms around him. He crumpled into me, burying his face in my shoulder. "It's okay," I murmured, holding him tight, "you're okay."

They were such easy, meaningless words. I said them anyway.

Chapter Twenty-Six

That week at school was one of the worst in recent memory. Which isn't an entirely illustrative statement, as I know most of my first year was a lesson in siege warfare. However, I can't *remember* most of my first year, so. The original statement stands on a technicality.

I showed up, Monday morning, knowing he wouldn't be there. Greeting his substitute as she dropped off Cheyenne and Joey still wrenched my gut. I checked my phone, over and over, waiting for updates. He sent them, of course. She was stable, she was okay, she was asleep. And then, about a hundred notifications from Sheets, telling me every time a teacher signed up for a meal train slot.

"Ms. Suré," Hugo asked, trying to read my phone screen over my shoulder. "Are we interrupting something?"

"What?" I wondered if my eyes looked as glazed as they felt. I dropped the phone and gave my darlings as much attention as I could muster.

"We were discussing the spring musical," Belen said, her pencil poised over her notebook, mid-page, as if she'd been in the middle of a major note-taking sesh. "And talking about how well last Thursday went."

It had gone well. So well, in fact, that half of my class was now sitting in a witch's cottage kitchen.

"The game was brilliant," I parroted, knowing not a thing about what they'd done besides the fact that Hedi had thought it had been cool.

"It was Noel's idea," Belen and Hugo said at the same time. Noel blushed. Angela looked up from the sketch she'd been working on. I wondered what it was of.

"Did you get good ideas for *The Queen's Will*?" she asked. It was Belen's turn to blush. Which was weird, because Belen didn't usually blush. That, and I hand't realized "ideas for *The Queen's Will*" was a topic of conversation capable of making people blush. I wondered if I should be concerned about next week's installment.

"There were some keepers," Hugo said, enigmatic, high on melodrama. He waggled his eyebrows at Angela. "There's a whole group of people stanning Oliver and the Warlock, though, which is a little concerning. We haven't seen the Warlock in, like, five weeks."

"Ya, and he's the *villain*," Belen added.

"Oh, like that's stopped stanners before," Hugo said, waving her words away with a hand.

He had a point.

"So Oliver's not going to end up with the warlock?" I asked casually. This was Paul's hopes for the story and I very much wanted to be the one to crush his dreams.

"He's the *villain,*" Belen repeated, her eyes wide, "why would we—"

"LA LA LA!" Claudia interrupted, staring, wide-eyed, from Belen to me and back. Belen frowned, then gasped, then scowled at me. I shrugged, a "what, me?" expression plastered across my face.

"Weak," Hugo muttered, falling into a bean bag as if he could no longer bare the weight of his mortal coils.

"Ugh. Whatever. She's not going to tell anyone."

Bold.

"It's not like we haven't all told her way more private stuff, anyway," Belen went on. "You never spill those secrets, either." Well, somebody was fighting dirty. What a scheming little fox. I rolled my eyes and guessed I wasn't going to be the one to let Paul down, after all.

"Anyway, we were talking about the spring musical," Noel called, probably wanting to change the subject before any other trade secrets were given away. She was pacing the poster wall—not an unusual way for her to spend a first period—and scribbling in a notebook.

"Yes, we need to get on that," I said, leaning back in my chair, one eye still on my phone. "I'm chatting with Paul during lunch about options. Do y'all have anything in mind already?" As if there was a universe where they hadn't already been campaigning for days in whatever group chat they and the tech students were all in. I wondered what the factions were, this year.

"Very much, yes," Hugo said, sitting up, his eyes wide and bright and brimming with youthful vim. Oh, to have energy. "But you have to hear us all the way to the end before you say anything."

"Well, before you say no," Angela clarified, closing her notebook, giving this conversation her full attention. Well, as full attention as a typecast dream girl can ever give.

"Um, since when am I a 'no' person?" I asked, huffily crossing my arms. "Who *taught* you 'yes, and?' Am I so easily forgotten?" I sank further into my chair, felt my every wrinkle and gray hair call out for filial justice. "Where is your honor? Where is your shame?"

"Somebody give her a muffin stat," Sophia said, rummaging around in her backpack. I grumbled, righting myself. Four students had dropped tributes of Halloween candy on my desk in the time it took to get myself straight.

"Thank you, thank you," I said, rubbing at my eyes, "but I'm okay." That, and I had actual tiramisu in the teacher's lounge. Hugo swiped a chocolate before Noel could reclaim it.

"I'm all ears and no nos," I said, glancing from student to student.

"Okay," Belen said, claiming the narrative. I wondered how many times she and Hugo were going to interrupt each other over the course of the next five minutes. "We were thinking, since it's our last year, and all—"

"It's *your* last year," Claudia called from where she was still pacing the poster wall.

"Yes, that's what I said," Belen went on, unphased, "that we could do something a little more…experimental."

Dear Judy. What had they been watching.

I suddenly understood why they'd felt the need to bind me to silence and judgement reservation.

"The spring musical," Belen went on, "it's the thing, right? The thing we do that involves the entire school. Anyone can audition, anyone can participate. Everyone comes." It was true. Each year, the musical cast was a fun mix of theater and choir students as well as lay students who simply wanted to try their hand at performing. A lot of times, it was because that year's particular musical was special to them, in some way. We had a fifty-person ensemble the year we did Wicked. Each year, a quarter of my Theater One class was made up of people who had been in the musical's cast, the semester before, and had subsequently converted into the department.

"We make most of our money from musical ticket sales," Noel added. I wondered why this was a relevant detail but, again, refrained from commenting.

"Each year, we have to pick a musical that we can actually pull off *and* that will get people excited. Each year, we pick musicals that we will live in, for three months, and learn to love. They become part of us, Ms. Suré."

This was taking a turn. I looked from face to face, hoping one would crack. They did not. This was very serious. I took a deep breath, stayed focused, and jumped back in.

"And so, this year, we were thinking... what if we did something that was already a part of us? That the student body was already very invested in?"

"And," Hugo interrupted, "that gave us an opportunity to expand our creative horizons? We've read and memorized dozens of scripts, Ms. Suré. We know how to tell other people's stories." Half the class was nodding vigorously, watching me with baited breath. This was, very clearly a rehearsed pitch.

"We want to try and tell our own, Ms. Suré, and we think we can do it, if we all do it together."

I refrained from telling them to get to the point.

"That, and it'll look great on college applications," Claudia pitched in. Belen nodded. Hugo glared at her, undoubtedly frustrated that she had punctuated the narrative arc with her mercenary, anticlimactic interjection.

"I'm still listening," I reminded them, genuinely curious. "Any day now."

"We want to turn *The Queen's Will* into a musical."

I'm sure you saw that coming from a mile away but, troubled as I was, and with the limited omniscience that I have, I did not.

"Oh," I said, reaching for my coffee cup only to discover it was empty. "Oh."

"We've already got most of the script written," Claudia hurried to say, "and wouldn't be doing all original songs, or anything. We were thinking Mamma Mia-style, you know? And let people try to write and score some songs, over break, and listen to them, and see if they'll work, and go from there."

Oh.

"And we'd wrap the story up in the weeks leading up to the musical," Belen added, "but not release the ending in the paper. If people want to know what happens, they'll have to come see the show."

Mer. Ce. Nar. Y.

"Sold. I'm in." Suck it, Maya.

Several jaws actually dropped.

"Wha—really?" Belen asked, looking a little cross-eyed.

"Why not? This is an excellent idea. I'm sorry I've never thought to give you opportunities to write your own scripts before." Theater rules, Newspaper drools. "Do you think the cast and crew will keep the ending a secret?"

"Yes," Hugo said, pulling himself to his feet and coming to stand by Belen. He looked as incredulous as she did. "Um… so it's a yes?"

"Well, I'll have to get Paul on board." I tried not to fantasize too much about the power trip we were about to go on. "Do you have a big enough cast? The story is mostly two characters, after all, but you're going to want to include a lot more people than that."

I've never seen a class of students nod so emphatically.

"We're at twenty-one and counting," Claudia assured me.

....twenty-one?

"Really?" How?

More emphatic nodding.

"Well, each of the main three characters gets an inner angel and demon," Belen said, ticking off people on her fingers, "it's funny, I promise. It makes sense. It's so we can punch up the jokes about romantasy. Like, the genre."

I felt like I had missed entire conversations. Which I had, of course. They'd been huddling up in their newspaper class for months, by this point, working on and arguing about their weekly installments with their fellow classmates. Not even Maya was sure about what all was going on behind the scenes. They'd become incredibly paranoid about spoilers.

"And then there's a whole bunch of people... um, coming up," Noel said, glancing from me to Belen and back. I tut-tutted.

"None of that, now. I can't green light a student musical if I don't know what you're planning on doing on stage."

Hugo looked ready to argue the point. Belen gave him a look, shrugged, and nodded.

"Fair," she said, "but you can't. tell. anyone."

"You already said it," I said, smiling. "I'm a steel trap."

"And we're also going to make a bunch of trees and bushes into fae characters, greek chorus style," Claudia went on, looking over her notes, moving all the while. I sometimes wondered how she'd gone her entire life without so much as a sprained ankle. "And there'll be warlock minions for the big villain song, and everyone will be in pleather, and—"

"So it's a yes?" Angela asked, interrupting Claudia.

"I assume the tech kids are already in on this?"

More nods.

"Then yes. So long as Paul's on board."

They actually squealed. I tried not to take too much offense that they had doubted. Because, at the end of the day, they'd written the script, planned the play, and prepped this proposal. They'd known I'd be supportive. Even if they didn't *know*, know. They knew.

Chapter Twenty-Seven

Dicky and I were helping Hedi's students make a giant "Get Well Soon, Carmen Dictine" card during their Wednesday art period. We'd just finished dumping an entire gallon of glitter over some glue-stripes when the man himself walked in, tired but alive.

Dicky and I didn't immediately notice him —students "helping" each other apply glitter requires maximum teacherly capacity—and our first thought when seven students screamed at once wasn't "their beloved teacher just walked through the door." Dicky went from sitting on the floor to standing on a table in less than five seconds, their gaze scouring the room for roaches, I assumed. I knocked the glitter over, in my surprise—Joey had hollered right in my ear—and thus became covered in thousands of flecks of shiny green plastic.

By the time I thought to look towards the door, most of the class had rushed to Hedi and was enveloping him in what must have been one of the more suffocating group hugs of his life.

"Is everything okay?" Dicky asked, breathless. "Has something happened, Hedi, what's —"

"All good!" he called from somewhere inside the hug. "Just came by to check on my students."

"It's about time," Chloe hollered.

"Ms. Suré, I thought you told us we weren't allowed to wear the glitter," Cheyenne said, studying me as she squeezed her teacher as hard as she could.

"It seemed like a good rule, at the time," I sighed. Hedi extricated himself enough to glance in my direction. He looked exhausted. That didn't mean he didn't also look wonderful. I'd seen him, the night before, when Maya and I dropped off that day's dinner. We hadn't stayed, though. Carmen's room had been full of family and friends and they didn't need two more bodies.

"If you need a change of clothes, I've got a spare set of newsboy trousers in my desk," he said, his face deadpan. I sort of laughed, sort of melted from the inside out.

His students had missed him. I mean, I already knew that. But knowing a thing is different than witnessing a thing. They told him every single thing they'd thought and done, in the past seventy-two hours, and got his feedback on every detail of the card they'd been working on for the past two days. Which was a relief, actually, because they'd really been wanting Dicky and I to text him and ask for his mother's favorite color, animal, phrase—you get the point—and neither of us really felt like that was an appropriate use of his airwaves, at present.

"Are you back, back?" Joey finally asked, a half hour later.

"No, not yet," he said, helping Chloe place a unicorn sticker in what had become the card's sticker corner. "I'm just here for a little while."

"When are you coming back?" Chloe asked.

"Soon. We should be going home tomorrow morning. I'll probably spend Thursday and Friday with her, too, to make sure everything's okay."

"But Monday?" Joey asked, looking at his watch.

"Hopefully," Hedi said. Dicky rested their hand on his shoulder, squeezing gently. Cheyenne did the same, watching Dicky's hand. Hedi, saint that he was, managed to keep a straight face.

"Thank you," he said, patting both Dicky's and Cheyenne's hands.

"That's good news?" I asked, tentative. He nodded.

"Her vision's back, as is most of the feeling in her hands."

"That's good?" I don't know why it came out as a question.

He looked up from his unicorns, smiling.

"You don't think so?"

I nodded my head.

"That's good," I repeated. He went back to his very important sticker-placing job, still smiling.

Julienne actually teared up, when the period ended and their substitute came to pick them up all too soon. Hedi checked in with the sub, getting a sense of how things had been going and answering a few of her questions. And then the class was gone, and it was just us. Dicky turned their kettle on.

"You left so quickly, last night," Hedi said. I shrugged.

"You had plenty of visitors already."

"Yes, but none of them were you."

I flushed, glancing to where Dicky was prepping maté at their desk. Dicky waved my glance away.

"I'm not even here," they said. I felt my jaw drop. And Hedi had had the *audacity* to insinuate *I'd* told my sister too much.

I looked back at Hedi, who had also followed my gaze to Dicky.

"How is your family?" I said, feeling awkward, all of a sudden. We hadn't so much as flirted, since our Saturday texts. Hadn't addressed the would-be date, hadn't mentioned the kiss, hadn't even touched in a way that wasn't simply comforting and supportive. It hadn't felt appropriate, all things considered. He'd been a little preoccupied. Busy. "Mother's sickbed" didn't seem like the best place from which to water a budding romance.

"Oh, they're…" he let it hang, sighing. "I haven't seen most of them in a while."

"Is it bad?" I tried not to assume the worst of his extended kin.

"Nobody's dead-named me yet, if that's what you mean."

"Always a start," Dicky said, carrying over two cups of tea before returning to their desk for the third.

"I certainly think so," he said. He stirred his tea, for a moment, before pulling his gaze back up to meet mine. "Bea, I don't know how to tell you this, but you've got a little something on your cardigan."

I hate to come off as petty or immature, but there is a solid chance I threw my arms around him for the sole purpose of getting as much glitter on his sweater-sweatpants combo as was humanly possible.

The problem with that, of course, was that we were suddenly touching, which reminded me of the last time we had suddenly been touching, which was not a school-appropriate memory. I stepped back, clearing my throat, and was pleased to see that his face was a little flushed, too. He ran his fingers through his hair and tried not to look too distracted. I smirked.

"You've got something in your hair," I said, studying his newly sparkling streaks. He glanced down at his hands, his sleeves, his shirt. They had all fallen victim to the glitter.

"Well, I did need a pick-me-up," he said, smiling. And then, "wait, don't you have a class, Bea?"

Shit.

"Dammit," I said, checking my watch. It had been going for ten minutes, by that point.

"I'm glad you came by," I said, waving like an absolute loser, "we miss you, Hedi."

He quirked a brow. Tapped his toe, too.

"I miss you," I amended. He smiled.

"I miss you too, Bea.'

Dicky muttered something in Korean under their breath. I didn't stick around to ask for a

342

translation, though. Some of us had classes to teach. Apparently.

Chapter Twenty-Eight

Paul and I tried to play it cool.

Tried.

"Do you also feel drunk on power, or…"

"Dear god, I *know*," I squealed, drumming my hands in front of me. I was in his choir room, sitting sideways on the third riser, a draft of *The Queen's Will* script in front of me. It was only the material adapted from what our students had written, so far. They said they were still working on the final arc and would "have it in ASAP." Whatever that meant.

Paul and I had more than enough material to come up with snippets of songs and monologues for the upcoming auditions, which would be announced the following Monday and take place the Monday after that.

"Maya is SO. MAD," Paul giggled.

"MAYA IS ALSO SO. RIGHT. HERE," she yelled. She only had twenty minutes before basketball practice started up. She'd decided that was more than enough time to haunt our afterschool planning session.

"How does it feel to have been so thoroughly betrayed by your students?" I asked, batting my eyelashes as victoriously as I could manage.

"They didn't *betray* me, " she pushed through clenched teeth, "they *pivoted.* For the sake of *money.* "

"Ugh. What yuppy scum," I agreed, giving her the "there, there" hand gesture.

"More seriously," Paul said, scanning the potential song list provided by our collaborating students. "We are going to nix Unholy, right? The vibes are a little too 'orgy,' right?"

"Are they?" I asked, running through the lyrics in my head. It felt mostly fine. "Besides, we did Chicago, two years ago. If they can do 'Cell Block Tango' in fishnets they can do Sam Smith." I thought some more. "But it wouldn't be a good audition song. It doesn't showcase range. Did you see the Queen's opening monologue? I mean, geez?" The thing had brought actual tears to my eyes. I suspected Angela had had something to do with it. The character's alienation and despair had been knitted into this whole bit about time and meaning and it was exactly the sort of "life is heavy but we carry it anyway" energy Angela brought to her creative endeavors.

"God, I know," Paul said. "And the Warlock's stage directions? I feel like they all got together, last weekend, and watched David Bowie highlight reels for three hours."

"Oh, that manna is already burned into their brains," I said, tapping my forehead. "They don't need a refresher."

"Everyone needs a refresher, now and then," Paul said, flipping through some of the pages. "I like the idea of making them audition as the hawk version of Oliver," he said, pointing to one of the earlier Queen/Oliver exchanges. "It might give us some ideas on how that transition could be embodied."

"Love it," I said, marking the dialogue. "Though, I will say, I'm kind of thinking they're thinking they're going to be co-directing this."

"Ha," Maya harrumphed, "good. We'll see how *you* like mutiny."

"Jealousy doesn't suit you, Maya."

"I've gotten that sense, too," Paul said, ignoring our aside. "How do you feel about that? I don't think I mind."

"Me, neither," I agreed. "They'll still need to be managed, I think. Something tells me they aren't always going to have the same artistic visions. Or, you know, the ability to direct their peers towards said artistic visions." For some reason, I didn't really think Hugo was the sort of person who would know to rephrase a directive if people didn't get it the first time.

"Damn," Paul murmured, reading through another few pages, "damn, damn. They really took the 'adaptation' process seriously. There's new material, longer speeches. They've punched up the drama. They've included notes on how we might do the Warlock's magic, on stage. Also, the Warlock is way more of a character?"

Maya sucked in a breath.

"What?" I asked, looking up from the lines I was bracketing in blue for later. Not everything was ready to go, after all, and, twenty students working together to create a coherent script aside, some parts still didn't quite make sense.

"What do you mean, 'more of a character?'" Maya asked, snatching some pages from Paul. A big no-no, by the way. We'd been sworn to secrecy, when they'd handed over these two scripts. They'd had us sign something and everything. No showing other teachers, no leaving copies laying about, no spilling secrets, accidentally or otherwise. I was pretty sure minors couldn't make legally binding contracts. I was also pretty sure that wasn't the point.

"He's less of a trope, here," Paul said, "he's given a more complicated motive. He—"

Paul cut off, his jaw dropping.

"You don't think—"

"Nooooo—" Maya groaned, sinking onto the piano's bench, next to Paul, "no, they wouldn't *do* me this *dirty*!"

"First things first," I said, flipping back to the bits with the Warlock, "you aren't allowed to know anything, Maya, so don't you dare get us in trouble. Second of all, I'm pretty sure the Queen won't end up with the Warlock. Don't ask me how I know, but—"

"—but *nothing*, you killer of dreams," Paul interrupted, pumping his fist in the air to some anthem I couldn't hear. "But *nothing*. Oh my *gosh,* I love theater."

"Stay in your lane," I muttered.

"I am a homosexual, Bea, theater *is* my lane. My birthright, my lover, my—"

But I wasn't paying attention, busy, as I was, reading and re-reading some lines between the Warlock and the Queen. Surely not… they wouldn't… they wouldn't do that to me, would they? Not after Belen had been so adamant, not after they'd set up such a love between Oliver and the Queen, not after they'd come so far together and

348

were now so close to declaring themselves anew, not after—

"Should I be concerned that I'm this invested in the serialized fairy romance our babies wrote because they didn't want to do an essay?" I asked the room at large.

"You're only just now asking yourself that question?" Maya asked, pressing piano keys at random. Paul eventually closed the lid.

"Don't worry, I already asked my sponsor," Paul said, circling another few lines, "they say it's perfectly fine to be interested in our students' creative endeavors. We're in the clear."

"I'm not sure this is 'interested.'"

Whatever.

Chapter Twenty-Nine

Carmen was discharged Thursday morning. Lena planned on making them dinner, that evening, but Carmen was already asleep. Instead, Lena, Penelope, Hedi, and I drank hot toddies on their mom's porch and watched the sun fall below their neighbor's roofs. Five boxes of picked-over takeout sat between us. Unfortunately, we had all liked the Bang Bang cauliflower the best. It had disappeared quickly, leaving us all to pretend like maybe we'd also eat the box of ginger green beans Lena had thought would be great.

They were not great. They were green beans.

"You're both staying here?" Lena asked, sipping on her toddy. Hedi nodded.

"For the first few nights, anyway," he said. "Until we're sure she's on the up and up."

"Thank you," Penelope said for the umpteenth time.

"Stop it," Hedi sighed, reaching over his sister and plucking a dumpling from a nearby box. "Or else risk another few hours of me crying and apologizing about waiting so long to come back even though I knew you shouldn't be doing this on your own."

Penelope started blinking an above-average amount of times. She wiped at her eyes, then. Hedi wrapped his arm around her and squeezed.

"She's okay. We're okay," he said, kissing her temple before letting go.

"Yeah, yeah," she sniffled, wiping at her eyes. "So, how's the case coming?" she asked, turning to Lena.

"Which one?" Lena asked, frowning, her eyes going a little crossed as she tried to remember what all she could possibly have told Penelope.

"I don't know," Penelope said, pulling the blanket from Hedi's shoulders and tucking it in around her legs. "You're a lawyer. I was just sort of hoping that there'd be a case you'd want to talk about. It was a conversation-changing tactic."

"Oh. Ha, ha. Very good." Lena smiled her crooked smile, which was her equivalent of an entire giggle-fit.

"So," Penelope prompted, leaning against the rail. "The case?"

Lena nodded, putting her serious attorney face on.

"Right, well, the world of special needs' trusts has been particularly rife, this week, and—"

She went on, for a while, and distracted us all with tales of estate law and guardianship disputes. At some point, Hedi came to sit beside me. At another, I rested my head on his shoulder.

"Thank you," he murmured after a while.

"For what?" I asked, pulling my attention from Lena's increasingly animated portrayal of this one quirky probate judge whom she, by this point in her career, could do an incredibly apt impression of.

"Well," he said. "The tissues, I suppose."

I smiled.

"I mean, it was a perilous quest. Do you know how many different brands of aloe-infused tissues there are?"

"We're in your debt, truly."

We both sighed at the same time. Which made us laugh, at the same time, which made Lena and Penelope look over and ask us what exactly was so funny. And so the moment came and went, and we were four once more.

***

The problem with Saturdays is that there is so much free time to just sit around and think. Sometimes that's okay, of course, but sometimes I'm no fun at all to be around and my inner monologue is the last person I want to be trapped in a room with, full stop.

That Saturday morning felt like the first space I'd had all week to just breathe and be and boy, did it have bad timing. The emotional exhaustion came crashing in. The guilt, too, at feeling emotionally exhausted—I barely knew Carmen, after all, and had no right to these feelings. Which are the sorts of thoughts I sometimes have that lead Lena to suggest I go back to therapy.

The actual exhaustion came next. It had been an intense week, at school, and Paul and I had stayed after almost every day preparing for the auditions. My students were gearing up for state competitions in speech and debate, too, and Monday practice had gone longer than usual. And then we'd been to the hospital, every evening, or Carmen's house. I'd gotten back late, each night, and then laid awake for an hour, trying to calm down enough to sleep.

And then, you know, there was the massive elephant in the room.

I had given Hedi all the space he did and didn't ask for. I fully understood, in my adult logic brain, that he was busy. That "mother getting hospitalized" was one of those things that gave people a fully reasonable reason for being emotionally AWOL. And he hadn't even really been emotionally AWOL. I mean, for a son panicking about his mother's health, he seemed incredibly "with it."

They'd been home for two nights, though. His mother was much better, too. By all accounts, she was stable and well and insisting they didn't need to be so smothering.

And Hedi hadn't texted yesterday. Which was totally fine.

This meant I hadn't seen him yesterday. Which was also totally fine.

Again, "being with family during a difficult time" totally trumps "fooling around with that chick who left me high and dry, months ago." Which I realize isn't what was happening, per se, but this Saturday morning wasn't a great look for me.

And then I'd woken up, this morning, thinking… well, that he might be a little freer, today. Maybe? Maybe we'd finally get around to having that chat. To discussing our feelings. To seeing whether or not he was already committed to some sort of Boston polycule. And I'd texted him. And my little "good morning" text had appeared just under my "how's your evening going?" text from the night prior. And the spiral had begun.

Because obviously he hated me. Obviously the timing was shit. Obviously we'd only been brought together out of desperation and convenience. Obviously the time he'd had, this past week, with his family had allowed him to get his priorities back in line. And, obviously, I had no place in that line. Because I was a vapid, fickle person—we were reaching far into the archives for these thoughts—and he and his deep thoughts and feelings could do so much better.

I decided, sometime around ten that morning, that I needed to let him off easy. We had to work together, after all, and I was pretty sure we could probably be friends, after a few awkward weeks. Yes, giving him an out was the best way forward. It was probably much better than making him pretend to be into me, for a few weeks, before finally letting me know he wasn't actually interested in pursuing a committed relationship, at this time. He would do that, too—date out of politeness, I mean—because he was just that sort of kind man.

He was also terribly earnest and faultlessly honest. This detail had no place in my current fantasy world, though.

Some time around ten thirty I also realized that his sister probably hated me as well—I would hate me, too—and wondered if she and her mother had begun telling him to run the other way. That I was a grasping opportunist, only in it for his money. I decided I probably owed Penelope an apology, too. Hers would have to wait, though, until I'd dealt with her brother.

Fifteen minutes later, and I had the message I'd drafted and redrafted no fewer than twelve times ready to go.

Hey Hedi! It began, *hope you're well!* Because I did. *I just wanted to let you know that I know that you've got a lot on your plate, right now, and "us" might not fit. I totally get it and just want you to know that we can be whatever you need, right now. I'm not going anywhere, of course, but I also don't want you to think you have to give me time you don't have. I don't want to add any stress to your life. All that to say, we don't have to un-raincheck that date, if you don't want to, and I won't bother you about it.*

I re-read it, nodded to myself, satisfied that I was doing the just and honorable thing, and clicked send.

The muted sound of a text alert cut through the quiet. I frowned, wondering if my phone had turned ventriloquist on me. A few seconds later, and

I reached the more logical conclusion that the sound hadn't come from inside my apartment. I rose from the couch and wandered over to the front door, wary. I peeped through the hole. Yanked open the door, then, and seriously considered admitting myself to a hospital.

Hedi stood there, a bouquet of flowers in one hand, his phone in the other. He was staring at the screen, reading something.

"I—"

"Hold on," he said, still reading. I don't really know where my mind went, just then. There were two entire seconds where I questioned whether or not he was actually real. I shelved those thoughts. Moved on to wondering what was in the cooler bag he had slung across one shoulder.

"Hedi, I—"

"One second."

He moved the flowers to the crook of his arm, freeing up his hands to type something out on his phone. He finished whatever it was he was writing, pocketed the phone, and looked up.

God, he was beautiful.

My phone vibrated in my pocket. He glanced down at said pocket, waited. I took out my phone, saw that he'd responded to my text.

Does this mean you don't want panettone?

I looked up. Words failed, in that moment. I'd spent all morning with my words, after all. They were tired and currently wracked with their own inadequacy.

"Is that a no?" he asked, raising one perfect brow. When I didn't say anything, he smiled. Sighed, too. "What sort of morning have *you* had, Bea?"

"In my defense," I tried. But I actually didn't have a defense. I stood there, my heart pounding, not quite believing that he was just... there.

"Mmhmm?" He stepped closer, then, his eyes crinkling, his lips quirking.

"I just ..." Just, what?

"Yes?" Another step. I could feel his body heat.

"Are those flowers for me?"

Another step, and then there was nothing between us at all.

"No." It was no more than a whisper against my skin. "I thought I'd get myself something nice. Apparently, I'm very stressed out right now."

I tucked my fingers through his belt loops and pulled him inside.

"Makes perfect sense," I murmured, one hand finding its way into his hair as he kicked the door closed behind him. His lips traced a line from my cheek to my ear to my neck and back. "You deserve something nice."

"Mmm." The soft cooler he'd been carrying thunked to the floor. "Bea?"

"Hmm?" I'd already gotten half of his shirt's buttons undone. Which was, perhaps, a bit forward on my part—not to mention the fact that my mental health required a DTR, stat—but I sort of assumed we all knew where this was going.

"How could you possibly not know that I want you?"

My eyes stung, suddenly. I pulled back, reeling, just a bit, and felt the inexplicable urge to laugh or cry or both. He was watching me, his black eyes bright with mid-morning sun.

"Because I never asked."

The bastard smirked.

"Funny how that works."

"What do you want, Hedi Dictine?"

He rested his forehead against mine, softly, sweetly. I refrained from grabbing his butt. Didn't want to ruin the moment.

"I want you to know that I am the bigger person, right now, and am in no way tempted to expound upon the virtues of karma."

"What could he possibly mean?"

His shirt fell to the floor. Some careless soul had loosed all the buttons, bless their hearts.

"I want you to know that I'm terribly into you, Beatrice," he went on, setting the flowers on the arm of the couch. His arms made their way around my waist, after that, and pulled me up against him. "I want you to know that I'll do my best to keep from leaving a text unread for longer than five minutes, apparently."

"It was a *day,*" I muttered, distracted, tracing the straps of his binder. He shivered.

"I want," he breathed, kissing me softly, "to date you, and learn you, and love you. So please, Ms. Suré, don't raincheck my raincheck."

His lips found mine again. And again, and again, and again, and I forgot everything there ever was or would be.

"Bea," he whispered against my skin. I tried not to huff. I thought we were done with the talking.

"What?"

"What do *you* want?"

I should think the fact that I'd gotten him out of his pants in less than ten seconds would have made the answer to that question extremely obvious. But then, that wasn't what he was asking, was it? I pulled back, a few inches, and studied his every line and lineament.

"Well, that bouquet would have been a nice place to start."

"Mmhmm." That comment, apparently, cost me my sweatpants.

"Baked goods, of course. I'm always hungry." The ratty t-shirt went, next. I'm not sure he understood the concept of cognitive reprogramming. And then we were kissing again, and I thought that was that and had very much assumed the matter was settled. But when I tried to pull him towards my room he paused, ever so slightly. I sighed against his neck. Cupped his face in my hands and pulled his gaze down to mine.

"I want you, Hedi," I said. He tried not to look too devilishly triumphant.

"Was that so hard?" He breathed, brushing his fingers through my hair.

"And only you," I went on, ignoring him. And then, because we were apparently getting everything off of our chests, right then, and it seemed like the time for radical candor, "you're not, like, already in some polyamorous quintuplet, are you?"

He blinked. Blinked again. Choked, a little. And then the laughter came forth, unchecked.

"I—what?"

I distracted him with my body and we never talked about it ever again.

Just kidding. He mentions his polyamorous quintuplet at least once a week.

Chapter Thirty

Hedi actually *had* made us panettone. I couldn't believe he'd gotten around to it. Except, obviously he had. Obviously he hadn't batted an eye at the "requires twenty-four hours of advanced notice" cake. Obviously he had thought it a more than appropriate offering for our first date. Second date? Was this even a date? Anyway. The cake was delicious. I 10/10 recommend tricking a hot man into baking you one and hand-delivering it to your bedroom.

I want you to know that I am actively refraining from making jokes about all of the other things said hot man could hand deliver in the bedroom. I want you all to know that I am choosing maturity, in this moment, and literary refinement. You're welcome. Moving on.

We fell asleep at some point in those quiet moments between midnight and dawn. I drifted off curled against him, his fingers drawing soft circles across my back. I woke up, some time later, cold and alone.

He wasn't there.

I stared, confused, at the space beside me, and wondered how I could possibly have so intensely misunderstood the situation. He didn't *seem* like a "sneaking out while I was asleep" sort of person. But then, what did I know? I'd spent the morning prior thinking his lack of texting meant he hated me, body and soul.

Maybe I was actually a terrible time, after all, and he had decided he couldn't spend another second in my pres—

—the toilet flushed, ending that particular train of thought. The faucet squeaked on, then off. A few more seconds, and then he was tip-toeing into my room.

"Oh," he whispered, noticing that I wasn't asleep. "Sorry, I didn't mean to wake you." He crawled back into bed. I rolled closer and let him pull me into his arms.

"It was so cold," I murmured. "I thought you'd left me to die."

"Has anybody ever told you that you're terribly dramatic."

"That's why they pay me the big bucks." And then, "well, the medium bucks." I thought some more. "The small bucks, but with a pension."

"Don't forget the pension," Hedi agreed, coiling a strand of my hair around his finger.

"I would never." I wrapped my arms around his waist and considered never letting go. "I thought you had left."

He propped himself up on one elbow, his frown barely visible in the darkness. "Was I supposed to?"

I tightened my grip in response. He sighed, dropping his head back to the pillow. "Bea, I wish you'd have a little more faith in me."

"I have nothing but faith in you."

"Okay, faith in us, then."

"But that would require me to see what you see in me." I hadn't realized how very much that was the problem until I'd said it out loud.

"Well, that won't do," he mused, tracing the contours of my face with one finger. "Not at all. Let's play a little game, Bea, called 'mirror, mirror.'" He was smiling, as he said it, and I knew I was about to be subjected to some tactic that had probably been learned in therapy.

"I don't wanna."

"No, no. It'll be fun, I promise. We get to talk about how some of your perceptions of me are actually reflections of your own insecurities."

"That doesn't sound fun at all."

"You'll love it. First on the list: what's this about me being a flight risk?"

"I don't think you're a flight risk," I breathed, wondering how in the world he expected me to focus on this conversation when his hands were doing such distracting things to my lumbar region. "I think you think I'm a flight risk."

"Are you?"

"I'd marry you tomorrow, Hedi Dictine."

His hands froze. I felt myself smirking.

"That's just your inner lesbian talking," he finally managed. I tried not to preen too much. I'd always wanted to be a lesbian.

"So he's dismissive, too," I said, ticking his imaginary personality flaws off on my fingers. "What's next? A dash of gaslighting, perhaps?"

"Hush, baby. It's all in your head," he murmured, pushing me onto my back, kissing that spot between my neck and shoulder. I shivered and snickered and a few other things, too.

"I'm sorry I'm unhinged." I finally got around to saying.

"Don't say such things about my girlfriend."

"Girlfriend?" I asked. He looked up from what he was doing, brow raised.

"Oh, so you're allowed to propose marriage, but I'm not allowed to call you my girlfriend?"

I fluttered my eyelashes at him and said not a word. He rolled his eyes and went back to kissing me.

"What *do* you think of me?" he breathed against my skin, "I don't go around doing what we're doing with just any 'ol pedestrian."

"Oh my gosh, he thinks I'm *old*."

He groaned. Pushed off of me, too, and threatened to go back to sleep. I rolled after him and showered him with kisses and promised I'd be on my best behavior, scout's honor, Lapone's living soul as my witness.

After, we sat against the headboard and shared a piece of panettone.

"I think," I began, trying not to let the idea of being honest and vulnerable for ten entire seconds give me palpitations, "I think it's because it's easy to see why you like a person, specifically, but hard to see why they like you for any reason other than proximity and convenience. I know why I like you, but it's hard to know why you'd like me, besides the fact that I'm who's here."

"Bea, are you… are you shaking?"

Maybe.

"Emotional vulnerability stresses me out."

"We just had, like, a whole bunch of sex, Bea."

"I said *emotional*."

He flicked my nose. "Oh, so you're one of those compartmentalizing fuckers."

I twisted to face him, chewing, waiting. For what, I don't know. But I felt like I'd said my piece.

"Bea, love and friendship have always been about the people who are there. We fall for the ones who show up." His gaze swept across my face, slow and thoughtful. "It's not convenience, it's community. It's the people who say 'yes, and,' when you ask them to do life with you. Besides, you're *hardly* convenient. I had to go to four different stores before I found the right kind of flour for this cake."

I smiled. Rested my head against his shoulder.

"But, if you need an itemized list of every single reason I'm in your bed right now I can provide one." He cleared his throat, which was when I realized he meant right there and then. "First —and bare in mind, this is in no particular order— first, I forgot to move my sheets from the washer to the dryer and didn't want to have to wait for an entire dry cycle before getting into my own bed. Second, I—" I shoved a piece of cake into his cake-hole, though, and that was that.

Chapter Thirty-One

There's nothing quite like going back to the job where you're surrounded by adolescents after you kissed the boy you've been crushing on for months and feeling like you might as well be wearing a scarlet "FYMF." Which, for all you offline folks, is "fuck yeah, mothafucka." I both felt extremely accomplished and also like the children were going to sniff me out within the first five seconds.

It's not like I was opposed to students knowing I was dating, or anything. Probably. Maybe. I don't know. I feel like I'm opposed to most people knowing I'm dating, which, I suppose, is a "me thing" that I should work on or something.

Point being, I felt super exposed, that Monday morning, and like my only task was to make it through the forest of high schoolers undetected.

By the end of the day, they would have been more likely to suspect me of drug use than romantic chicanery. I'd slightly overcommitted to "playing it cool." And "I'm not paranoid, you're paranoid." And also a little bit of "this isn't twitchy, this is just my face."

I don't know why I was so convinced they'd find me out. I made up such a small piece of their lives, after all, and even less of their brain space. That, and I was pretty sure they thought I lived at the school. I'd heard Sophia telling her aunt over the phone that I was "probably mid-forties or something," so I also had that going for me.

This was the false sense of security I'd lulled myself into by the middle of the day. And so there I was, walking into the teacher's lounge at lunch time, minding my own business and thinking I was doing a very good job of it, when Paul's voice cut across the room.

"Wow, *somebody's* glowing. Is it just me, or are you a little light on your heels, Bea?"

How. *How.* I tried to glare at him. Ended up smiling a terribly smug smile. Anita looked up from the game she'd been playing on her phone, frowning.

"What?"

"Nothing," I said, opening the fridge and taking out my Tupperware of soup.

"How *dare* you," Paul gasped, "we are *starving*, Bea. You would *deny* us this opportunity to *sustain* ourselves? So much for solidarity. I thought you were an *ally.*"

Anita looked down at her half-eaten sandwich, clearly trying to figure out why she was hungry.

"What do you think you know?" And how, I wanted to add. Paul waggled his eyebrows at me.

"I think nothing, my lady," he said. "I *know*, however, that you had a very… satisfying weekend."

"You disgust me," I said, a grin giving me away more surely than any spoken confession. I looked down at my outfit, wondering if I'd somehow accidentally written the words "just had sex" across my dress.

"What am I missing?" Anita asked, trying not to look too eager.

"Bea got laid."

"Dammit, Paul," I muttered, pinching the bridge of my nose.

"What?" Anita asked, frowning. "But I thought you were sort of trying to have a thing with Hedi? Oh. Oh. *Oooh.*" And then Eager Beaver was grinning, too.

"Dear god," I muttered. "Don't *say* anything. *I* didn't say anything. You don't know *anything*. Stop *smiling,* Paul." And then, "*how?*"

"He told me."

"*What?*" That pervert. "*When?*" When had there possibly been time for that little heart to heart.

"We both had bus duty, this morning."

I squinted at him.

"I don't believe you."

"You can look up the schedule, you'll see —"

"Paul."

He rolled his eyes.

"Bea, I'm trying to sew chaos in the garden of your infant relationship, stop thwarting me." I kept staring. "Fine, we were simply exchanging 'how was your weekend' pleasantries and he said 'fine' and I said 'what did you do' and he didn't technically tell me he'd done you but he did say he'd been over and watched Sinbad at your place."

Dammit, Hedi.

"What?" Anita asked, lost again. "Did you not actually watch Sinbad?"

"Oh, we watched it," I said. We'd put it on after the first slice of cake. Who doesn't love Michelle Pfeiffer as Chaos?

"Sinbad is a mood, Anita," Paul said, patting me on the head as he walked by and returned his

372

bowl to his bag. "And there's no way Bea could make it through that sort of mood, next to that sort of man, without making a move. I know that. Bea knows that. Everyone knows that."

"Except Hedi, apparently."

Paul turned the electric kettle on, his sachet of earl gray already out and ready to go.

"I can't believe you sealed the deal to the sound of Brad Pitt voice acting an animated pirate."

"To be fair," I said, sniffing, deciding I was going to take my lunch break somewhere else, thank you very much, "we'd already sealed it. A few times. So, ha."

Paul was cackling as I turned on my heel and left.

***

"Ms. Suré."

I jumped out of my skin. Realized I'd been fully zoning for the past ten minutes. That I was safe, in my classroom, and that nobody was attacking me. No, it was just Belen, her hands clutching her notebook. "Ms. Suré, I think we've got our ending."

I sat straighter in my chair, anticipation leaking through my bloodstream. I held my hands out. She shook her head.

373

"It's not ready, yet," she said, "We haven't finished writing it. We're still working on getting the words just right."

"Makes sense to me," I said. The bell rang, her classmates left. She watched them go. Waited for them to go, too. I wondered what it was she didn't want to say in front of them.

"It's been kind of hard to write," she finally admitted. "The end, I mean."

"Oh? Why?"

She looked down at her notebook, her dark hair falling in front of her face.

"It's just… well, it's the love bits. Like, the bits where they declare their love. It's…we want to get it just right, but it's hard. Which is weird. All the other bits were just getting words on the page and helping each other edit. But now our lovers have to tell each other why, you know? And we're like… well, why? Why does it work, for them? What is love? And their romance was the whole point, so now we have to state the point, outright, and make people believe it. And now all of Newspaper Club is super in their heads about it. It's really breaking down group morale. Everyone keeps going on about how they don't know, anyway, because they've never been in love, and is it even real? Well, except Becky, who's pretty sure she's going to marry her floozer boyfriend—pardon my language—but she's been banned from making suggestions ever since she tried to kill Oliver at the Hedge of Darkness."

"She *what*?" Who was this person and why was she trying to steal my joy?

"I know, right?" Belen shifted from foot to foot. "Anyway, we're still working on it. We can give you the outline, though, if you really, really need it before moving forward with auditions. But it's just...it's not there, yet. And we want it to be... well, perfect."

I smiled. Belen sighed.

"You're about to go into Sage Mode, aren't you."

"Listen, wee one," I said, pitching my voice into that gravelly register so often used to caricature the elderly. "Love is never perfect, probably, but that doesn't mean it isn't good. And good is good enough. Boom. Done."

Belen rolled her eyes.

"More seriously," I said, grinning, "you can change the dialogue up until opening week, if you want. You aren't locked in with what you have. I'm not saying you should give into your inner perfectionist demons—because, bad—but I am saying maybe lower the stakes for this draft, a little? The words might come easier if you know they don't have to be the final cut. Because writing, like love, is a process, not just a product. You don't have to be perfect. You don't even have to be good, at first. You just have to want it, and work towards it, and be willing to ask for help, along the way. Which I feel like you mostly already know, anyway. You and your friends have done something truly special, this semester. I mean, for Garland's sake, a *musical?* I don't think I've ever met a group of high schoolers who would *think* to try. And here you are, *doing.*"

Belen waved the comment away, clearly very secure in how awesome she was.

"Thank you," she said, her gaze dropping back to her notebook. "I…thank you." She didn't make a move to leave, though, which was when I realized I'd 1) missed the mark and 2) would have to hold my bladder for at least another ten minutes.

"What is it, Belen?" I asked, sitting back in my chair.

"I…" She actually started shaking. I panicked for all of two seconds before realizing I knew exactly where this was going.

"Belen, you don't have to say anything, if you don't want to. But I am here, and safe, if you feel like sharing."

She huffed.

"What? Too out of a can?"

She sort of laughed, which made me think I" d still succeeded at cutting a little bit of the tension.

"I just... we made this whole big love story, and... and a lot of people really like it, and are going to keep liking it, and we're doing an even bigger production of it, and..."

Wait for it, wait for it, wait for it—

"And I feel like a fraud, is all. Like, what do I even know? I've never been in love. I've never even tried. I'm about to be released into the world, Ms. Suré, and I don't have any actual experience, and—"

'Hold it, hold it, hold it," I interrupted. "'Experience?' What? You've got seventeen years' worth of living under your belt, Belen, that is nothing *but* experience. There are plenty of ways to love, in this life. It's not all about romance." Geez, these children had grand expectations of high school. "First of all, never let anyone infantilize you because you haven't gotten around to dating yet. Kissing someone doesn't turn you into some wise elder. Second, you're seventeen. You're not supposed to date until at least forty. Third... actually, I don't have a third point."

Belen looked unconvinced.

"It's easy for you to say, Ms. Suré. You've had plenty of girlfriends."

"I wouldn't say *plenty,*" I said, sniffing, pulling my cardigan tighter around me. And then I decided to just put her out of her misery. "Belen,

you have nothing but time to date. Now, later.
Whenever. And, when the time comes, you don't
have to be afraid of what others will think, either.
Like who you want. Date who you want. It really is
going to be okay."

She finally got around to looking at me.

"Is it…is it, like, obvious or something?"

"You're in theater, Belen. It's expected."

That wasn't true—mostly—but I didn't want her to
spend her afternoon overanalyzing four years' worth
of potentially gay behavior.

She sighed.

"I… I don't know how to… how does one…
am I even gay? Like, if I never date, do I still
count?"

I'd asked myself that same exact question
too many times to laugh it off now.

"Yes."

She held my gaze, thinking.

"Okay." And then, "do you think… um… do
you think anyone else is? Gay, I mean. I mean, in,
um… class?"

I nodded.

"Pretty sure Hugo might be into boys."

She rolled her eyes.

"Belen, I don't think I'm allowed to go
around making guesses about other students'
sexualities. I might be wrong, but that feels like the

sort of thing that would be used as an example in an HR training video." She huffed again. "However, you could always ask *her.* I don't think the person you may or may not be thinking of is the sort of person who would be offended by the question."

She covered her face with her notebook, groaning.

"Oh my gosh, it *is* obvious," she wailed. My bladder began to herniate.

"It is not," I tried, "and who cares, if it is? There's nothing embarrassing about having a crush." I was very glad, in that moment, that no adult friend of mine was there to witness my absolute hypocrisy.

"Easy for you to say," she mumbled into her notebook. "*You* know that your crush likes you *back.*"

Well. So much for that.

Chapter Thirty-Two

We didn't call it a "dinner." Penelope said her mother was too tired for the idea of a "dinner." She wasn't too tired for friends, though, and if they happened to be eating while over? Mores the better.

Lena, my mother, and I showed up at Carmen's house, that Saturday, salads and soups and one very-layered cake in hand. Hedi opened the door, smiling, and let my mother and sister in. He stepped in front of me as I tried to pass, brow raised.

"Can I help you?" I asked, handing him a crockpot of vegetable soup. It was too heavy.

"Demonstrably, yes." He looked me up and down. I was wearing my fourth green dress of the week. "Sage looks good on you."

"Oh? Do you like it?" I hadn't noticed.

His gaze returned to my face. "Were you about to just walk right in?"

"Is this a troll under the bridge situation?" I asked, peaking over his shoulder to where Penelope had already put mulled wine in my mother's and sister's hands.

"Do I look like a troll to you?"

"Well, I don't know what trolls look like, now, do I?" I said, reaching forward and pretending like his collar needed fixing. "Maybe they look like really hot argyle-wearing teachers from SoCal."

He rolled his eyes, resting the pot against one hip.

"I suppose I wouldn't mind levying a toll," he said, his black eyes rimmed with the coral light of the falling sun.

"Mmm?"

He leaned forward, proffering one cheek. I ignored the cheek, instead taking his face in my hands and pulling his lips to mine. He laughed against my mouth. Kissed it, too. For perhaps an amount of time that was inappropriate, present company considered.

"Gross," Penelope called from the kitchen. "Some of us are trying to eat, here."

I kissed him for another two seconds and gave his sister the bird from behind Hedi's back. And then we broke apart, smiling and sighing, and joined the not-dinner.

This time when Penelope asked, Lena really was working on "a case." So much so that she had to put her spoon down. Rare were the cases whose explanations involved both of Lena's hands. I frowned, wondering why she hadn't said anything about it before now.

Besides, you know, the three obvious reasons. Two of which were sitting in this very living room.

"Anyway," Lena was saying, "we're suing the company for the client's records, first, but Joseph—" her law partner—"is gearing up for a class action suit."

"Damn," Penelope said between spoonfuls of soup. "Damn, damn, damn."

"Lope," her mother said, tsk-asking her. "Is that how I raised you?"

"Yes?"

Carmen went off on her children to my mother, who matched her story for story. I sort of paid attention. Sort of vibed, too, and stole dessert from Hedi's plate.

And so the night wore on. Nursing school was hard but good, in Penelope's estimation. Lena had finally convinced the office manager to stop buying anise tea. Our mothers' opined the warmth —"each year, hotter and hotter, longer and longer" —and Hedi regaled our families with the latest

382

sagas from his classroom. Joey, apparently, had needed to make a poster for geology, and had deputized the entire class in his pursuit of the perfect igneous rock. The center table in Hedi's classroom had been overtaken with rocks the students kept finding and bringing in for Joey's perusal.

And Carmen. Well, she was well. She laughed, and talked, and watched us all. She looked tired, yes, but not in the bloodless, exhausted way she'd been, days earlier. She was getting better. The relief of that reality had been hitting me in waves over the past several days. And I barely knew her. I could only imagine how Penelope and Hedi felt. But then, I suppose I didn't have to imagine. I suppose it was written all over their smiling faces.

At one point, Carmen saw me watching her. I smiled. She winked. Hedi, apparently, witnessed the entire exchange. I didn't realize he'd seen it, in the moment, but it was one of the first things he brought up when we got around to being alone, later that night.

We were sharing a cup of chamomile tea, sitting on my kitchen stoop, and pretending like the sky was clear enough for stargazing.

"It's a game, you know," he said, sipping from the tea, "the winking, I mean. We used to play it, growing up. Sort of like hot potato, I guess. Or tag. You're it."

"Oh?" I tried to take the mug back—my hands were cold, regardless of what the mothers had to say about SoCal's unseasonable warmth—but he wouldn't let it go. I rolled my eyes and kissed his cheek. He grinned, relinquishing the mug.

I should never had said anything about troll tolls.

"Do I want to be 'it?'" I asked.

"Only on Wednesdays," he said, pulling me onto his lap. And before you get too "oh, how precious" or "geez Bea, we get it, you're honeymooning," I would like to say that the gesture was motivated mostly by his desire to use me as a blanket. He tucked his frigid fingers into my pockets and I almost yelped. He might as well have stuck ice cubes into my pajama pants. "Don't take this the wrong way, Bea, but she hasn't winked anybody in in years. I checked with Penelope, just to make sure it hadn't made a resurgence while I was away."

"How could I possibly take that the wrong way?" And then, "and how do I win?"

He laughed against the back of my neck.

"You know. I don't know."

I laughed, leaning against him.

"Are there any rules?"

"Oh, probably," he sighed, resting his chin on my shoulder. "Obviously you can't 'get' somebody if they didn't see you getting them. Oh, and you can't get the person who just got you."

Made perfect sense to me.

"What happens on Wednesdays?"

I felt his smile against my neck.

"The person with the wink got to bring Abuelita her rum raisins."

I burst into laughter.

"Did you also get to do the dishes for getting all As," I asked, twisting around, handing him the last sip of chamomile. He didn't immediately take the glass, tapping his cheek with his finger instead. I rolled my eyes and kissed him again. He smiled, took the glass, and finished the tea.

"I'm not sure you understand the cost of things," I muttered, realizing, belatedly, that I'd just been rum raisined.

"And I'm not sure you understand how fun it was to sneak an alcohol-soaked raisin with your grandmother."

He made an excellent point.

I turned around until I was facing him. I brushed the hair back from his brow, slowly, softly. There wasn't any rush. Wasn't anything we were hurrying away from or running towards. No, in that clear, cool darkness, his arms wrapped around me, his eyes bright with my neighbor's kitchen lights, it was so abundantly easy to just breathe, and be, and know that this moment was real, all by itself. Wonderful, all by itself. That we just *were*, in this moment, and didn't have to pay any heed to the strings of narratives wrapping around it, stitching it into our pasts and futures. I wondered why I felt so incredibly free, just then.

It wasn't happiness, per se. Wasn't that fleeting feeling of "oh, this is nice, time to catch my breath while I can." I wasn't sucking in air while I knew I could, wasn't dreading some inevitable reality that would spin me back into the suffocating chaos. We were simply here, no more, no less, and together. And we had all the time we had to keep doing exactly that.

It would never have occurred to me to want this feeling. I'd never felt it before. I wouldn't have known how to ask.

I wondered why love felt so much like peace. I chalked it up to the affects of aging on a person's priorities. Thirty had done all sorts of weird things to my body.

"Hedi," I whispered, cradling his face in my hands, staring him down. And then I winked with all the melodrama I could muster. Which, as you know, is quite a lot. "You're it."

Epilogue

I would wax on about "The Audition: High School Musical Edition," but I won't. Mostly because I had never orchestrated an audition for a musical my students had written that half the school subsequently showed up to try out for. There was no back catalogue of precedent to wax on *about*.

Paul and I walked through RAG Hall the Monday of auditions and tried not to panic. No fewer than fifty students had crowded themselves into its embrace. They stood in a wide, chaotic line, chatting with one another, their hands twisting around the pages of audition pieces. The shortest clips of monologues, dialogues, and song snippets that our board of directors—what our theater, choir, and newspaper club students who very much thought they were running this show had begun to call themselves—could manage while still showcasing range. Some students rehearsed their lines with their friends. Some had simply deputized the nearest wall or door. Some were merely there for moral support. Surely. Garland, I hoped some of these people were just here for moral support.

The line snaked out of RAG Hall and into the school's main corridor, adding another hundred or so to our list of auditioners.

"Kill me now," Paul muttered, holding the door to the PAC open for me as we both hurried through. The door snicked shut and the roar of hopefuls fell into a muted din.

"Oh, you love it," I said, grinning, sipping on the espresso Pete had just handed me. I almost spat it out. It more or less tasted like acid mud. If acid mud could also give you a heart attack. I swallowed, though, because Chris and Lu were standing within spotting distance and I didn't want to be rude. The tech students had bought the classroom an espresso machine with their Halloween proceeds and were still fully in the learning phase of the craft. I could swallow a few dozen health hazards if it meant I'd be sipping on perfected cortados by Christmas.

Bowie, I hoped it was only a few dozen.

We sat in the fifth row, the sole audience to what was about to be an hours-long show. Well, not the *sole* audience. My tech students were pacing the PAC like shepherds—the dogs, not the people—somewhat wanting for jobs but mostly convinced that their general, vigilant presence would keep anything from going wrong. They barely trusted *theater* students in the PAC. The open auditions for each year's musicals just about gave them heart attacks. And this was *before* the espresso machine.

"Are we ready?" I called to Pete, who actually did have a job, just then, working the light booth. Was he taking the task of "keeping a few low-lit spotlights on stage" a little too seriously? Perhaps. Did he have any other mode? Not even a little.

"Ready," he called back.

"Ready?" I asked Lu, who had just taken a seat beside me. She opened the laptop and nodded, ready to enter each student's information into our auditions spreadsheet.

Belen, Hugo, and Frances—a senior in choir who was also on the "Board"—burst into the auditorium, clambering over three rows of chairs before collapsing into the seats in front of ours. I raised a brow.

"Change your mind?" I asked.

"Not even a little," Hugo said, rolling his eyes. "Though, if I don't get to be the Warlock I will be wresting full directorial control from your nepotistic hands."

"Um, excuse," Frances said, flicking Hugo's nose. They'd competed for the same role in every musical since they'd started at this school, four years ago. "These are supposed to be fair auditions, Hugo. You can't threaten the directors."

"As opposed to that time an hour ago when you told me you were going to get a cold during

State competition if you didn't get cast as a lead?" Paul asked. Frances picked at his nails and said not a thing.

"Did you need something?" I asked Belen, selecting her as the most likely to get to a point.

"We just came from outside," she said, her eyes wide. "There are...so many people?"

I tried and failed to raise a single eyebrow.

"What did you think was going to happen?"

"I—not this. My palms are sweaty." She wiped her hands on her pants. "Do we need to add in a few more parts or something? There's so *many* people, Ms. Suré, and not everyone's going to get a role. I don't want anyone to be sad, or—"

Paul and my's cackling laughter cut her off. She scowled. We just kept laughing, though. Paul even snorted a few times.

"Welcome, my darling, to the joys of casting," I said, wiping my eyes.

"Oh, dear," Paul said, massaging his diaphragm, "she's worried about hurting people's feelings."

"No," Hugo corrected, "she's worried about people being mad at her."

"And the affect that will have on the *project,*" she added, still scowling. "I don't want them to like it less because... because we made it personal, or something."

I wondered how much time I had to soliloquize on how all stories were personal. How narratives were always relational. How the meaning we got from them was relative and ever-changing, depending on our relationship to the storytellers and their audience.

"We don't have time for whatever it is you're about to rhapsodize about," Paul said, interrupting my internal rhapsody.

"I guess you're right," I said, checking my phone's clock. "I was just giving Maya a few more minutes."

"She has one hundred and eighty seconds."

One hundred and sixty-two seconds later, Maya walked in. I would say "rushed"—she gave all appearances of having been hurried—but she ambled in at her usual pace, which in no universe, known or otherwise, can be confused with "rushing."

"Have you seen the line?" she asked, sitting on Paul's left. "Dear God, y'all. That's insane."

"Yes, which is why we're trying to start on time," Paul said. "Now, shoo," he said to our seniors, "it's not good to look this cozy with the directors, children. If you do get good parts, people will accuse you of nepotism."

"But it *would* be nepotism," Maya said as they scrambled off.

"No, it would be a complex system of merit, seniority, and ability to emotionally rally and regulate," Paul clarified. "Shall we?"

"Let's," I said, opening to the first page of a brand new notebook. "Send them in, Lex."

And so it began.